HEALING OF THE HEART

RUBY SCOTT

Thank you to my beta readers, Pattz, Nellie, Sharon, Jules and Monna. You are an awesome team who make my heart sing.

And to A, every day I love you a little more...

JUST A THOUGHT

"The mystery of human existence lies not in just staying alive, but in finding something to live for."

— Fyodor Dostoyevsky

"Hope is the thing with feathers that perches in the soul and sings the tune without the words and never stops at all."

– Emily Dickinson

ONE

The buzz of the lunchtime rush filled the hospital cafeteria. Doctors, nurses and patient families flitted around the room with full trays looking for empty tables as those already seated swapped stories as they ate.

For the families of patients, this was a chance to take a quick break from the stress of bedside vigils. For the medical staff, it was a reprieve from a constant barrage of questions, problems that needed solving, and the mountain of paperwork that seemed to be overtaking their time with patients. Out of all of the spaces in the hospital, the cafeteria offered some stolen moments of respite.

The hot topic of conversation for the day was the upcoming audit. It had been years since the hospital staff had been submitted to a full, formal audit, and no one was looking forward to it. Some of the staff were familiar with the process that could follow a difficult patient, or a procedure that had an unfortunate outcome. Lawyers might be called in, interviews conducted, depositions taken.

The conference rooms would be a hive of business suit activity, behind drawn blinds. For a few days, the staff of one department or another would walk on eggshells, with everyone holding their breath and having hushed conversations in quiet corridors and then it would all be over. Everyone would relax back into their regular routines, happy to still have their jobs; until the next unfortunate incident and the whole thing would start again in a different department.

The audit would be like that, but with the dial turned up to ten. A full team was being brought in to conduct interviews with every member of the medical staff. All of their patient files and records over the past few years would be reviewed, they would be required to give their opinion of *other* members of their department, and their fitness to carry out their duties would be critically evaluated in a way they'd never struggled through before. To make matters worse, there would be no break from it; the whole hospital would be audited, all in one go.

Whether they were talking about it or not, the audit was on everyone's minds, and a group of nurses huddled together to talk about it;

"Why do you think they're doing it?" One of the younger nurses, a pretty girl of about twenty-five leaned in close to her friends. "Do you think someone filed a report or something?"

"Businesses are audited all the time." An older woman with steely hair held captive in a strict bun, rolled her eyes. "Don't be so dramatic."

"I'm not being dramatic. I'm just saying; there has to be a reason for this, right? Something must have kicked this off. What if one of the doctors screwed up?"

Her older co-worker shot her a withering look, and the young nurse slouched back in her seat, folding her arms over her chest. "What? Maybe we've had a few too many complaints, they thought it would look good to have someone go over the place. You know, weed out the uh... the weaker members of staff."

"Maybe they're coming to interview nurses who'd be all too happy to gossip about their co-workers," the older woman said pointedly, sipping her coffee.

"So why do *you* think they're doing this then?" the younger woman snapped. "If you don't think someone's screwed up."

"I think this is a business. I think they want to run it as effectively as possible, and to do that, sometimes you have to *trim the fat.*" The older woman looked at her co-worker out of the corner of her eye, and cocked an eyebrow. "You know, to increase efficiency?"

"Why are you looking at me like that?"

"No reason." She looked away, smiling to herself as a young man joined the table. "Jason, what are you thinking about all of this?"

"All of what?" He dropped into the seat across from them. "The audit team?"

"Mm. Erika here thinks that she's living in the middle of a whistleblower fantasy—we've killed off too many of our patients, and there's a team coming to smoke out the murderers."

"I didn't say that!" Erika protested, sitting up straighter. "But the doctors have to get a lot of complaints, right? Maybe they brought a team in because they think there's more to it than that. Maybe they think there are more complaints that are being covered up. Don't you think that's a *possibility?*"

"If the hospital was covering up malpractice, why would they have hired a company to dig into all our files, and interview us?" Jason asked, picking up a french fry from his plate and waving it around as he spoke. "You know, if you're driving around with weed in the back of your car you're not going to speed in front of a traffic cop, are you?"

The table fell silent for a moment as the other nurses peered at him suspiciously. Jason cleared his throat and looked down. "Hypothetically, I mean."

"*Anyway,*" The older nurse continued, narrowing her eyes at him momentarily. "It doesn't matter *why* they're doing the audit. The only thing that does matter is that it's happening, and we need to be ready for the team when they get here. The last thing we need is to have those people turn around and say that the nurses aren't organized enough, or that we don't have all of our files where they're supposed to be. If the nursing staff gets a bad report we'll *never* get that pay rise."

There was a murmur of agreement around the table at that, followed by a sombre moment of silence. Then, out of the corner of her eye, Erika saw a flash of white as a lab coat whipped past their table, and her eyes lit up as she leaned in again. The others around the table mimicked her as she peered across the room, tracking the doctor who had walked past them.

"What?" Jason asked, stuffing another handful of food into his mouth.

"What do you think they'll make of *her?*" Erika whispered, pointing to the figure in the white coat who strode purposefully past their table, before weaving between the groups of gathered doctors until she finally found a spot on her own by the window. In unison, the group turned their heads to look at the lone woman, before huddling together again.

"I mean her record's got to be spotless, right?" Jason murmured.

"Yeah, but it's not just her record that they're going to be looking at, is it? They have to make sure she can work and play nicely with others. And if there's one person in here that *can't*, it's her. Besides, if they're asking us all to snitch on each other—"

"They're not asking us to snitch on—"

"*Whatever.* If they're asking us to give our 'professional opinion' on everyone else, who's going to give her a glowing report? None of the nurses from Neuro like her, doctors think she's an asshole and even the surgeons think she's arrogant. She's probably got more complaints from patients than the three of us *combined*! I mean seriously, she's going to be screwed when it comes to—"

"Erika!" The older nurse cut across her sharply, and Erika shrank back in her seat with a sigh. "Stop it. Whether you like it or not, she's a part of the hospital and she's a good surgeon. You don't need to go around spreading gossip about how much of a toxic, stuck up bitch she is."

There was a pause around the table while the older nurse sipped her coffee, and glanced in the solitary woman's direction. "Even if it *is* true."

They all looked over towards the lone figure watching as she raised the sandwich to her mouth. Just as she was about to take her first bite, the chime of the intercom cracked into life. "Doctor Asquith to surgery, please."

The nurses watched as she let out a low groan, tilted her head up to the ceiling for a moment, and then stood up. She left her sandwich, untouched, on the tray, and pushed past a couple of doctors on her way to the doors. As she walked out of the cafeteria, the nurses exchanged knowing glances with each other before silently returning to their meal.

———

It had been a long day.

It was *always* a long day, working at City General. But any day that ended with an emergency surgery certainly felt longer than most. As Meredith Asquith made her way out of the OR, disposing of blood-soaked gloves in the infectious waste unit, she let out a soft sigh of relief, and rolled her shoulders in a slow, languid stretch.

"Thanks for the assist back there," a voice called from inside the OR. She didn't bother turning back to face them, instead she released an incoherent grunt and held up her hand in an attempt at a wave. It was all she could manage, given the day she'd had.

Meredith made her way through the halls of the hospital, glancing out of windows as she passed them. The sun had already set, and the sky outside had melted into an inky navy hue. It must have been getting pretty late.

So much for leaving early. Crossing one arm over her body, she grasped her elbow, stretching out the muscles. A late finish last night, followed by an early start meant that she hadn't gone for a run. She was starting to get a little antsy, just like she always did when it had been a little too long since she'd gotten some exercise. It was like there was a little pot of nervous energy inside her, and someone was dialing the heat up; watching it bubble to the rim and threaten to overflow.

If that stupid kid hadn't been speeding on his motorcycle this afternoon, she'd probably be out on that run right now, rather than heading back to her office to finish up on paperwork she'd had to postpone. Hot-headed teenagers with high powered bikes were the bane of the state, in her opinion. The kids had too much money and not enough sense to be driving something that powerful. Today's surgery was testament to that.

He'd live, of course, and at the end of the day that was the most important thing. Stupidity wasn't a death sentence after all. He'd need months of physical therapy and rehab. He'd likely never ride again, and he might end up living with a few cognitive problems, but he'd been wheeled into a recovery room rather than the morgue. And when all was said and done, even if she complained about being interrupted, that was what was important.

Meredith made a right at the end of the hallway and unlocked her office door, before turning on the overhead light. It flickered and then came to life, illuminating the mess of paperwork she'd left behind. Patient files, along with progress records and consent forms dropped off by the nursing teams filled her desk. Three stacks loomed high, one of which looked dangerously close to toppling over.

All I want to do is go home. Her heavy sigh filled the room followed by the click of the door closing behind her. The low hum of noise from the rest of the hospital, and for a few moments, Meredith's office was completely silent. Then, with a groan, she crossed the room, threw herself down in her chair, and eyed the piles of case files, demanding her attention.

The idea of a late night run in the park to clear her head and cool off had *never* appealed to her more, but she knew that wouldn't be happening any time soon. No, instead she had paperwork to tend to, and if she left it, she would only have to come back to it in the morning.

Audits were coming up.

Meredith, like every doctor and surgeon, was about to have auditors peering over their shoulder and poking around in their personnel files to unearth malpractice lawsuits. If you were squeaky clean, you weren't doing your job right but if you had complaints, well then there were just even more questions. You could be damned no matter what and that made everyone uneasy. Audits were a pain in the ass, and although she knew they were useful for *some* people, Meredith didn't exactly see the point of scrutinizing everyone.

Like I need some corporate asshole who faints at the sight of blood to tell me I'm a good doctor, she scoffed, tossing another patient file back onto the desk. Sure, there were some doctors in the hospital who had to have a lawyer on retainer given their likelihood of screwing up, and there were others who she suspected *might* have just bought their way through medical school, but she wasn't one of them. Anyone could see that, and she didn't need a whole goddamn audit to be sure of it.

The worst part was that *everyone* was going to be on edge for the duration. Everyone was going to be extra careful, and *careful* translated to *slow* where most people were concerned. That meant every piece of paperwork would need to be double-checked to make sure there were no errors, and everyone was going to be asking for second and third opinions. All for an audit.

The team hadn't even set foot in the hospital yet and they were giving her a headache. They were due to arrive at the beginning of the next week, and in anticipation for that, every single doctor and surgeon had to have a complete summary of their patient files ready, just in case they were one of the chosen. Everything had to look perfect.

Even if it wasn't.

TWO

There were four days until the audit was due to begin, and the tension around the hospital was palpable. Meredith felt like she'd spent most of her day weaving between people who were chasing down lost paperwork or stressing over what would be facing them on Monday morning, rather than actually doing the work in front of them.

Her fears about how much the audit would interfere with the daily workings of the hospital hadn't been unfounded and even though it hadn't started yet, she wished the whole thing was already over. She'd just finished surgery and headed to her office, still dressed in her scrubs. It was the end of *another* long day—not that any of them ever felt short—and even though she just wanted to head home and have a hot shower, she had a pile of patient correspondence to get through before she left.

Thankfully it wouldn't take too long which was mainly down to the wonder of Julie, the Neurological Department secretary. Julie was a one woman miracle; she could read the hieroglyphics of a surgeon's handwriting, decipher the most obscure notes and juggle a host of unwieldy diaries all at the one time. Meredith was almost done when she heard a knock on the door to her office. Before she could even answer, the door swung open, and Phil Squires appeared.

"Evening."

Meredith glanced up from the file for a moment, glaring at him. "You know you're supposed to wait for me to tell you to come in, right? That's usually how it works."

"Well, *usually* you don't let me come in, do you?"

"Ever thought there might be a reason for that?" Meredith muttered, turning back to her file. There were few people on the medical staff that she could tolerate, and Phil was one of them, but that didn't necessarily make the two of them *friends*.

He was a decent surgeon but that was just about the only redeeming quality he had, so outside of work Meredith tried her best to ignore him. He was a thin, balding man in his late forties who spent half his time flirting with the nurses, residents and families of patients; or any female with a pulse. And when he wasn't fooling himself into believing he was Chris Hemsworth, he spent the rest of the time bragging about his sports car and sprawling suburban paradise. Sometimes he really stretched himself and did both simultaneously.

Meredith thought he was an ass, and he probably thought the same about her, but there was a degree of professional respect that they managed to extend to each other. That respect didn't usually translate into Meredith inviting him into her office though.

"What do you want, Phil?"

"Melanie wants to see you."

"Oh really?" Meredith didn't bother looking up from the file. "what does she want this time?"

"She didn't say." Phil leaned against the door frame lazily, folding his arms. "She didn't look happy, what have you done to piss her off this time?"

"I don't think I have to actively *do* anything to piss Melanie off." She closed the file and tossed her pen onto the desk with a sigh. "I get the feeling my sparkling personality does that for me."

"Yeah, well she wants you in her office. Said if you were free now, you were just to pop up." Phil glanced around Meredith's office, and his gaze fell on the stack of files she'd piled up on the floor beside her desk. "Is that for the audit?"

"Sure is." She grabbed her white coat from the back of her chair and swung it on. "I'm tired of hearing about the damned thing and it hasn't even started."

"You're telling me," Phil gave her a wry smile. "I was hoping we'd get a pass and they'd just audit the Fellows and the Residents, but everyone's getting the same treatment. It's bullshit; all this time worrying about the damn thing, and we could be spending it looking after patients and who knows maybe even saving a few lives."

"Mmh," Meredith grunted, "You are preaching to the converted here. So did you have an audience with Melanie too?"

"Yeah, although I'll let her break the surprise to you. You are going to love it."

Meredith eyed him slowly. The smug look on his face suggested she wasn't going to like whatever she was about to be told. Ushering Phil out of her office as she walked into the hallway, locking up behind her. "The quicker this is over the quicker I can head home for the day."

She walked off in the direction of the administrative wing without bothering to say goodbye to Phil, who still wore a disconcerting smile. Nestled between two meeting rooms, Melanie's office looked out over the main hospital entrance, giving her a view of everyone who walked in and out.

The chief administrator's secretary had already gone home for the day when Meredith made her way to the office, and her desk was left empty, except for the bowl of complimentary mints she offered to anyone who passed by. Meredith dipped her hand into the dish, picked a mint out, unwrapped it and popped it into her mouth before knocking on the door to Melanie's office.

"Come in." Melanie called from the other side.

Meredith opened the door and poked her head in. Melanie Saunders was alone, seated behind her desk with piles of paperwork around her. At the sound of the door opening, she looked up to see who was there.

"Evening," Meredith closed the door behind her. "What did you need me for?"

"Meredith, good. I was worried you'd already left for the day." She smiled, and raised her hand to beckon Meredith over with a friendly wave. "Why don't you have a seat?"

She would rather have not. She hated conversations with Melanie; she reminded Meredith of every teacher she'd hated in high school. She had a simpering falsetto voice that sounded just a *little* too high to be real, and no matter who she was speaking to, she always seemed to manage to talk down to them. She also had a bad habit of prying into the personal lives of the other members of staff, in faux concern, but it was all so insincere. Mix that with that godawful women's suits she wore, in every pastel shade imaginable and it was fair to say she didn't feature highly on Meredith's Christmas card list. But then again nobody did.

"Do I have to?" Meredith eyed the seat with a frown.

"Please." Melanie pointed to the chair in front of her, a little more insistently this time. "Take a seat. I want to talk to you about the audit."

Of course, the fucking audit.

"You want to talk to *me*?" Meredith sat, folding one long leg over the other. "You think I'm going to be your biggest concern here? What about Adams, he nearly lobotomized that cyclist last year. Or Denner, refusing to admit her patient was dying of cancer and pushing ahead with the surgery anyway? Or-"

"This might surprise you, Meredith," Melanie interrupted her with a thin smile. "But I'm actually aware of the histories of every doctor who works for me, including Adams and Denner. *Their* patient histories shouldn't concern you."

"Fine," It was probably for the best that she dropped it. It wasn't worth dragging this conversation on for any longer than absolutely necessary. "What do you want to talk about? I'm already looking at my patient files, so don't worry. The bureaucratic wheels will continue to turn for another day."

"Do you have any idea of *why* we have our doctors audited, Meredith?"

"So we don't kill people?" Meredith shrugged. "I mean I assume. That's a big part of the job."

"It's important that doctors are able to perform their jobs to the best of their ability at all times. Part of that involves psychological evaluations from a team of unbiased individuals, who can help to give the hospital a profile of the best doctors. And, of course, of the *worst*."

A long silence followed Melanie's words, and she folded one perfectly manicured hand over the other, shooting Meredith a pointed look.

A hush filled the room.

"I hope you're not lumping me into the second category," she said finally. Melanie raised an eyebrow and smiled again, but it was that same thin, cold smile as before.

"The hospital and indeed the audit won't be making their judgements on statistics. Your mental fitness to carry on doing the job also comes into play. The board wants to make sure we keep the best surgeons and that doesn't just mean a steady hand holding a scalpel."

There was another long silence, even heavier than the first. Meredith cocked her head to one side, looking across the desk at her boss. "So should I consider this conversation some kind of friendly warning?"

"I'm just letting you know how important this audit is. Well that and the fact that the board has decided that the neurosurgical team undergo psychological interviews. Every member of the surgical team will be receiving a report based on a series of interviews and evaluations the team are conducting, and that report will become a large part of your employee file, and an important factor in your position here." Melanie had dropped the pretense now; it was obvious she was just speaking directly to Meredith. "I don't just judge my doctors by their skills in the OR, Meredith."

Meredith clicked her tongue and leaned forwards so that her elbows rested on the desk. "What would you rather have, a doctor who plays nice with everyone, or a doctor who gets results?"

"You know it isn't impossible to have both, right?"

"Maybe it isn't. But you know as well as I do that there are far too many doctors in this place who care about how much other people like them, and don't care enough about patient care. I don't really think you need another one. We *both* know how that ends up for the family."

Melanie opened her mouth to respond, but couldn't come up with anything and fell silent instead, looking uncomfortable. She shifted around in her seat, avoiding Meredith's gaze for a moment before speaking again. "Everyone has to go through the audit process Meredith. I'm just making you aware of what's coming."

"Thanks for the heads up." She stood up with a sigh. "Can I get back to my job now?"

Melanie pursed her lips for a moment, but she swallowed whatever comment had been on the tip of her tongue, and waved Meredith away instead. "Sure. Thanks for the chat. Close the door on the way out."

"Any time." Meredith smiled but made little effort to hide her contempt. The next few months were not going to be fun.

THREE

Emily was a long way from California.

It was one of the things she liked the most about her job. A lot of her friends hated the idea of traveling from work, and were more than happy to take the same route to work every day, staring at the same scenery out of the window as they got stuck in traffic. They liked routine, they liked familiarity.

Routine got boring though, for Emily at least.

When she'd graduated from the college she'd attended halfway across the country, her mom had been ecstatic. Psychology wasn't a profession known for a nomad lifestyle, and she'd probably figured that her daughter would settle down, work within a practice, and then one day open up her own. In other words, she would *stay* in California.

For a couple of years, Emily had done just that. She'd worked at a breezy ocean-view office, listening to rich middle-aged men complain about their new young wives, and talk about how unfair the world could be. She listened, she nodded along, she offered solutions that would never actually be followed through on. And then she'd do it all over again with another client, and then another. And then, eventually, she got bored of the whole thing, and she'd looked for something new.

That was how she found herself at Wells Consulting Agency, thousands of miles from California, her mom, and her friends. She was heading to a hospital on the east coast with the rest of the team, ready to get to work auditing their surgical staff.

It would be a long job. They were going to be working at the hospital for a few months, taking time to build up a detailed report of every member of staff, so as compensation for being away from home for so long, the company had put them up in condos around the city. Emily was sharing her condo with Angela, a data consultant in her late forties.

They'd arrived that morning with their luggage, and set about making the place feel a little more like a home instead of the sterile showroom it appeared. The condo came fully furnished, which was good, but everything just felt so... generic. They had shared a condo on a few previous assignments so they quickly fell into a pattern of making the place feel a bit more welcoming; books on the coffee table, their own mugs and Angela even brought framed photos of her family which she placed around the place.

"At least it feels like people are actually living here now." Angela joked, once they'd stepped back to appreciate their handiwork that night. "It doesn't feel like a hotel anymore."

Emily nodded slowly, although to be honest, she wouldn't have really minded if they *had* just been put up in a hotel. The chances were, she wouldn't be spending a whole lot of time in the condo, and even when she was there, she'd be glued to her laptop. She'd already seen the list of medical staff that they were going to have to make their way through, and she knew she was going to have her work cut out.

Angela clearly knew that too, because she was all too happy to spend the evening just relaxing in front of the TV, letting some crappy reality show wash over them while they ate takeout. It would be one of the few evenings they would have left where they weren't also up to their eyeballs in paperwork and data.

The audit wasn't supposed to officially begin until Monday morning, but when they landed on the Thursday morning in an unfamiliar city with nothing but time on their hands, it only made sense that they would start getting ahead with their work.

Emily headed to the hospital on Friday morning. She'd already been told that an office had been prepared for the team in the administrative wing, so she figured it would be a good idea to find it and familiarize herself. There was going to be a lot that she needed to prepare for, after all.

With a latte from the hospital cafeteria in hand, Emily made her way through the halls to the office that had been set up for her. It wasn't very impressive, just a box with a few tables squashed together, and a handful of tiny windows that let a little sunlight in. Obviously *this* wasn't where the hospital's massive budget had gone.

Emily unlocked the door and flipped the light on, wandering around the desks. A few were already organized, likely by team members who had already arrived in the city with the same train of thought as her. Some even had their desks set up with pen pots, their own hardback folders and even a few personal items, but the rest were just a mess of documents.

She found a desk towards the back of the room stacked high with boxes, and on top of it, she found a scribbled piece of paper with her name on. These three boxes of files were hers to work through, and if her last few jobs were anything to go by, they wouldn't be the last she would see.

The hospital staff had already been notified of their arrival in advance, so they'd taken the time to put together some preliminary information for the team. Some of her co-workers had spreadsheets and timecards to look at, others had detailed notes on surgeries that they had to make sense of. Emily's specialty was psychological profiling, and so she had pages and pages of personal information to leaf through.

"No rest for the wicked," she murmured to herself, setting her coffee cup down on the desk before she dumped the boxes on the floor. Once she was settled in her lumpy office chair—probably discarded from someone's office after they'd upgraded to something with padding— she pushed the lid off the first box, picked out the top file, and started reading.

Emily knew just how guarded doctors and surgeons could be over their privacy. They made for notoriously bad patients, and nowhere was that more true than when it came to their psychology. Emily had heard of doctors yelling at members of their team, storming out of meetings, and even once they had threatened to have a psychiatrist thrown out of the hospital because they didn't like the questions.

It was something she had been told when she'd first started working with the consultancy. They'd explained to her in no uncertain terms that the audit team would be unpopular from the moment they arrived, and it was just all well they weren't there to win friends. It was something she'd just understood to be part of her job, and although it could be frustrating, it was just something they all had to deal with.

City General would be no different, and she knew if she was going to make any progress, she was going to need to know more about who she was up against. Once the workload was divided up between the team, Emily got started reading up on each of the staff members she would be reporting on.

Surgeons tended to be the worst to audit. It was probably something to do with the power trip they had in the OR—they held people's lives in their hands, and that made a serious impact on their psyche. It was no secret that surgeons tended to be arrogant assholes, and they didn't exactly enjoy it when an audit team poked around inside their head, questioning their every move.

Most of the medical staff she would be reporting on were specialist surgeons – three neurosurgeons, four members of the cardiothoracic team, and a couple of plastic surgeons. In the past, she'd realized that the more senior a doctor was, the more likely they were to be difficult. Nurses seemed to understand the process for the most part, junior doctors were almost apologetic when they were questioned, but surgeons nearly *always* behaved like the whole thing was beneath them.

Specialists like the ones she would be handling were probably going to be particularly hard to talk to. They'd climbed the ranks at the hospital, dragged themselves through the years of training to get to where they were, and they probably thought that they were too smart to be questioned.

They weren't, and they were going to find that out.

Emily spent most of her morning leafing through thin manilla folders, trying to get a vague sense of the people she would be interviewing. It was interesting to see why some doctors had been slapped with complaints, and to see where some of them had been praised in turn. The more she found out now, the easier the hunt would be.

There was one particular file that grabbed her attention as she made her way through the boxes. It belonged to one of the Neurosurgeons, Dr. Meredith Asquith. When Emily pulled it from the box, she saw a purple sticky note shaped like a leaf, that someone had attached to the front. There were only two words written on it; *Good luck.*

"Good luck?" she read out loud with a small smile. "That's not ominous at all."

She wasn't sure why this doctor in particular had come with a hazard label attached, not at first. At first glance, she just seemed like the rest of the people Emily would be talking to. She was accomplished, she had come with good recommendations. There was nothing to indicate that she would be particularly troublesome.

And then, Emily turned the page to see a list of complaints that had been lodged against Doctor Asquith, from patients, family members and medical staff alike. Most doctors had a few complaints made against them over the years, but even for someone with as much experience as Meredith, it was a long list.

Most of the complaints against her told the same story. She was rude, she was abrasive. She didn't take criticism well, but she was more than happy to dish it out to anyone she worked with. Apparently she'd even struggled with an ill-fated team-building exercise the hospital administration had pushed at one point.

Doctor Asquith questioned the validity of my Medical Degree in front of a patient family when I disagreed with her findings. It later turned out that I was incorrect, and Doctor Asquith was correct, and she used this to excuse her behavior. However, I believe it was wholly inappropriate of her to behave in this way in front of patient families, and undermine my authority.

That was one comment, and it didn't exactly paint Meredith in a favorable light.

Doctor Asquith was rude and blunt when talking to my wife about her operation. My wife was very nervous before the operation, and she was worried about the complications and long term effects that it might have. Doctor Asquith didn't offer her any comfort or reassurance before the operation, and probably made her feel more nervous.

That was a second comment, from a family member this time. The complaints continued like that, down the page in a long list. She had a terrible bedside manner. She seemed "desperate to leave the room once she had my consent form." She "refuses to treat other doctors as equals in the OR, and sees them as assistants."

The more she read, the more Emily realized that Meredith was certainly going to be challenging but equally she could prove to be interesting. If she didn't care about the opinions of the other doctors on the staff with her, how was going to respond to Emily's presence?

She looked down at the sticky note, at the two words of warning someone had very kindly left for her. *Good luck.* Perhaps she would need it.

FOUR

It was late—or rather, it was early—by the time Meredith returned home. The streets were mostly empty as she made her way back from the hospital, and when she parked her car in its normal bay and slowly made her way up the stairs, she didn't pass another soul. It had become her normal routine when coming home from work now; she finished so late most days that it was actually stranger for her to see someone on her way home than not.

Today's surgery had been complex and lengthy. The position and depth of the brain tumor had meant that both she and Phil had been required to work together and whilst the outcome had been better than anticipated it had taken its toll on both surgeons.

When she finally walked through her front door, Meredith dropped her bag on the floor by the couch and flopped down onto the cushions with a low groan. There was a dull ache in her feet from the hours she'd stood by the operating table, and her neck hurt from craning it down to see what she was doing, but at least she could relax at home, at least for a little while.

It was quiet, and after the day she'd had, that was all Meredith really wanted. She'd spent the whole day focused on weaving and cutting her way through tissue, being careful to avoid the myriad of blood vessels with the constant low hum of machines whirring in the background, and gentle footsteps from the team of OR staff. Finally, she was somewhere dark and quiet, where she could switch her brain off.

She didn't lay on the couch for long, even though it felt good to just sink into the cushions for a while. A few years ago she would have just melted into the couch and let her eyes slip closed to sleep through the rest of the day, but not now. It was a little after five, so if she left for a run now, she could be back home by six, and then she could wake up again around midday, to start the whole process again.

Maybe some people would have hated this life; waking at ungodly hours of the day and night, spending close to sixteen hours of the day at work sometimes, rarely getting to have any human inter-action outside of the hospital. For Meredith though, it suited her just fine. It wasn't like she had a social calendar that was bursting at the seams anyway, and she had enough downtime to go for a run and curl up on the couch to read. That was all she wanted from her free time.

Right now, she had some of that free time to use however she wanted, so she decided to throw on some shorts and a tank, and head out for an early morning run. It always helped her to unwind after a long shift, and given the stress of the day ahead, Meredith figured she could do with a chance to clear her head.

Pulling her hair back from her face in a tight ponytail, she then grabbed her running shoes. As she stooped to lace them up, Meredith thought she heard someone moving around in the apartment beside hers.

The walls were thin in the building—she'd been able to hear the last tenants arguing late into the night before they'd split up and moved a few months earlier, and the place had been nice and quiet since they'd left. It had lain empty, but from the sounds of things, she had new neighbors. She could hear someone moving around, and then the door swung open. Footsteps passed by Meredith's door as her new neighbor headed down the hall, and then they faded away.

Strange, she thought, checking her watch. It had just gone quarter past five, so it was still early for most people to be awake, but she'd definitely heard someone leave the apartment beside hers. Perhaps they worked unsocial hours like her, and they were heading out for the day, or maybe they were heading out for a run too.

Just in case that was what was happening, Meredith decided to hang back a little and give them a few minutes to get out of the building, and do whatever it was they wanted to do. She wasn't really in the mood to stand around and make aimless small talk with someone new, chatting about property prices or the weather. After the day she'd had, she wasn't really in the mood to talk to anyone about anything.

So she waited there for a few moments, poised outside the door just in case the neighbor decided to come back for something. When she heard nothing, Meredith decided it was safe to head out undisturbed, so she slipped out of the apartment and headed downstairs for her run.

Whoever they are, I just hope they aren't as annoying as the last ones, she thought to herself.

———

It was just before nine on Monday morning, and Emily's first session with Meredith Asquith was due to start at any minute. Saying that Emily was actually looking forward to meeting with Meredith might have been overstating her feelings somewhat, but there was a certain morbid curiosity about the woman. She probably had the best employee record of any doctor Emily had interviewed before, and she had to wonder how that might impact her personality.

Emily had been set up in one of the unused offices to conduct her meetings. With the exception of the desk, two chairs and the paperwork she'd brought with her, the office was bare. *It's not exactly the warmest place I've ever worked,* she thought to herself, setting her laptop on the table. *But it's probably not the worst place either, in all fairness.* That said it was hardly an environment conducive to getting people to open up emotionally.

Over the course of her career, Emily's job had led her to work in some fairly uncomfortable offices. Although the plain white walls and navy carpet were pretty boring, at least it was clean. Even that wasn't always a guarantee during these interviews.

Emily took out the top files from the box—Meredith's—and settled down in her chair to go over it one last time before she met with the doctor. As she opened the slim manilla folder, the sticky note that had been attached when she'd first seen it fell out and fluttered to the ground, landing at her feet.

"Good luck..." She read aloud as she picked up the sticky note, before tucking it back into the folder neatly with a smile. Part of the fun of her job was figuring out what made people tick, and she liked a challenge—she wouldn't have gotten involved with auditing doctors if she didn't. If the sticky note was anything to go by, Meredith would certainly be a challenge, and then some.

Her employee file shone. Meredith had come to City General with a shining recommendation from the Royal London, and it looked as though she had lived up to her reputation once she'd arrived. She had an impressive record in the operating room, but that wasn't what interested Emily, not really. She was more concerned with what happened *outside* the operating room, and that would be hard to get a feel for until she actually sat down and talked to Meredith.

"Guess I won't have to wait long now," she murmured, pulling her phone out of her pocket. It was 9:03, and she had a text from her mom: *Missing you!*

There was a picture attached with the text, and when Emily opened it, she couldn't help but smile. Her screen was filled with a blurry shot of a white Labrador, the latest in a string of out of focus photographs she'd received since leaving California. Even though her mom was enjoying dog-sitting for her while she was out of state, it looked like she was having a little trouble getting the dog to sit down for more than thirty seconds.

I miss you too! She sent back, just as a knock at the door drew her attention from her phone. She tucked it back into her bag, and took out a little notebook instead. That had to have been her first interviewee of the day on the other side of the door.

"Come in!" She called.

The door swung open, and a woman strode in, her hands shoved deep into the pockets of her white lab coat. She was tall and slender, with dirty blonde hair that she'd thrown back into a high ponytail, and if Emily had to guess, she'd have said the woman was in her mid-forties.

"Doctor Asquith?" she asked, standing up quickly. The woman pursed her lips, looking from the table, to the box of files by Emily's feet, before her icy gaze finally settled on Emily herself. Her eyes narrowed, just for a moment, and Emily realized with a start that the woman was judging her, taking in every detail she could before she went any further.

"You must be the psychologist." She kicked the door shut behind herself using the heel of one of her scuffed trainers, with her hands still in her pockets.

Yeah, Emily thought to herself, *this has to be Meredith Asquith.* Meredith was the only doctor Emily was due to interview who hailed from London, and there was no mistaking that clipped British accent when she spoke.

"I'm Emily Porter, I'm here with the audit team." She offered her hand, but Meredith didn't take it. She glanced down at it, almost like it was a piece of trash someone had tried to hand to her, and then slumped down in the spare chair without a word.

Off to a great start then. Emily lowered herself into her own chair with a small smile, clearing her throat. "Shall we get started?"

"Unless there's something else you'd rather do instead. It's not like I'm busy." Meredith's tone was frosty, and Emily couldn't help but bristle at it, just a little.

FIVE

The first sessions at hospitals were always the worst, so Emily wasn't entirely surprised by Meredith's attitude. No one enjoyed being audited—the idea of strangers coming into your place of work with the sole intention of poking holes in your methods was enough to make anyone squirm—but doctors hated it more than most.

Emily had prepared herself mentally for this. It was part of her job description to not allow people to get under her skin when they were resistant to the audit, and she was used to it. But even with all of her hours of training and experience behind her, Emily couldn't help but be just a *little* surprised at how cold Meredith was straight away. Most people at least *pretended* not to be bothered by the audit team, for the sake of common courtesy if nothing else. Once the questions began they would inevitably end up getting defensive, but Meredith seemed to have skipped that step entirely.

"Is it alright if I record these sessions?" Emily asked, placing the digital voice recorder on the table between them. Meredith looked down at it for a few moments, and then, with her brow furrowed, she looked back up.

"Do I have a choice?"

"Of course. I'll be making notes either way, the only difference is, if there's a recording of the conversation then there's no way for me to misremember anything you've said, or misquote you." Meredith still didn't look convinced, so she spoke up again. "The device is secure and fingerprint-protected so no one else can access the files. Plus it'll mean I don't have to keep asking you the same questions over and over again. I won't take up as much of your time. "

That was the argument that spoke to Meredith, clearly. She still didn't look happy about the prospect of her interviews being recorded, but she nodded, albeit hesitantly. "Okay."

"Great." Emily hit Record on the device. "This is the first interview with Doctor Meredith Asquith. Doctor Asquith, can you just confirm for me that you've consented to have these interviews recorded?"

"I have."

She certainly isn't going to be the most talkative subject I've ever interviewed. Emily thought to herself, eyeing the older doctor up and down. Everything about Meredith's body language screamed that she thought this whole affair was just a huge waste of her time; she was lounging back in her chair, staring up at the ceiling rather than bothering to make eye contact, and her arms were folded over her chest.

Closed off, resistant to interview. Emily scribbled down on her notebook, before clearing her throat. "People don't tend to enjoy this process."

"That's shocking."

She smiled gently, leaning back in her own chair to mirror Meredith's body language. "Why do you think that is?"

"Shouldn't *you* be telling *me* that?" Meredith said coldly. "I thought that was your job, figuring out why people do things?"

"Well, you're the one who doesn't want me here," Emily pointed out, "I was hoping you could give me some insight."

"Well that would hardly be fair, would it? Then I'd just be doing your job for you."

Emily couldn't help but smile a little at that. She'd sat across the table from a lot of people during the course of her job, and everyone reacted differently to her questions. Some people were genuinely helpful—they figured if they just told her what she wanted to know then they'd be able to get out faster. Some were aggressive, and when they didn't like a question they made sure Emily knew it; that was why she opted not to be part of the prison audit team any longer.

Meredith didn't fall into either of those extremes. It didn't seem as though she was going to be what Emily would consider *helpful* by any means, but she wasn't aggressively standoffish either. She was just... cold. And Emily didn't mind cold.

"Most of the time, people don't enjoy audits because they're worried someone will find out about the thing they did that they would rather no one ever knew about." She explained, even though she suspected Meredith was smart enough to know it already. "Maybe they're worried a second glance at the patient who died on the table will show they're more culpable than they first thought. Perhaps they haven't kept on top of their paperwork, and they know we're going to find discrepancies, or shortcuts they shouldn't have taken."

She paused, tilting her head to one side as she looked the doctor up and down. That wasn't the case with Meredith though. Her employee file was outstanding—she had the highest success rate in her department, had the fewest days out of the hospital on sick leave or vacation. She was a model employee (although potentially a workaholic). Meredith wasn't concerned about her shortcomings being exposed, because as far as she could tell, the doctor didn't *have* any. That meant it was something else.

"You think this is a waste of your time, don't you?" she said finally. The corner of Meredith's mouth twitched into what might have become a smile, and then she met Emily's gaze finally.

"Yes."

"Why? You don't think there's some merit to making sure the hospital and its staff are as effective as possible? I'd argue that should be at the top of your priority list, wouldn't you?"

"I think saving people's lives should be at the top of my priority list," Meredith said sharply.

"You don't think we should be identifying the weak links in your team? Surely that would only help. Patients would get better care; other doctors wouldn't have to run around picking up the slack for their less competent co-workers... Doesn't that appeal to you?"

"If you're looking for a weak link in the surgical staff, you're wasting your time talking to me," Meredith said coolly. "You'd be better off looking at the guy who's getting sued for malpractice, or the Fellow who screwed up blood work, and nearly ended up telling the wrong patient he was positive for Hep C. Don't you think that would be a better use of your time?"

"Are you telling me who I *should* be interviewing?" Emily cocked her head to one side. "I thought you weren't going to do my job for me."

Meredith sucked in air through her teeth, looking Emily up and down slowly for a few moments before she continued. "If you asked anyone in this hospital who the weak links are on the staff, they wouldn't point the finger at me. Take a look at my file, you'll see."

"Oh, I already have," Emily assured her. "I know if I ever need brain surgery, you're the doctor I'd want operating on me."

"Why do I feel a 'but' coming?"

"*But,*" Emily continued. "I don't really care about your record in the OR. I'm not a doctor, I'm not the one who'll look into your past surgeries. To be honest, those case files don't really interest me, not for the purpose of these interviews."

"So what *does* interest you?"

"What's underneath those scrubs," Emily pointed to the pale blue scrubs Meredith was wearing under her white coat. A beat of silence followed her words, while Meredith looked down at herself, and then back up at Emily slowly.

"Under *these* scrubs?" she repeated, tugging the fabric. "These ones specifically?"

Emily pursed her lips, realizing the double meaning of what she'd just said. She could tell from the hint of a smile on Meredith's lips that the older woman was trying to get her flustered, but she wasn't going to let it happen, and she pushed on ahead. "You know what I mean. Medical skills aren't the only thing you're being judged on. Surgery is a team sport, so your relationship with other people in the department, and in the hospital in general, is important."

She scoffed, rolling her eyes. "So what, do you want us to do trust falls in the OR before we cut the patients open? Maybe we should hold hands and sing a few campfire songs together."

"You don't think there's some merit to building trust with the people you work with? You're in a high stakes job; when people screw up, lives are on the line."

"It's a good job I don't have a propensity for screwing up then, isn't it?" Meredith said coldly. "Otherwise we'd be in trouble."

"I wasn't accusing you of making mistakes in the OR," Emily assured her. It was obvious Meredith cared a lot about her own reputation in the operating room, even if it was one of the few things she *did* seem to care about, so Emily knew it would be a bad idea to imply she wasn't pulling her weight.

"Then *what are you saying*? What's the point in me being here? You said yourself you're looking for the weaker links, so unless you want me to point them out to you then I think I'm done here."

That was the second time in only a matter of minutes that Meredith had brought up the shortcomings of other doctors. "You're pretty quick to throw your fellow doctors under the bus."

"I'm not throwing anyone under the bus," Meredith snapped. She hadn't raised her voice yet, but in only a few short minutes, she'd gone from acting like the interview was a mild inconvenience to getting seriously annoyed by Emily's questions. "It's not like you won't find this out anyway. It'll come up in your files.

Eager to talk about the problems with her own co-workers while performing surgery. Emily noted, before looking back up at Meredith. "I'm not interested in the surgical files, I told you that. Someone else handles that side of things, and when all of this is over, the hospital will have a nice shiny chart showing the top performers and the biggest liabilities. Don't worry, I've got no doubt you'll get glowing reviews from that side of things."

"If you don't care about my surgical history, then what's this audit about? What else matters?"

Cares about the medicine, the facts and figures. Doesn't care about the human aspect of being a doctor. Likely little to no patient interaction, unlikely to have friendships with fellow doctors.

Emily looked up from her notebook. "Some people would say there's a great deal more to being a doctor than just cutting someone open and peeking at what's inside."

"And *that's* what you're going to critique me on?" Meredith laughed, shaking her head in disbelief. "This is ridiculous."

Ease up, Emily thought to herself. This was only the first session —of many—that she would be having with Meredith, and she didn't want to ruin any shot she had of making a connection with the woman. If she pissed her off too much now, there would be no way she would actually manage to get anything meaningful out of her.

"Why is it ridiculous?" she pressed gently, closing her notebook and laying the pen down on top. She'd learned from experience that some people were a lot more receptive to these kinds of meetings if they didn't feel like everything they said was going to be noted down. It made them uneasy, watching Emily scribble down their words onto the page, and she figured perhaps Meredith was one of those people.

"I have an impeccable record as a doctor. Ask anyone in this hospital, even the people who hate me, and they'll tell you I'm a good surgeon. But because I don't chat around the water cooler, or run around after patients to hold their hands, I'm going to end up with a bad review after all of this?"

There it is.

Every interview was a little different, and over the past few years, Emily had learned that she needed to adapt her meetings with people depending on who she was talking to. Some people needed a little guidance to get the information she wanted. With a little poking and prodding here and there, they would end up giving her the information she needed.

Some people let on more than they were aware of when they answered questions, unconsciously letting information about themselves slip through without even realizing it. Other times, it was best to just ask an open-ended question, and let the other person do the talking. They'd end up revealing something sooner or later.

Meredith, as it turned out, was that person.

"I never said anything about giving you a 'bad review' because of your interpersonal relationships," Emily reminded her, leaning in. "Just that I'd be looking at them. Why, are you worried that's going to be the blemish on your report?"

"No."

That's a lie. Otherwise you wouldn't have been so defensive about it.

"Now that we're on the subject, what *is* your relationship like with the other doctors?" Emily asked, leaning back in the chair again. Meredith offered a half-hearted shrug, saying nothing. The action spoke volumes though—she'd been at the hospital for eight years, and if her first response wasn't to mention at least one person she got on with, that was a good indication that she didn't have many relationships with the rest of the team.

"A shrug doesn't show up very well on the audio recorder," she reminded Meredith, who pursed her lips.

"It's... fine."

"Fine? Eight years of working here, and all you can give me is 'fine'? Is there no one here you like, no one you get on with especially well? No friends? No confidants?"

"Confidants?"

"It's a stressful job, being a doctor. I imagine you must see a lot of things in your job that are hard to deal with emotionally. Surely there must be someone you talk to about all of that? Someone you feel you can lean on?"

"Well there isn't."

"*No one?*"

"Trust me, once you meet the rest of the doctors, that won't seem so surprising to you."

"You don't hold your colleagues in very high regard, do you?"

"They're capable enough in surgery. None of them have cut their own fingers off instead of cutting into a patient." Meredith paused. "Yet."

"Okay..." Emily changed track. "How do you think your colleagues view you?"

"View me?" Meredith seemed genuinely surprised by the question. Her brows shot up, and her eyes widened for a moment as she thought about it. "I... Well, probably not well."

That wasn't completely surprising, given the way Meredith had talked about them so far. Some people were able to hide their real feelings about others when they were around them, but she suspected Meredith wasn't one of them. It was very likely her co-workers knew that she wasn't exactly warm to any of them, and they in turn probably didn't appreciate her attitude.

"Why do you think that—" Emily wanted to probe a little deeper, and try to figure out if Meredith had any ideas on why she might be so unpopular among the other doctors, but just as she spoke up, Meredith's phone began to ring.

"Hold that thought." She pulled the phone out and answered it. "Asquith. What's wrong?"

Someone else was speaking on the other end of the line, and by the look on Meredith's face, it was something to do with a patient. For the first time since she had walked into the office Emily saw something other than irritation or boredom on her face. She was listening intently to whatever was being said on the other end of the line, her brow furrowed as she concentrated.

"Alright, I'll be there in a few minutes. No, no, don't do anything until I get there. I'll take a look at the scans, and then we'll see if we need to operate. Yeah, just put them in my office."

She stood up, stuffing her phone back into her pocket. "I have to go."

"Don't let me stop you." Emily motioned towards the door. It was strange to watch the sudden change come over Meredith like this; she'd sauntered into the room like nothing mattered to her, as if Emily should have considered herself lucky that the doctor would have taken time out of her hectic schedule to talk to her.

When she walked out though, it was like she was a different person entirely. There was none of that arrogance or haughtiness, she didn't roll her eyes or act like she was too good to run out of the room. She walked out without another word, swinging the door shut behind her before Emily could even thank her for her time.

When lives are at risk, Meredith is nothing if not professional.

Emily leaned over and hit the "stop" button of her audio recorder, staring at the seat Meredith had pushed out behind her when she'd rushed out of the room. She'd only made a few notes during the course of their short meeting, but it was enough to get a general overview of the woman.

She didn't work and play well with others, she had little to no respect for the rest of the doctors she worked with, regardless of their actual experience or skill. She didn't seem to care about medicine beyond providing her surgical skills in the operating room, and it was unlikely that she would have any kind of a relationship with patients or their families. She was cold, abrupt, and rude.

Ordinarily, Emily might have just dismissed her as another asshole surgeon—they were a dime a dozen in hospitals, and she'd come across more than her fair share of them over the past few years. Even though everything Meredith had said so far seemed to point to that conclusion, Emily wasn't sure she was ready to write her off as that just yet.

SIX

Meredith made her way to the doctors' lounge with her hands stuffed deep into the pockets of her white coat. Denner was an idiot, it was a wonder he'd even managed to get a license, let alone get board certified. He'd called her because of a dark spot on a brain scan, and he was *convinced* that it was a tumor.

When Meredith arrived, all she did was order the scan to be redone. There was no point in telling a patient that they had a life threatening tumor if they weren't certain it was just a mistake on the part of the radiologist. Sure enough, when the second scan came back, it was clear. Either the tumor had magically disappeared, or it had been an issue with the print out.

The one small miracle that had come from Denner's screw up, of course, was that she'd been called away from her meeting with the woman from the audit team, and she hadn't even needed to come up with an excuse to do so. She'd had a genuine reason for slipping away, and if anyone asked, she could tell them honestly that there had been a patient emergency.

The doctors' lounge wasn't busy when she made her way in, thankfully, and she could grab a coffee for herself without being disturbed. She didn't have long until she had to scrub up for an actual surgery, so a few minutes of peace and quiet was what she really needed.

Of course that couldn't happen, could it? She hadn't even managed to make a coffee for herself before the door to the doctor's lounge opened, and Phil Squires poked his head in. He peered around, locked eyes with Meredith, and beckoned her over with one hand.

"Asquith," he called, "got a patient here for you."

"In the hall? What do you want me to do, scrub up?" Meredith tossed the magazine aside and got to her feet, shoving her hands deep into the pockets of her white coat as she wandered over.

"Don't be an ass," Phil snapped. "It's an *ex*-patient, I think they might even be here to thank you."

"To thank me? For what?"

"Probably saving their life. I assume it wasn't your bedside manner that brought them crawling back here." Phil held the door open enough that Meredith could walk into the hallway, and when she passed him he pointed to where a young mother and her child were standing.

She recognized the girl immediately. It would have been hard to forget her, given that everyone in the OR had been making comments about how young she was. Her name was... Tina. Or Tyler. Or Tasha, maybe? It definitely began with a T, she was sure of it. She'd come in for a Craniotomy about half a year earlier, and back then she'd been pretty sick. She didn't look that sick anymore though.

"Can I help you?" she asked, looking up at the girl's mother.

"Doctor Asquith, I'm so sorry to bother you. You probably don't even remember us, but five months ago, you operated on my little girl, Tamara." The woman smiled nervously, patting the girl's head.

Tamara, damn. I knew it began with T.

"I remember. If there's a problem with her post-op recovery, you're better off heading to the walk in clinic on the ground floor."

"Oh no, there's no problem!" the woman assured her. "No problems at all. I actually... I came here to thank you."

"You wanted to thank me?" she echoed, glancing back over her shoulder. Phil was still lounging in the doorway, his arms folded. "Why?"

"Well, Tamara's starting third grade this year, and... well after all the problems we had last year, it seemed like a miracle that we would be able to see her do that. But you made it happen, and I just wanted... to thank you, to tell you how grateful I am for you helping my little girl."

Meredith looked from the mother to the daughter, who was half hiding, staring up at her with big brown eyes. She looked more than a little confused, and a little scared, which was understandable. The last time she'd seen Meredith, it had been right before they'd cracked her head open.

"You're welcome," Meredith said quietly, before turning around to head back to the doctor's lounge.

"Tamara actually has something for you." The woman called, trying to get Meredith's attention one last time.

Jesus lady, I get it, she thought, turning back to look at the two of them. The little girl was clutching a card in her chubby fist now, which she held out to Meredith.

"Thanks," she opened it to see the words 'Thank you Docktor' scribbled in messy pink pen. "You're welcome. Good to see you're... you know. Better."

"She's even getting back into soccer." The girl's mother beamed at Meredith. "She's joining an after school club and she's—"

"That's great." Meredith cut across her with a tight-lipped smile. Of course the girl was getting back into hobbies she had before the surgery; that was part of what recovery was supposed to be about, wasn't it? "I'm sorry, but I'm busy. I've got to go."

"Oh." The mother's face fell. "I understand. I'm sorry, doctor. You must be busy, we're taking up a lot of your time. I just wanted to make sure you knew how grateful we are to you for what you've done for us."

"Well, you're successful. Now I know."

With that, Meredith turned on her heel and walked off, heading back into the doctor's lounge, closely followed by Phil.

"That might be the first time I've seen a family actually thank you," he said, joining Meredith as she walked over to the coffee machine. "I take it they didn't really talk to you much before the surgery."

"Why'd you think that?" Meredith dropped the card on the countertop as she poured herself a coffee, not bothering to offer one to Phil as well.

"If they had done, they'd have known this was a waste of time," he murmured, picking the card up to have a look inside.

"Kid misspelled 'doctor'." Meredith stirred one sugar into her coffee and blew on it to cool it. "Unless she's German, in which case she actually spelled it right."

"Shocking," Phil deadpanned. "A six-year-old who can't spell doctor. That must have ruined the whole card for you."

"Shut up." Meredith snatched the card back from him and stuffed it into her pocket. "I don't know why they're giving it to me anyway."

"I mean you saved the kid's life. People tend to be grateful for that kind of thing. Well, at least... I know *my* patients tend to be grateful. I get why yours aren't so quick to offer up their thanks, on account of you being an asshole and all."

Meredith scowled at him over the top of her coffee. "Phil, shut *up*."

"Alright, alright." He held his hands up in mock surrender. "I'm sorry I even brought it up. I've got to go anyway, I've got my meeting with the audit team."

"Oh?" Meredith cocked an eyebrow. "I had my meeting with the psychologist this morning."

"How was it?"

"About what you'd expect." She shrugged. "She didn't get the chance to ask much, I had a pre-op consultation to rush to before she could get through the questions."

"What did she ask you? What's she like?"

Meredith sighed heavily, rolling her eyes. Phil was obviously considering the best way to start his charm offensive. "She wanted to know about my relationships with the rest of the staff here, kept asking if I got on well with the other members of the team, if I trusted them."

"Do you?"

"Depends on what I'm trusting them *with*. Some people here I wouldn't trust to change the tires on my car."

"That's fair." He snorted, shaking his head. "What a waste of time... Do they think this micromanaging crap is going to help us at all?"

"Emily told me she wanted to help us find the weaker links in the team, so we can be stronger when we come out the other side. Or... Something like that."

"Great." He snorted again, rolling his eyes. "I can't wait."

"Yeah, you have fun with that." Meredith turned away, not bothering with a goodbye. Unlike most people in the hospital, she knew Phil wouldn't be offended by her abrupt exit. He was used to it, after the years they'd worked together, so he didn't even bother to call a hurried "bye then" after her as she left the room.

SEVEN

Emily had a long list of preliminary meetings to get through once she was done with Meredith. Each one went by fairly smoothly, especially compared to the battle she'd expected to fight on arrival. At the end of each meeting, Emily moved on to ask each staff member a handful of questions about their co-workers, trying to find out how they worked together.

It didn't seem like the hospital had a big problem with teamwork and cooperation. Most of the doctors and nurses Emily spoke to were pretty complimentary when it came to the rest of their team, with one notable exception.

Meredith.

Emily was curious to know what other people thought of her. From the comments in her file, it seemed like no one on the staff could stand her, but she figured surely that wasn't true. There must have been *someone* who liked her, at least a little, otherwise she would have struggled to maintain her position for as long as she had done. As it turned out though, there really wasn't anyone who was a fan of the neurosurgeon.

Everyone had said similar things to say about the woman. Whenever Emily asked specifically about their thoughts on Doctor Asquith, they'd struggle to hold back a groan, or they'd roll their eyes and shake their heads. One nurse even snorted and let out a withering sigh.

Without fail, they'd all respond in the same way. Once their initial gut reaction was out of the way, they'd try and find something complimentary to say about her, but they'd come up against a brick wall in an instant. They couldn't even bring themselves to lie about her to give her a real compliment.

"Doctor Asquith is..." They'd say, looking around the room like that would be able to help them find *something* kind to say about her. They'd falter, stutter for a moment, and finally land on the fact that she was a brilliant surgeon. If there was some kind of surgical Olympics, she would have the gold.

But that was it, the only thing any of them could say. Emily would press them for a little more information, and then, somewhat hesitantly, they would admit that she was a difficult person to get along with. Most of them rattled off the same reasons that she had already seen in Meredith's file. There was only one doctor who didn't seem to struggle with finding a compliment for Meredith in the way that the rest of the staff did; Phil Squires, the other neurosurgeon.

He reminded Emily of every drunk middle-aged divorcee who'd hit on her in bars during college, and when he flashed her a smirk and winked at her from across the table, she felt her skin crawl. He was the most stereotypical surgeon she could have come across, from his smarmy, self-confident attitude to the way he bragged about his achievements.

"I graduated from Johns Hopkins." That was one of the first things he told her when he sat down, like he thought she might have missed it in his file. He just wanted to make sure that she knew how impressive he was, it seemed.

Out of all of the people she spoke to that day, he was probably the least interesting of the bunch. He was self-absorbed, self-aggrandizing, and other than the school he graduated from, nothing really stood out about him. The one thing that *did* get Emily's attention though, was the way he spoke about Meredith. Unlike everyone else, Phil didn't seem to struggle to find a way to describe her, and he didn't start with a compliment.

"Oh, *Meredith*? Yeah, she's a real peach. The uh... Belle of the ball, here at City General." he chuckled, shaking his head slowly. "You know that British stereotype, of the stiff upper lip? I'm pretty sure they got the idea for that from watching her."

"What do you mean by that?" Emily asked, leaning in a little bit.

"Oh, you know... She's not really interested in making small talk and isn't interested in gossip. She eats alone in her office most days, and when she *does* sit in the cafeteria, she doesn't eat with anyone else. Not even others from the surgical staff. Except me, sometimes." He flashed another grin at Emily. "I won her over with my stunning personality."

"Clearly. Are you two friends?"

"Friends?" Phil laughed at that. "No. No, we're not friends. We're colleagues who work together, that's all."

Emily frowned, a little confused. "But you said..."

"We eat together sometimes, that's all. That doesn't make us friends. We're two of the best doctors on the staff, we see things the same way most of the time, but that doesn't make us buddies. We don't go out for beers after work, we don't have barbecues at each other's places on the weekends. Sometimes we sit at the same table, we eat food, and we talk about cases or procedures."

"So who *is* she friends with?" Emily asked. "It doesn't seem like many people here are fond of her."

"That's because they aren't. And that's the way Meredith wants it. She's here to do her job, and that's it. She's worked in this hospital for eight years, if she wanted a friend here, she'd have made one by now."

"What about outside of work?"

Phil shook his head. "I've got no idea. I don't even know where she lives," he admitted, chuckling. "I don't think anyone does. She never talks about herself, never talks about family. I don't think she's got any kind of a life outside this hospital, and she probably knows it. It's probably why she never talks about herself; there's nothing *to* talk about."

"Mm." Emily leaned back again in her seat, nodding.

"She said she met with you this morning."

"She did?"

"Yeah," Phil grinned. "I can't imagine she gave you much uh... information on anything especially anything personal."

Emily shot him a thin smile and nodded, more at how he responded rather than at the answer itself. She had gotten just about everything she could out of him, and she wasn't really in the mood to spend any more time with him than was totally necessary. "Thanks for answering those questions, Phil. I think we're done here."

There was more to Meredith Asquith than she was being told, Emily was sure of that. It wasn't that she was asking the wrong questions but perhaps these were just the wrong people to ask. The lack of information was intriguing. That in itself told a story but she wanted to know more.

————

Meredith was already stewing by the time she drove into the parking lot that evening. Auditors and these independent consultants were a part of the job, a necessary evil that she and the rest of the medical staff were simply going to have to accept, and Meredith knew that. It was important for the welfare of the patients to make sure none of them were about to go postal in the OR. All of that had been explained to her, over and over again.

But that didn't mean she had to *like* it.

As Meredith made her way up to her apartment, she passed by a few of her neighbors who were heading out for the evening. They exchanged a few nods, a wave here or there, but other than that she was left alone. Maybe they could see just how exhausted and pissed off she was, and knew that it was better not to bother her.

She came to a stop outside her apartment, and leaned against the wall as she fished her key out from the depths of her purse. She knew that it was somewhere in there, she could remember tossing it in as she'd left for work that morning, but it was lost amongst the mess of tissues, band aids and at least two chap sticks.

"Ugh!" She groaned loudly, dropping to a crouch outside her door. She put her bag on the floor to dig around inside with both hands, peering in for a better look. Those keys were *somewhere* in there, surely. Surely she hadn't accidentally thrown them in her locker at the hospital, had she?

Please don't tell me I have to drive all the way back to the hospital. Just then her hand closed around the key. "Thank *god.*"

Meredith straightened up and shoved the key in the lock with just a little more force than was completely necessary, but before she could open the door, she heard a voice from down the hall, around the corner where the stairwell was. A woman's voice.

There were only three condos on her floor; hers, the elderly man at the end who had that asshole of a Pekingese, and the condo that had been empty for months. The condo that no longer seemed like it was completely empty, with what she'd heard a few days earlier. Were these her new neighbors coming up the stairs?

As much as she wanted to just get inside her apartment and hide away from the rest of the world, Meredith's curiosity got the better of her. She never had guests over, and the man at the end of the hall was only ever visited by his son, so she wanted to get a glimpse at the strangers. Who was it?

She got her answer only a few moments later, although she wished that she hadn't. Two women rounded the corner, chatting away together, and as they got closer, Meredith realized that she recognized them.

Oh god... No. No way.

It was an older woman, probably in her early sixties, who was accompanied by a younger woman that Meredith had already seen *far* too much of.

Emily.

"What are *you* doing here?" Meredith asked, her voice coming out far colder than she had intended. Emily stopped abruptly in the hallway at the sound of her voice, and when she recognized Meredith, she blinked in surprise.

"Oh, hello."

Meredith glanced over her shoulder at the unoccupied condo next to hers, the wheels in her head spinning as she tried to make sense of this. There was *one* explanation that made sense...

"Are you... Are you living here?" she asked, jerking her thumb in the direction of the other condo. "I thought you said your team wouldn't be here for long."

"We won't be." Emily smiled. "But we still need a place to live. The company rented out a few properties for employees. It's cheaper than hotels and allows us to be more comfortable. It's just for a few months."

A few months. Meredith looked at the potted plant in Emily's hands, and the box that the other woman was holding. They really did look like they were moving in.

"You live here too?" Emily either hadn't picked up on Meredith's less than thrilled expression, or she was choosing to pointedly ignore it. "We're neighbors!"

"Apparently so."

"Well," Emily passed by her, still smiling. "this'll be fun, won't it?"

Fun wasn't exactly the word Meredith would have used to describe this situation. A gross invasion of her privacy, maybe. Fun? Absolutely not.

This building may not have been much, but it was far away from where most of her co-workers lived. She could wander the streets freely without bumping into anyone that she knew, she didn't have to worry about making awkward small talk if she came face to face with another doctor while in line at Starbucks. This apartment, this building, this neighborhood—all of it was hers, and she didn't have to share it with anyone else. And now the woman who would be poking around into her personal life was moving in right next door?

Of all the buildings in all the world... she thought bitterly, looking between the two women. How was this fair? There were doctors living all over the city, most of them much closer to the hospital than Meredith. How come none of *them* were getting housed right next to the audit team?

"Don't worry," Emily said with a small smile. She must have seen the look of horror on Meredith's face. "I'm off the clock when I'm here. I'm not going to bug you about the audit . I'm just... your neighbor. That's fine, right?"

Not really, no.

"I suppose I don't have much of a choice in the matter, do I?" she said pointedly, motioning between the two women. "You both seem like you're settling in just fine."

"We are." The older woman's tone was just as clipped as Meredith's. She probably wasn't happy with the frosty welcome the two had received. "I'm sorry, I don't think we've met."

Emily hurried to introduce them, somewhat apologetically. "This is Doctor Meredith Asquith, she's one of the surgeons at City General. I actually had my first interview with her today. Meredith, this is Angela Thompson, she's one of my co-workers at the agency. She's a data analyst."

"Neurosurgeon," Meredith corrected, as Angela stuck out her hand to shake.

"Sorry?" Emily asked.

"I'm a *neurosurgeon.* I spent three extra years in training to get that title, I like it when people use it," Meredith said, without taking Angela's hand, which was still extended out to her. There was a moment of silence while the three women looked at each other, and then slowly, Angela pulled her hand back in.

"Sorry," Emily murmured.

"It's fine." Meredith glanced at Angela again before she pushed her door open. "It was nice to meet you, I'll see you around."

As she stepped inside her apartment, Meredith heard both women say goodbye, but she didn't wait for them to finish talking before she let the door swing shut behind her, cutting them off sharply.

She waited there for a few moments with her back pressed to the door, listening to the sound of Emily and Angela as they headed into the apartment through the wall. Then, once their door closed, she let out a low, mournful groan. All she'd wanted to do since she'd set foot in the hospital that morning was to come home. She just wanted to sit in her front room with a blanket pulled up around herself and a book in her hand, and forget all about the audit, and Emily.

How was she supposed to do that now?

EIGHT

It had been a week since the audit had started, and Meredith had managed to do a pretty good job of avoiding Emily during that time. Their shifts rarely coincided, and when she met the dark haired, younger woman on the stairwell they were both far too busy for much more than a quick "hello." At work, Meredith could pretty much forget about the audit when she was locked away in her office; sometimes someone would pop their head in to ask her a question about a file she'd handed over, but that was about it.

The rest of the hospital was a different matter entirely though. If she risked stepping foot into the hallways, she'd be met with the nervous whispers of doctors and nurses alike, who were all worried they were going to be caught out for something. Even when she scrubbed up for surgery, Meredith heard about doctors who'd been pulled in for meetings with the psych team, spending hours in there with them going over their files. She had to listen to constant gossip about who was the most likely to have mistakes on their record, who was the weakest link out of each department.

It never seemed to end, and she was sick of it.

Thankfully, no one bothered to ask her what she thought of what was going on. Conversations whirled around, but never actively included her, because folks seemed to have realized that there was no point in asking her opinion. No one asked how *her* meetings had gone, or whether she'd been asked to answer questions on an old surgery, so she just had to listen to them swapping their own stories.

As the week wore on, she was getting more and more desperate to spend time away from the hospital. If she was lost in a book or on a run then she didn't have to think too hard, and she wouldn't risk dwelling on the audit, their intrusion, nor their findings. So, rather than going for a run a few times a week, she found herself using it as an outlet for all her frustrations most days, and sometimes more than once a day. She'd head out in the early morning, long before the sun was up, and then head to work. Once it was over, she would come home, go for another run, and then when she was suitably exhausted, she'd pass out and begin it all over again.

It was a routine. It might not have been a very exciting one, but it was one that worked for her. So on the Friday after the audit had started, Meredith rose early, headed out on a run, and came back before sunrise, ready to start the day. It was a cold morning, especially when it was dark, and as she ran down the street towards her block, she felt the cool air whip against her cheeks.

She came to a stop outside her apartment building, and bent over for a moment to rest her hands against her knees, bracing herself. Her heart rate began to slow, and her breathing started to return to normal after a few moments, and once the blood seemed to be flowing the way it was supposed to, she straightened up again to look around the deserted street.

The sky was *just* starting to get a little lighter. The first few rays of sunlight were poking out from the horizon, and in the distance, she could see the heavy blanket of darkness start to fade out into the pale blue of a morning sky. It wouldn't be long until the streets around her were filled with people going about their day.

Meredith raised her hands up above her head and gave a long, full stretch. She had time for a quick shower before she headed to work, and then she'd need to get going, ready for another session with Emily. Another meeting where she'd have to listen to some psycho analysis garble as she tried to tell her how she was feeling.

And then, as if Meredith's thoughts alone had summoned her, she spotted Emily through the double doors of the building. She'd just come out of the stairwell, dressed in running gear of her own with a bottle of water in one hand, and when she spotted Meredith on the pavement outside, she waved, smiling. Even her small pert breasts moving rhythmically as she stretched a little didn't make her any more welcoming to Meredith.

Fantastic, she thought to herself as the young woman walked through the lobby to join her in the crisp morning air. *As if I don't have to deal with her enough today already, here she is again.*

"Morning." Emily rubbed her hands together as she stepped outside. "Are you going out for a run?"

"Just coming back from one, actually."

"Ah, that's too bad." She smiled brightly. "I was hoping you'd be able to give me a little tour of the best spots in town to run. I'm still figuring out a good route for myself."

Meredith inhaled slowly, looking the younger woman up and down. Was this sunshiney Californian attitude supposed to be another way of making her feel at ease, so that she could come to Emily with some sob story for her report? Or was she just genuinely asking? It was difficult to tell either way.

"Depends on when you're running," she admitted. "If you're going alone, and it's dark? I'd stay away from the river. The running path isn't well lit, there have been a few problems down there. The park's pretty good for a run, and at this time of the day you're prob-ably going to meet some other people too."

"Ah okay. Which way's the park?"

Meredith pointed back down the street, in the direction she had come from. "It's down there, about two blocks, and then on your left."

"Uh huh…" Emily looked down the street, nodding slowly to herself. "You think there'll be many runners?"

"There's going to be a few, probably." Meredith had actually passed a handful on her way back to the apartment building.

"Is that why you go out so early?" Emily asked, her gaze flickering from the near-empty street to Meredith herself. There was a smile on her lips as she spoke, almost like she was teasing her. "So you can avoid the other runners?"

"I have an early shift. So by extension, I had an early run," Meredith explained, cocking an eyebrow. "You know there isn't a *reason* for everything, right? There isn't some deep dark psychological reason for everything people do."

"I never said there was," Emily pointed out. Meredith faltered at that, and pursed her lips. In fairness, Emily never *had* said those words, but that didn't mean she wasn't thinking them.

"Anyway," she murmured, moving on. "The running path opens up from the entry to the park. You can't miss it."

"Great. Thanks for the help." Emily smiled gently, and held up one hand in a wave. "I'll see you later, shall I?"

"Yeah, sure." Meredith watched as Emily started to run down the road, the young woman's body was fit and she moved with grace but she couldn't help but roll her eyes. Not only had the audit team invaded her place of work, but two of them were living in the condo next to hers. Even worse, one of them was a runner. Slowly but surely, that damn team was creeping into every facet of her life, taking root in every part of her day. Sooner or later she wasn't going to be able to turn around without bumping into one of them.

"Is nothing sacred anymore?" she sighed, before heading into her apartment building. "*Nothing?*"

————

When Meredith walked into the hospital an hour later, things were just as chaotic as always. She had a surgery booked in for that day, on top of her meeting with Emily. Between the preparation, meeting with the patient, and then actually *performing* the surgery, she was hardly going to have the time to sit down, let alone meet with a psychologist.

She wasn't due to meet with Emily until nine, which meant she had time to familiarize herself with the patient's scan's and notes and prepare herself for the day ahead. From there, her day was probably just going to be one long blur.

She was only in her office for an hour or so when a knock at the door interrupted her, and she looked up to see Emily standing there, with her folder and recorder in hand. "Good morning."

"Hi." Emily smiled. "I know you're busy, so I figured I'd come to you for our meetings, to make it a little easier."

"That's thoughtful of you." Meredith leaned back in her chair. "Or you're worried I just won't turn up."

"Well there's that too, to be honest," she admitted, taking the seat across the desk from Meredith. "I mean, you did run out of our last meeting."

"That was an emergency."

"Mm, so I gathered." Emily set the recorder down. "I noticed how quickly you ran off, so I figured it must have been serious. I was curious, so I went to check what had happened, and found out that it was actually just a problem with the image machinery."

"I didn't know that at the time," Meredith admitted. In fairness, she really had thought there was a serious problem that needed her attention.

"No, that's true. But when you found out that you weren't *actually* needed, you never came back to finish our meeting, did you?"

"I—" Meredith faltered at that, and smiled ruefully. "I guess I didn't."

"I didn't really get much out of you last time, given how short our session was and part of my job is to get an understanding of how effective the behavior of teams are in the hospital so I've been asking other staff about their coworkers. Needless to say that means I've gathered some thoughts and information that relate to you."

"And what did they tell you?"

"You are a good surgeon. Albeit you're hard to get to know. You don't have any friends here, you don't really like to interact with anyone. No one knows anything about your personal life, they don't even know where you live." She paused, and grinned at Meredith. "Except for me, of course."

"So what do you need to know?"

"I guess I want to know why." Emily shrugged. "I want to figure out why you don't seem to want to connect with any of your team members. Why your dealings with them are perfunctory. "

"I'm not a football player, they aren't team members. They're colleagues, and sometimes they assist my surgeries. That's the extent of our relationship, and that's how I want to keep it."

"My surgeries," Emily repeated with a nod. "Why?"

Meredith shrugged. "Maybe I'm just a difficult person to get to know."

"I guess that might be it. I just..." Emily laughed, shaking her head slowly. "I guess I'm just intrigued, that's all. A lot of the doctors I meet can't wait to talk to someone about all their skills in the OR, but not you. You're very guarded."

Meredith tapped on the desk a couple of times. "Is that your professional conclusion? I'm guarded? Your report looks like it's going to be very short."

The corners of Emily's eyes creased a little into a smile. "Do you think anyone on your team is up to your standard of medicine?"

Meredith snorted and rolled her eyes. "I'm board certified. You know what that means, right? I'm the only board certified Neurosurgeon in the hospital. So no, I don't think anyone matches my standards."

Emily nodded along slowly. "I'm only asking because... well, to be honest, you don't seem very ready to talk about yourself, but you jumped at the chance to talk about the shortcomings of other people. I just found that interesting."

"Are you saying I should play nicely with the rest of the doctors?" Meredith asked, tilting her head to one side.

"I'm saying it might not be a bad idea is all. It doesn't seem like anyone here really knows you. I can't help but feel like that might impact your work negatively."

"I promise you, it hasn't," Meredith assured her. "If you'd like, we can go through my history?"

Emily laughed, and shook her head. "No no, that's fine. I might pop back later to have another chat with you, Meredith. I just wanted to... Drop in, say hi."

She stood up and gathered her things, before heading for the door. Meredith watched her go, a little confused—she'd made a big show of coming down here to see her, and now she was just going to turn around and leave? What was even the point of showing up?

"Oh!" Emily paused at the door, and then turned to smile. "I was actually wondering, are you busy this evening?"

"Why?"

"Are you?" she pressed.

Meredith hesitated for a moment before she answered. "I'm... not. Why?"

"I was wondering... I know you went out for a run this morning, but I was hoping maybe you could show me one of the running routes around the city. The park was pretty nice, but you mentioned the river, and I was thinking..." Emily trailed off, before shaking her head. "Never mind. You don't want to, do you?"

Meredith didn't, not really. She liked running alone, focusing on nothing but the feeling of her feet hitting the ground over and over again, but then again, she didn't like the idea of Emily going out onto the running path alone at night. The trail that ran parallel to the river wasn't always the best place to be when you were a woman. Besides, she'd been planning on going for another run that evening anyway.

"That depends." She cocked her head to one side.

"On what?"

"On whether you can keep up with me or not. I don't like waiting around for people, I don't want you slowing me down."

Emily looked surprised that Meredith was even considering her suggestion but a smile blossomed across her features. "You're okay with me joining you?"

"How good are you?"

Emily walked back over to the desk, grinning now. Meredith had never seen anyone look so happy to be invited on a run. "I'm very good."

"Then you can come along. Six o'clock, my place. If you're late, I'll just go without you."

"Then I won't be late," Emily assured her with a smile, before turning on her heel and heading out of Meredith's office.

NINE

At precisely six o'clock, Emily stood in front of the door to Meredith's condo, eager to go out on a run. There was a part of her that was hoping that outside of the hospital setting the older woman would relax a little bit, and maybe the two would be able to have a real conversation, but she wasn't holding out a whole lot of hope for that, given how poorly their sessions had gone.

It took Meredith a little longer than she expected to answer the door, and when she finally did, she was wearing a bathrobe, holding a towel over her head. Water dripped from her damp locks onto the floorboards in front of her, and her skin still glistened with moisture—she must have only just gotten out of the shower.

With her hair free falling around her face and in her natural environment, Meredith had a different air about her. She seemed softer and dare Emily admit it but attractive. And then Meredith spoke.

"You're early."

"Don't think I am, actually." Emily smiled at her. "I think we agreed on six, didn't we?"

Meredith groaned gently. "Yeah, we did. It's six already?"

"I'm afraid so. Do you want me to come back later?"

"No, it's alright." Meredith sighed. "Come in, I'll just get dressed and dry my hair off."

She opened the door properly, and beckoned Emily to come inside the apartment. During their sessions, Emily had always wondered what Meredith's home life looked like, and now she had the chance to take a peek at the way she lived. A person's home said a lot about them, but Emily's job never afforded her that luxury. She only ever got the chance to talk to people on neutral ground, or if she was lucky, their office.

As she walked into the apartment, Emily had no idea of what to expect. With some of the people she talked to, she could make an educated guess—some of the more arrogant doctors were likely to have their medical degree somewhere where every guest would have to see it, some were so busy and unorganized that it wouldn't have been surprising if their houses looked like a college student's room. There were doctors who were in it for the money, who owned luxury houses in gated communities, and there were first year residents who were barely making rent and probably ate instant noodles for dinner most nights.

But through their interviews together, Meredith had remained an enigma. She hadn't given up any indication that she even had a personal life, and none of her colleagues had been able to shed any light on it either. Emily hadn't even known whether or not she was single.

When she walked over the threshold and heeled off her running shoes, Emily took a quick look around, and couldn't help but be just a little disappointed in what she saw. It was very—plain. She couldn't see any art on the walls, no photographs to decorate the place, no flowers to brighten up the front room. Nothing.

"I'll be back in a few minutes," Meredith murmured, before walking across the front room towards the closed door on the other side of the apartment. This place had the same layout as Emily's, so she assumed it was Meredith's bedroom.

When Meredith's door closed behind her, Emily took the chance to look around the condo a little more, although she quickly realized there wasn't all that much worth seeing. There was a shoe rack pressed up against the door, with a couple of pairs of old sneakers, a single pair of ballet flats, and her running shoes. A single rain jacket hung from the hook above the shoe rack, and a lone umbrella hung beside it.

She wasn't married then, or in a serious relationship. Emily had wondered if part of the reason Meredith had been so resistant to making friends with her coworkers was due to a hectic home life, but it didn't exactly look like that was the case.

If Emily was honest, the apartment felt like something out of a showroom, or like one of those places she sometimes saw on real estate sites—the ones that hadn't yet been built and furnished, so the developers just mocked up an idea of what it would look like when the furniture was in place. It didn't look like a *home*, like someone lived there.

The kitchen was off to the side of the front room, just like Emily's. She poked her head through the doorway into the kitchen, trying to see if there was anything interesting to be found. There wasn't. Other than a half empty glass of water on the side, there was nothing in there. No mugs of coffee that had been sipped and abandoned, no dishes in the sink.

It looked so... cold. She'd only been living in the place next door for a week, and it was temporary accommodation anyway, but that apartment *still* felt more like her home than Meredith's place.

Emily wandered back into the front room with a sigh, trailing her hand along the back of the couch. There was a box of tissues on the coffee table, an unlit candle, and the TV remote, but that was all. Curious to try and find out *anything* about Meredith, Emily stooped low and sniffed it.

Hm, lavender. She wouldn't have pinned Meredith as the lavender type, but then again, she reminded herself, she really knew nothing about the woman other than her job.

Her gaze fell on the bookcase that lined the back wall, behind the television. That was the one part of the room that actually made the place look like someone lived there. The shelves were lined with books, and not just medical journals, judging by the covers. Emily wandered over and began to browse, trailing her fingertips along the spines of some of the books.

Meredith had built up quite a collection, and it looked like it was a few years in the making; some of the books were new and shiny, but others were older and looked well-worn. Emily saw cracked spines, faded titles, and when she pulled one book out to peek at it, yellowed pages.

She's a reader... Who likes lavender candles.

It wasn't much, but she knew more about Meredith than she had done when she'd walked into the apartment. More importantly than that, she had managed to get a little more information than *any* of their therapy sessions had produced so far, so it was a start.

"Looking for book recommendations?"

Emily turned at the sound of Meredith's voice, and found her standing in the doorway to her bedroom, pulling on a pair of socks. She grinned, and went back to looking at the bookshelf. "I've actually got quite a few of these myself."

"You do?"

"Mm. It looks like we've got similar tastes. I never took you to be much of a romance fan," she admitted, tapping the spine of one of the books. "*The Price of Salt* is good."

"You're a fan?"

"It's not my favorite, but it's definitely good." She smiled gently, before stepping away from the bookshelf. Meredith cocked an eyebrow.

"What's your favorite?"

"*Desert of the Heart* by Jane Rule. I actually..." Emily trailed off with a laugh, shaking her head slowly. "It's kind of embarrassing, actually. I uh, I named my dog Reno because of the book. It's set there, and I... Yeah."

"*Desert of the Heart...* I've seen the film. Years ago, but I've never gotten around to reading the book. I'd heard it was better than the film."

"It is! Plus the woman who wrote it was actually a lesbian, which is good." She grinned over at Meredith. "I always get suspicious when I see lesbians written by straight men. I actually just get suspicious when I see *women* written by men in general."

To her surprise, Meredith cracked a small smile at that. "Yeah."

"It's the same with TV and film, and the uh... what's it called? Kill Your Gays trope." Emily grimaced. "It's gross."

"Yeah, I'm bored of watching straight people killing off gay characters for the sake of shock value," Meredith agreed, smiling gently. "Just so they can pat themselves on the back for including a character who's not straight."

For the first time since they had met, Emily realized Meredith wasn't scowling at her, or barely concealing her irritation. The two were actually having a conversation, and Meredith wasn't just responding with a sarcastic quip, or a one word non-answer. Her eyes were shining and engaged causing Emily to smile back brightly.

"Oh, and don't get me started on the sex scenes that straight guys put in shows," she carried on, shaking her head. "You can tell straight away when it's a guy that's written it, and women weren't consulted."

Emily paused as she said that, realizing that she had probably overstepped a professional boundary or two. It wasn't like she hadn't talked with clients about sex before—she had done, plenty of times—but that usually came up in a purely professional context, not... whatever this was. Although she couldn't say for certain, she thought the last time she felt like this had been on a date.

"Uh, yeah," she finished lamely, managing a nervous laugh. "Anyway—"

"No, you're right." Meredith joined her at the bookshelf, dragging her fingertip along the edge of a series of books. "You can always tell when it's been written by someone who doesn't have experience. There's always something off about it."

Her voice dropped just a little, bordering on an almost husky tone as she looked over the volumes of books on her shelf, and as she did so, Emily followed her gaze. "Something off?"

"Oh, they've never experienced it, so they don't know how to describe it. They're just... mimicking what they've seen in badly acted porn. There's nothing real about it. When you read a book, you're reading for immersion. You want to feel what the character feels, to know what they want, and it's hard to get that when the author has no idea what they're talking about."

Meredith paused, and then met Emily's gaze with a small smile. "So I agree. Lesbian sex should be left to the lesbians."

A silence followed her words that Emily never would have expected. Something was keeping her locked in place, staring into Meredith's eyes, and for a moment, she swore she saw the other woman's eyes flicker down to her lips, just for a brief moment, and then back up again. Her throat went dry. She cleared her throat. "I uh... I think we should probably um..."

Run. You're supposed to be going for a run.

"I was going to show you the running trail, wasn't I?" Meredith pulled her hand away from the bookcase and let it hang by her side. "Come on, let's head out."

As it turned out, Meredith was a pretty serious runner.

Emily had always prided herself on her physical fitness. Ever since she was a kid she had been sporty; she'd joined the hockey team, the volleyball team, ran track and field in college. She'd never struggled to keep up with another person before, until she ran with Meredith.

The woman was like a machine. She hardly seemed to break a sweat as they ran through the park and up to the river, even though her "warm up" speed was way faster than the pace most people set for themselves. She hardly needed to stop for a break as they made their way along the path either, and it wasn't until Emily begged for a time out that they eventually came to a halt.

"Hold on a moment." Emily called out, coming to a stop by the railing that ran the length of the river. "I need a second. Gotta... gotta catch my breath."

Meredith obliged, and with a wry smile, she wandered back to Emily. "You know you're struggling to keep up out here, right?"

"Yeah," Emily leaned on the iron fencing heavily, panting. It was unbelievable how out of breath she was, and how *fine* Meredith seemed to be. "I noticed that."

"I'm starting to think you're not actually a runner, you know." Meredith rested her elbows on the top of the fencing, glancing at Emily out of the corner of her eye. "Maybe you just keep inviting yourself out with me because you're trying to get me to talk to you more."

"You're very cynical, has anyone ever told you that?" Emily asked, dropping to a crouch as her breathing began to settle a little bit. Her heart was still racing almost impossibly fast though, and the night air was so cold that it hurt her throat. "Is it working?"

Meredith actually chuckled at that, shaking her head. "No. You're going to have to try a little harder than that."

"Do I not look like I'm trying to you?"

"You do." Meredith conceded, looking her up and down slowly. "Just not hard enough."

"You know, none of the other doctors are this difficult to talk to. They don't tend to torture the audit team, just because we're trying to ask them a few personal questions."

"I thought I told you before, I'm not making your job easier for you. Where would the fun be if I did that?" Meredith held out her water bottle as she spoke, offering it out to Emily. "Here, drink."

"I'm fine, thanks." She waved it away as she straightened up, but that only made Meredith roll her eyes.

"*Drink*, for god's sake."

After another moment's hesitation, Emily accepted the bottle of water, popped the cap open, and downed half of it in one go. "Thanks."

"No problem." Meredith took the bottle back and wiped around the rim with her thumb and forefinger, before finishing the rest of it off. "You know there's no need to martyr yourself just to keep up with me, right?"

"Why'd you say that? Are you feeling guilty, putting me through this?"

"No." Meredith shrugged. "It's not my fault you can't keep up. Besides, you're the one that invited yourself on my runs, I've never asked you to join me."

"Well I guess that's true," Emily admitted, looking out over the river for a few moments. The city looked beautiful at night, with the light of restaurants and tower offices reflecting off the dappled surface of the water. There was a certain beauty to urban life that only a handful of people could really appreciate; it wasn't just smog and traffic when you lived in a city.

She turned back to Meredith, who was waiting for her expectantly, tapping her foot against the ground. "I take it you're ready to go?"

"Only if you are. I don't want to stop again in five minutes because you've got a stitch or something."

"Yeah, yeah." Emily waved her hand dismissively. "I get it, I'm a weak mortal, and you're the pro athlete here. Let's go."

Just as she was about to set off again though, Meredith stopped her when she dropped to a crouch. "Hold on. My laces are undone, give me a moment." Emily hung back to wait for her for a few seconds, leaning against the railing yet again.

She closed her eyes for a few moments as she leaned backwards, just allowing the cool breeze to wash over her for a few moments before they started running again. As she did so, she heard the pattering of footsteps coming from further up the path, distant at first, but then quickly growing louder and louder. Emily opened one eye just a crack, to see a young blonde girl tearing down the path at full speed, her bag flying out behind her as she giggled.

Meredith had obviously heard the girl too, because she looked up just in time to see her mother *also* running down the path, chasing after her daughter. "Megan! Megan, stop running, you know I can't keep up!"

"Come on mommy!" The girl skidded to a halt dramatically, and swung around to look back at her mother without falling over. "Come on, quicker!"

"Alright, alright." Her mom caught up, panting the same way Emily had been only a few minutes earlier. She put a hand on her daughter's shoulder—probably to stop her running off, more than anything else—and shot Emily and Meredith an exhausted smile.

"Evening." Emily grinned, looking between the two of them. "She's quite the sprinter."

"Oh she definitely is. Especially when there's an iHOP dinner at stake." The mom laughed, jostling her daughter's shoulder gently as they passed by. Emily watched them go with a small smile, before looking over at Meredith, who was also tracking the pair with her eyes.

"I used to do the same thing," she said. "For me it was Denny's though. If I saw a Denny's sign in the distance no one would have been able to catch me. Hey, if you want to motivate me to keep up with you, maybe you should put a Denny's sticker on your back. I bet I'd run faster then."

Meredith was still watching the mother and daughter walk away, as if she was in a trance. It was almost like she hadn't even heard Emily, and she didn't turn around until Emily tapped her on the shoulder gently. "Hey, Meredith?"

"Huh?" She turned sharply, brushing Emily's hand off as she took a step away. She looked startled, like she'd forgotten Emily was even standing there beside her. "What?"

"Are you alright?" Emily looked past her at the mother and daughter, who were fading into the darkness of the evening, melting off into the shadows. "What, do you know those two or something?"

"Know who?"

"The..." She pointed down the path. "Them. The mom and her daughter, the ones who just went past."

"No," she said quickly. "Why would you think that?"

"Because you…" Emily trailed off, confused. Meredith's voice was oddly defensive for such an innocent question, like they were back in the hospital in the middle of one of their interviews.

Did I touch a nerve, perhaps? She wondered, looking the older woman up and down slowly. She certainly looked worked up about *something*, but Emily wasn't sure what it was. "Are you okay?"

"I'm fine. I'll be even more fine if we actually start moving again though, you know."

Her voice was sharp and pointed, like every sentence was an attack, and the sudden shift in her mood took Emily by surprise. Only a few moments ago, the two of them had been getting along just fine, but out of nowhere it seemed like Meredith was just annoyed with her. She knew it wasn't going to be a great idea to press Meredith any further. The older woman was already looking at her like she was intruding on something, and she knew if she kept pushing, she'd only end up annoying her even more.

Save it, she told herself sternly. *You can talk to her about it some other time.*

Emily drew in a breath, and shrugged as if nothing had happened at all. "You know what, never mind. I think you're right, I won't be able to keep up with you, so I'm going to just… head back to the building."

"Suits me."

"Are you coming too?"

"No." Meredith shook her head. "I'll see you around."

And with that, without even waiting for Emily to respond, she took off down the running path, and quickly faded off into the distance. Emily stood there on the path in silence, watching her shrink as she ran further away, and then slowly turned her head to look back the way they'd come, the direction the mother and daughter had walked. Slowly, she began to retrace her footsteps, heading back towards her apartment.

Meredith wasn't in that bad of a mood when we headed out

tonight, she thought to herself. *She wasn't really in a great mood either – she wasn't singing and dancing, but then again, she never is. But then she saw those two, and something in her changed. What though? What could have made her go so cold and distant all of a sudden?*

Emily picked up a stray stone from the path and tossed it out into the river, pausing for a moment so she could listen to the splash as it hit the water. Then, she continued along the path, glancing back over her shoulder to the spot where the two of them had stood together.

"Did one of them remind her of someone?" She wondered out loud. "A patient, maybe?"

But then, why would she have reacted the way that she did? Meredith was proud of her success record in the OR, her history was impeccable. Unlike some of the other doctors whose files were riddled with malpractice lawsuits and complaints about ethics from other members of staff, Meredith was spotless. There was nothing in there that would dredge up bad memories for her.

Unless there's one buried far back in her file that we haven't seen yet. Or maybe one from her time back in England? Given that she's got so few screw ups on her record, the ones she does have probably stick out to her. Maybe I could ask someone else, get a little insight on her.

With that, Emily decided it was time to head home. She grabbed another bottle of water for herself from the bodega that she passed, and then went back to her apartment.

TEN

Angela was still awake when she arrived back, looking through files of her own to write up her reports, and she looked up at the sound of Emily coming home.

"That was a short run," she called. "Did something happen?"

"Mm..." Emily gave a non-committal hum in response. "What are you working on?"

"NICU nurses. So far it all looks good, but we're waiting to hear back from your side. Have you interviewed any of them?"

"Nope, NICU isn't my department. I've got surgeons, mostly." Emily flopped down on the couch with a heavy sigh looking across the room at her coworker. "You aren't looking through any of their files, are you? The surgeons, I mean."

"I've got a few of them. Why? Is there someone in particular you're looking for some information on?"

"Meredith Asquith. She's from Neurosurgery, transferred out of a London hospital about eight or so years back."

"Asquith..." Angela slipped her reading glasses off her nose, thinking about it for a moment. "You mean the woman who lives next door to us, the one who looked like she'd seen a ghost when we showed up? Yeah, I've got her history. Her stats are impressive, if she's the one I'm thinking of. One of the lowest fatality rates out of the whole surgery team."

"But she does have them, right?" Emily knelt up on the couch to look over at Angela eagerly, her interest piqued all of a sudden. "Fatalities, I mean."

Angela shot her an odd look, but nodded slowly. "Of course she does. Everyone does."

"Have you got a summary of any of them that I can take a look at? Do you remember anything about any of the cases?" Emily peered at the box on the floor by Angela's feet. "Or have you got anything on her in there?"

"You're eager, aren't you?" Angela turned back to her laptop. "No, I only brought the NICU folders home with me today."

"Oh." Emily dropped back down onto the couch again with a sigh, drumming her fingertips against her knee. "Never mind then."

"What are you looking for anyway?"

"I just wanted to know about the patients she's lost over the years, that's all. I wanted to know if any of them you know—stood out. People she knew, people who reminded her of someone she knew... Maybe even kids?"

"Well, I can't tell most of that from my files," Angela reminded her. "All I can tell you is an anonymized patient number, and what went wrong. You're supposed to deal with the personal aspects, remember?"

"Yeah." Emily sighed, looking up at the ceiling. "The only problem is, she never tells me anything personal. All she talks about is her spotless record. She's never been found at fault for any of the deaths that happened during or after surgery... Do you remember if anyone who died on her table was a kid?"

"A kid? No, why?"

"No you don't remember, or no there were no kids?"

"No I don't *remember*. Why do you want to know so bad?"

Emily sighed again, looking at the wall that connected with Meredith's apartment, as if she could see into it. There had to be *something* buried under all those layers of iciness, something that had triggered such a sudden shift in her mood. She knew Meredith wouldn't tell her outright, so she was going to have to figure it out for herself.

————

The next morning, Emily left for work before Angela was even out of her bedroom, and headed to the hospital alone to get a head start. She set herself up with a coffee and Meredith's record, and started flicking through it, looking for any fatalities.

There was an elderly woman who reacted poorly to anesthesia, there was the man who'd had a stroke. There was the woman who caught MRSA after surgery, and passed away a week after the operation. Then there was the guy who'd died in the OR before they'd even put him under. Meredith hadn't even picked up a scalpel, but she was the one to call the time of death, so he was in her file too.

Over the years, there had been a few investigations by the hospital board, but she was never found to be at fault in any of the deaths. In fact, just as she had suspected, the only blight on her record at all was her personality; the compliments all stopped when it came to that.

And no children. Emily thought to herself with a heavy sigh, finishing her mug of coffee in one gulp. None of the patients who had died during or following an operation were under the age of eighteen, so perhaps she'd made a mistake. Maybe it wasn't the little girl who'd upset her so much, but it had been her mother instead.

"Oh god it would be so much easier if I could just *ask her...*" Emily groaned, resting her head on her forearms. "But nooooo..."

————

"Miss Porter." Melanie smiled at her. "What a nice surprise. How's everything going with our doctors? I hope no one's giving you any trouble."

"No, no," she lied. "They're all great. I did... I did have one question for you though, and it might seem a little bit strange."

"Strange?" Melanie beckoned to the seat opposite her own. "Well, I'm all for that. Who did you want to ask about?"

"Doctor Asquith."

An emotion Emily couldn't quite place flickered across Melanie's features. It almost looked like she was trying to conceal a smile as she leaned back in her chair, nodding slowly. "Doctor Asquith... I see. And what's Meredith done to get herself on your radar?"

"Well, I mean..." Emily trailed off, uncertain of where to start. "She's not exactly the easiest person to talk to. I understand, some people are more open to talking to someone like me, and some people..."

"Are Meredith," Melanie finished for her, smiling openly now. "I have to admit, none of this is surprising me so far."

Emily was about to continue when she spotted something on Melanie's desk that made her pause. It was a stack of lilac sticky notes, in the shape of a leaf. "Did you write the note on her file? The one saying 'Good luck'?"

"Maybe I did. It sounds like you needed it."

"Mm."

"Is there something I can help you with, Miss Porter?" Melanie asked, smiling kindly. "Or are you just here to vent about Meredith?"

"I'm not and I'm sorry if it has appeared that way, although from your reaction I assume it is something which often happens?" Emily watched as Melanie nodded. "I'm not though. I have an actual question, about her medical record, the files you gave to our team"

The smile slipped from Melanie's features, and at the mention of the audit, she went back to the professional head of the hospital Emily had first met. "Fire away."

"Is there any way that a case file could be missing? Maybe it was struck from her official record? Perhaps a case that went wrong? Maybe... Maybe it was a younger patient?"

"Are you suggesting that we've falsified our records, Miss Porter?" Melanie asked, visibly bristling at the mere suggestion. Emily backtracked quickly.

"No, no! Nothing like that. I was just thinking, maybe it was done through official methods, I don't know. Maybe for some reason or another, there was a patient case, a death that was wiped from her record?"

"I can assure you there wasn't. Not at this hospital, at least. What makes you ask that? I thought another member of your team was evaluating her surgical skills."

"They are. It's—well, It's something that I saw. Yesterday, there was this mother and daughter who walked past us and Dr. Asquith seemed to respond to the interaction between them in a... I don't really know how to describe it, but she just seemed... strange, I guess."

An expression Emily couldn't quite place flickered across Melanie's face at that. At first she thought perhaps it was shock; the older woman's eyes widened a little, and her mouth went slack into a small "o." Then she cleared her throat, looked down at her desk for a moment, and shook her head. When she looked back up at Emily, she didn't seem surprised, but her brows were pulled together in a frown. It was almost... almost a look of pity.

"Would you know why that happened?" Emily asked after a few moments. A muscle twitched in Melanie's face, below her right eye, almost like she was wincing and then she shook her head again.

"I don't think that's relevant to your report, do you?"

That means she does. "You never know what might be relevant, especially given the way Meredith reacted. If you know something that you can tell me, then it might help me to—"

"I don't think it's a good idea to be talking about my doctors like this, Miss Porter." Melanie interrupted her sharply. "I'm more than happy to give you my professional opinion on Doctor Asquith, which I've already done, but if you want to know about Meredith's personal life, then you're going to have to ask Meredith."

"So there *is* something to ask her about? There's a reason she reacted the way she did?"

Melanie looked uncomfortable at that, and twisted in her seat for a moment. She inhaled slowly, and her gaze flickered to the framed photograph on her desk, before she looked back up at Emily again. "Your job is to evaluate Meredith from a more humane perspective, so I understand that it's only natural you would want to ask these questions. I'm also not going to tell you how to do your job. *With that being said*, I think this is the wrong place to look for answers. If I were in your position, I would just leave this alone."

Emily frowned, looking Melanie up and down slowly. Since she had started working at the hospital, she had expected some kind of resistance from the members of staff, but not from the administration. "What do you mean 'leave it alone'?"

Melanie sighed heavily, and her professional demeanor slipped away. She leaned back in her chair slowly, rocking back and forth as she thought about it for a moment. "This is... Not an official conversation, right?"

"Sure."

"Some things are better left untouched. I agree that it's important to make sure all of our doctors are completely prepared to be in the OR – there's no way I want anyone in there who could put a patient at risk. But I also think that we're all entitled to a little privacy when it comes to some parts of our lives, Dr. Asquith included."

There was something in Meredith's past that she wanted to keep hidden, Emily was certain of that now. Whatever it was, it was something *Melanie* wanted hidden too – could it have been an operation gone wrong, a medical mishap that had been quietly swept under the rug?

Emily's stomach turned at the thought. She didn't want that to be the case – Meredith's behavior wasn't great, but at least she seemed to hold herself to *some* kind of moral standard when it came to medicine. It wasn't much, but it was the one thing that everyone agreed on when it came to Meredith, and the one compliment she received. Emily didn't really want *that* to be taken away too.

ELEVEN

Over the last couple of weeks Meredith had warmed—slightly—to her new neighbors. While she enjoyed the peace of her solo runs, she had to admit that there was something nice about knowing there was another person by her side, taking the same path. After giving Emily a hard time about her fitness and being so offhand with her the first night they had gone running, Meredith had uncharacteristically felt bad.

After having built the courage to invite Emily along a few evenings later, she had just kept inviting her. Sometimes they went out in the early morning together, and caught the sunrise on their way back to the apartment building, but most of the time they went on night runs together.

When Meredith returned from the hospital, she'd swing past Emily's door to tell her she was back. She'd get changed quickly, and then the two would head out together into the evening, before coming back home a little while later. It was on one of those later evenings that Meredith knocked on Emily's door, and heard her calling from inside.

"Meredith, is that you?"

Emily sounded panicked. Her voice was high and strained, and the tone immediately set Meredith on edge. "Are you alright?"

Footsteps approached the door quickly, and then Emily wrenched it open. Her eyes were wide when she looked up at Meredith, and she seemed anxious. Before Meredith could even ask what was happening, Emily grabbed her hand and tugged her inside, slamming the door behind her.

"It's Angela," she explained, pulling Meredith through the apartment. "Something's wrong."

"Something? What do you mean *something*?"

"I don't know! I think she's sick, she doesn't look right, or feel right. Look." Emily pointed to the sofa where she saw Angela propped up with a cushion.

She was right, something was wrong with the woman. Her skin was pale, almost grey in the dim lighting, and when she looked up at Meredith it was through bleary, unfocused eyes. As she approached Meredith saw sweat beading on the woman's forehead. She dug her front door key out of her pocket, and tossed it to Emily. "In my apartment, under the sink."

"What am I looking for?"

"A black bag. It's got my stethoscope in it, and a few other things. Go, and call 911 while you're at it."

Emily did as she was told, all but running from the room in her panic to get to Meredith's apartment. As the door closed behind her, Meredith turned back to Angela, and checked her pulse.

"What's wrong with me?" Angela asked quietly, her breathing strained. "My chest feels... it feels heavy."

She's having a heart attack. Meredith realized, pulling out her own phone. There was no point in waiting for an ambulance, not when she could drive to City General just as quickly and have someone waiting for them.

She called City General, and warned them she would be arriving soon with a patient. By the time Emily came back into the apartment,

Meredith was hauling Angela up from the sofa, and helping her to stand.

"What's going on?" Emily looked between them. "Where are we going?"

"The hospital." Meredith grunted. "Grab her other arm, help me get her to my car."

Thankfully traffic was light, and Meredith was able to weave her way to the hospital without any major disruptions. She might well have run a red light, and she was almost certainly speeding, but no one tried to stop her, and when they pulled up to the hospital there were two nurses waiting.

Emily and Meredith helped Angela onto a gurney, just as a doctor from the ER appeared in the doorway. Meredith explained the situation, told him that she was almost positive it was a heart attack, and then Angela was gone. The whole thing was over in only a few minutes, and as the gurney disappeared down the hallway, Meredith and Emily were left standing by the doors in silence.

Everything had happened so quickly that Emily didn't seem to have had time to really process what had happened. She was staring at the doors Angela had gone through in shock, shaking her head slowly. "I just... I can't believe it. She seemed fine this morning."

"These things happen quickly," Meredith explained, trying to be gentle. Emily looked shell-shocked, and she knew it must have been difficult to see a coworker so ill.

"One minute we were just talking, and then she said her chest felt funny. She got out of breath, and then she just... collapsed. She was... shaking and pale and... she kept insisting she was okay but... I didn't know what to do," Emily whispered. "Thank god you arrived when you did."

"You'd have called 911. You knew something was wrong, and you'd have coped," Meredith assured her.

"Maybe."

Emily still looked like she was in shock, so Meredith found her a seat while she went to find out how Angela was looking. Luckily, it seemed like the heart attack was minor, and they'd managed to get her to the hospital fast enough to minimize the immediate impact. Meredith waited until they were certain they'd stabilized her, and then decided to take Emily home. It would be no good for her to just sit in the waiting room all night long.

She didn't say a word on the way back. As they drove home, Meredith kept chancing glances at the younger woman out of the corner of her eye, but every time she looked over, Emily was just staring straight ahead into the middle distance, unblinking.

I should say something. I should... comfort her.

Meredith had no idea of what to say. Bedside manner had never exactly been her strongest suit, and she was a little rusty on dealing with issues like this. When it came to dealing with worried friends and family, she usually just gave them the facts and let a nurse do the hand holding.

There was no one else to turn to in the car though, no one who could comfort Emily or make her feel even a little better. So Meredith cleared her throat and tried her best. "She'll—be okay."

"Yeah." Emily's voice was distant and soft, barely audible over the sound of the city flying by outside the car. Still, she didn't look over at Meredith.

"They stabilized her, and it wasn't a massive heart attack like some of the ones we see. There'll be some damage to the heart muscles, probably some scarring. Luckily she isn't a smoker and she doesn't drink regularly, so the risks of long term effects are going to be pretty low. Once she's out of hospital she'll—"

"Please," Emily interrupted, closing her eyes for a moment. "Meredith, please stop."

She fell silent, gripping the steering wheel a little tighter. Her palms were starting to sweat, and she could feel her heart racing in a way it hadn't done for a long time. Even though she hated these conversations, they never normally made her nervous, but tonight with Emily... the stakes felt higher, for some reason.

"I'm sorry." She said finally, letting out a low sigh. "I'm not good at these conversations."

"I understand."

They pulled into the parking lot, and Meredith shut off the engine. Emily was still rigid in her seat, staring out in front of her, but now she could see a muscle jumping in the younger woman's jaw. She was straining, tensing up, almost as if she was trying to keep from crying.

"Come on," Meredith whispered, unbuckling her seat belt. "Let's get you inside."

When Emily moved, it was more like she was a marionette on a string than her normal self. She was acting on muscle memory without really thinking about what she was doing, and as they got out of the car, she still had that same spaced out look on her face. Meredith led her up the three flights of stairs silently to their floor, keeping a hand on the small of her back to guide her.

"And we're home." She said quietly, stopping outside Emily's door. It had been a long night, and she knew Emily must have been exhausted, so the best thing to do was to get her into bed and let her rest as much as possible. But as she looked back at the younger woman expectantly, waiting for her to open the door, she realized that wasn't going to happen.

Emily had stopped a few feet from her front door, and she was as white as a sheet, her eyes blown wide. She'd taken her key out at some point in the trip from the parking lot to their floor, and it trembled in her hand, before slipping from her grasp and hitting the floor.

"I don't want to go in there." She whispered, shaking her head slowly. "I don't... I don't want to go back in."

Meredith stooped to pick up the keys, and looked over at the younger woman with a frown. It was understandable that she didn't want to go back in there after seeing what had happened; a lot of people had the same reaction to things like that.

"Alright," she said quietly. "Alright, why don't we go into my place? You can sleep there."

She didn't need to ask twice. Emily nodded her head eagerly, obviously desperate to go just about anywhere but her own place, so Meredith took out her own key and let them into her apartment.

"Come on," Meredith eased her onto the couch as gently as possible. "It's alright. It's okay now."

As she sank into the couch cushions, whatever resolve Emily had been clinging onto seemed to evaporate, and her shoulders began to shake. Tears welled in her eyes, and before Meredith could even jump up to grab her a tissue, she was sobbing into her hands.

She was never around for this part of the job. This was always the bit that she handed over to a junior doctor or a nurse, and they had the task of mopping up tears or consoling families. So when she heard Emily begin to cry, Meredith froze.

She'd never wished that she was anyone else on the surgical staff before that moment, but now she wished she was Squires or Michaels, or just about *anyone* who went misty-eyed at the sight of a crying family member. She wished that comfort and empathy came naturally to her, and that she could do something more than just pat Emily's shoulder awkwardly.

"I'm... sorry," she managed to get out between sobs, trying to draw in a deep breath. "I'm sorry—it was just so..."

"Take your time," Meredith said gently. "I'll get you some water and some tissues, okay?"

"Thank you," Emily whispered. Meredith hopped up from the couch and went to the kitchen to pour her a glass of water, and came back with a box of tissues too. When she returned, Emily was a little calmer, and took them from her with a grateful smile.

"She'll pull through," Meredith assured her with a small smile. "So don't stress yourself too much, okay? She'll be back to bossing you around in no time."

"Thanks." Emily let out a quiet, teary laugh and dabbed at her eyes. "That just isn't something I've ever really seen before, and it was... god, it was so scary. Although, I guess all of this must be pretty normal for you, huh?"

"Well, most of my patients are unconscious when I get to them, so it was a bit of a surprise for me," she admitted, relaxing back against the couch. Emily sniffled again, nodding.

"I just... I didn't know what to do when I saw her there. I thought I was going to see her die in front of me," she shuddered. "god, I know I sound so dramatic. I don't even want to go back in there. I don't think I'll be able to sleep. It was just such a fright."

Meredith frowned, rubbing the back of her neck. She was all too familiar with that sensation, knowing that sleep wouldn't come no matter how desperately she needed it. She also knew that one of the worst parts about going through something like this was to be alone.

"You know, if you want..." she offered, patting the couch cushion beneath them. "You could stay here? I've a spare room or I've pillows and blankets if you'd prefer the couch. At least you won't be alone, right?"

She didn't have to ask twice. Emily seemed desperate not to have to go home alone, and she nodded eagerly. "Yes, please. I'd appreciate that. The couch is fine, if that is okay for you?"

Meredith patted her shoulder gently and got up to grab some spare things for her, setting her up in an impromptu bed. Emily curled up on the couch gratefully, tugging the blanket up to her chin, and she managed a small, shaky smile in return.

"Thanks for this." She whispered.

"It's nothing. Just uh... just try to get some sleep tonight, alright? I know it'll be difficult, but you need to."

With that, Meredith turned out the lights and headed to her room, leaving the door ajar as she stripped off and got into bed. As her head hit the pillow, she frowned to herself, wishing that she'd been able to actually offer up some form of comfort to Emily, rather than just spouting off facts.

She wanted someone to hold her hand and tell her everything was going to be alright when she was scared, and Meredith hadn't even been able to do that.

Jesus Christ, Asquith, she thought, staring into the darkness. *What kind of a person are you?*

TWELVE

When Emily woke, it was to the smell of cinnamon.

Breakfast?

She stretched out languidly, raising her arms up above her head as she did, until her feet hit something solid, and she froze. Normally she could stretch out as far as she wanted in bed without hitting the footboard. And there was something pressed against her back too – not as soft as a pillow, but not hard enough to be a wall either.

The blanket that was draped over her didn't smell like hers, and she was cramped up uncomfortably too – she wasn't waking up in her bed.

So then where the hell am I?

She opened her eyes a crack to see an unfamiliar coffee table in front of her, a TV up against the far wall, and a bookshelf, stuffed to bursting. This wasn't her apartment, but she'd been here before: it was Meredith's place.

And then, in an instant, everything that had happened the night before came flooding back to her. The heart attack, the ride to the hospital, coming back to Meredith's apartment and just staring listlessly at the wall. Meredith had let her stay the night on the couch, so that she didn't have to go back to the empty apartment.

Emily sat up and stretched, wincing as her muscles began to relax after a night spent curled up on the couch. She probably hadn't been able to get that much sleep given how late they'd gotten back from the hospital, but it was certainly long enough for her body to protest. No matter how good a couch was, it was no substitute for a real bed.

"Oh good, you're awake."

Emily turned at the sound of Meredith's voice, and peered across the apartment to see the other woman in the entryway to the kitchen, holding a plate in one hand and a coffee in the other. She lifted them up, offering them out to Emily, before walking out to join her on the couch. "Are you hungry?"

"Not really."

Meredith ignored her, and pushed the plate into her hands. "Well, you should eat something."

Emily looked down at the plate. It was a cinnamon pastry, still steaming from where it had come out of the oven. "Did you... make this?"

"No." Meredith smiled gently. "I ordered some breakfast in, I put yours in the oven to keep it warm. I figured you didn't eat at all last night, you'd need something once you woke up."

"I..." Emily paused, surprisingly touched by the gesture. "Thank you."

"Don't mention it." Meredith was silent for a few moments, watching Emily pick at the pastry. "How are you feeling?"

"I don't know," she admitted. "I guess I'm just scared. I've never gone through anything like that before. I once took my mom to the ER when she cut her hand on some broken glass, but that's the closest I've ever come to something like... what happened last night."

"It's scary," Meredith acknowledged. "I get that."

"Not for you. You see patients all the time, it must have been like a... drop in the ocean or something."

Meredith sighed and looked down at her hands for a moment.

"Yeah. Well, it's different when it's someone you care about. I know that much."

There was something about her voice that made Emily pause. It was something about the low, almost throaty way she spoke, almost like she was getting a little choked up. Coming from the woman who always sounded so emotionally removed from every situation she found herself in, it was strange to hear.

Is she speaking from experience? Emily wondered. She put the plate down on the coffee table, and tilted her head to one side, before coming out with the question. It was better to be upfront with Meredith, she knew that.

"Have you ever gone through something like this before?"

"Yes."

Meredith's voice was so soft, Emily might have missed it if the apartment wasn't so silent. She hadn't expected to get a straight answer from Meredith, especially not about something with any kind of emotional attachment. During their sessions she'd been so closed off, Emily had just expected her to shrug off the question like all of the others, but this time, for some reason, she didn't. Emily pushed a little bit further.

"What happened?"

"It was..." Meredith paused and drew in a deep breath, before straightening up. Emily thought for a moment that she was just going to stop talking and change the subject, but then she cleared her throat and continued. "It was a car accident."

"A car accident?"

"Mm..." she hummed. "Head on collision. It was this stupid, one in a million accident, and in a moment, my whole life was ripped away from me. Everything changed. My wife, Jennifer... and our daughter. I was left with nothing. We were in an accident, taken to the hospital that I worked at, and... I was the only one still alive."

In her career, Emily had heard a lot of horrible things. People had opened up to her about things that had happened that *no one* should have to suffer through. They'd told her stories of abuse, broken down when they talked about addictions or abuse, or confessed their deepest, darkest fears to her. Platitudes were the worst things you could offer and Emily didn't. Instead she sat quietly, before saying "I'm sorry."

"So am I."

"That is a lot to deal with."

Meredith simply nodded.

"Was that the reason you came to the U.S.?"

"You catch on quickly," Meredith offered up a small, mirthless smile. "Yes. I couldn't walk back into that place after what happened. I took a few weeks off after the crash, but the first day I stepped back into the hospital, I felt like... I don't even know how to describe it. My heart was pounding, I felt like I was going to throw up, my hands wouldn't stop shaking. It wasn't the place I worked any more, it was the place they died. I looked through their files, found the doctors who worked on my wife... And when I saw them for the first time after the crash, I couldn't even look them in the eyes."

"You blamed them for what happened, didn't you?" Emily murmured. It made sense, during their sessions, Emily had only learned a handful of things about Meredith, but one of the things she *had* learned was that she was hypercritical of others' work.

"My daughter was dead before the paramedics could even get her to the hospital. The impact was too much for her and she..." Meredith stopped talking abruptly, and swallowed hard, shaking her head. It was too much for her, recounting her daughter's death in detail, so she changed the direction of the conversation quickly. "Jennifer though, my wife... she slipped into a coma, I had to turn off her life support machine."

"That must have been an impossible decision."

Meredith shrugged listlessly. "She was gone. By the time I turned off the machine she was brain dead, she wouldn't have been able to survive without help. But that wasn't the case when she arrived at the hospital—there was a chance for her when she was wheeled into the ER. Brain surgery."

"They didn't operate?"

Meredith snorted, rolling her eyes. "Of course they didn't. Brain surgery is risky at the best of times, and Jennifer's chances of surviving were slim even if they did operate. There was an inquest after her death, at my request, of course, and they said that they didn't think there was a point of getting her into the OR. She *probably* would have died on the table."

"But you didn't see it that way?"

"The way I see it, no one wanted to be the one with a scalpel in their hand when she died. Her chances of making it were so slim they just figured it would be easier to let her die without lifting a finger to help." Meredith pursed her lips into a thin line and shook her head again, looking disgusted. "They didn't even try to help, they were too worried about it going on their record, making them look bad. There was a *chance* for her if they operated. It was small, but it was there. Without the operation though, she was dead. They knew that, and they still just... turned away."

"That's why you left for the U.S.?"

She nodded, swallowing hard. "Yeah. I couldn't work with those people any more, not after what had happened. I trained in Neurotrauma, came to the U.S. and I haven't looked back since. And now... here we are."

Meredith gestured between the two of them, before running a hand through her hair. "I've never told anyone that."

"Never?"

"Well, I told Melanie. She wanted to know why I'd left London, and I figured she'd find out once she called them, so I told her, and then asked her to keep it to herself. Surprisingly, for someone who's always poking her nose into everyone's business, she not only agreed, she kept her word."

"And you haven't told anyone else?"

"Not until now, no."

"Well... thank you for sharing that and trusting me with it. It goes without saying I won't repeat what you've told me." Emily nodded in assurance but she wanted to go on, if Meredith would let her. "That night, when we went on the run together…"

"We've been on a few runs together now."

"You know which night I'm talking about though, don't you? The first night." Emily cocked an eyebrow. "That mother and daughter passed us by, and you just… took off. Is that the reason why?"

Meredith frowned, and then nodded slowly. "The little girl, the one we saw? Her name was Megan. The same as my daughter."

Oh.

It made sense now, all of it. Meredith's sudden change of demeanor, like she'd seen a ghost. Melanie's secretive, uncomfortable reaction to Emily's questions, when she'd been so forthright until that point. All of it was falling into place, and now that she knew the truth, Emily couldn't help but feel a little guilty.

"Anyway," she cleared her throat again, trying to muster up some kind of bravado for Emily's benefit. "My point is… I understand how you felt last night. I may not have acted like it, but I understood. I know how difficult it is to sit there and worry about someone. I also know what it's like not to have anyone to support you."

"I had you."

Meredith laughed coldly. "I wasn't much help though, was I? You don't have to lie to me. I just drove you to the hospital and back, I rattled off a few facts and stats about heart surgery. I didn't… I didn't comfort you, or hold your hand or hug you. I didn't do what normal people do in that kind of a situation. I didn't give you what you needed, and that was shitty of me."

It was the first time Emily had heard Meredith be even slightly critical of her own actions. Every time they'd spoken before, she'd been so haughty and arrogant that it was borderline infuriating – in her mind, Meredith could do no wrong. She must have felt *really* bad if she was actually apologizing.

"You made sure I didn't sleep alone in the apartment though." Emily reached out and laid her hand over Meredith's, squeezing gently. "You got me breakfast, you took care of me. You might not be good with this kind of thing, but... you were there. And last night, to be honest, that was the only thing I needed. I don't think I'd have paid attention if you'd rattled off some big emotional speech. All I needed was someone to be *here*, beside me. So thank you, Meredith."

Emily had expected that if she was ever to get this close to Meredith, the other woman would have just instinctively pulled away from her. Given how cold and standoffish Meredith always seemed to be, it wouldn't have surprised her if the older woman had just shrugged her off and walked away. But to her surprise, Meredith didn't move away. Instead, in the silence that followed, Emily thought she felt the pad of Meredith's thumb graze over her knuckles, with the lightest of touches.

Finally, after all the conversations they'd had, it seemed like Emily had worn down the walls Meredith had built up, exposing the kind of person she'd never imagined her to be. Underneath that icy armor, it seemed like she was... vulnerable.

Meredith looked up from their hands slowly, and met Emily's gaze. It was at that moment that they both seemed to realize just how close they were sitting, and how little was actually separating them. All of a sudden, Emily found herself becoming acutely aware of Meredith's thigh, pressed flush against her own. She could feel the warmth of Meredith's hand in her own, she could hear the other woman's gentle breathing. They were just so close, with almost nothing separating them.

She wasn't sure who started to lean in first. Maybe they both did at the same time, reacting to an unspoken instinct, but the next thing she knew, her lips were pressed to Meredith's in a gentle, *barely there* kiss. She tasted like cinnamon and coffee, and as Emily's lips ghosted over hers, one of Meredith's hands came up to nestle into her hair.

It took her a moment to even register what was happening, and the realization hit her, just as her phone began to ring on the coffee table. The two sprang apart like they'd been shocked, and Emily rushed to grab her phone, hiding her face as she answered.

"Hello?"

"Hello, Miss Porter? I was told to call you with updates about the patient you brought in last night." She heard a woman's voice on the other end of the line.

"Yes, yes. Angela, how is she?"

"She's been stabilized, and she's doing well. We think she'll need another few nights for observation, and then we'll send her home."

"That's fantastic news, thank you so much." Relief flooded through Emily at the news, and she turned to Meredith with a grin. "She's going to be alright."

"That's good." Meredith smiled gently, her reaction just a little more muted than Emily's. Their eyes met, and Emily felt her cheeks flush—was Meredith thinking about what had just happened too? The kiss had come out of nowhere, and it should have felt like a mistake, but somehow... It didn't. Not at all.

It should have done though.

There was a strict code of conduct Emily had to follow in her job, and one of the many unspoken rules was that there were *no* romantic entanglements or relationships allowed between the audit team and those they were auditing. The kiss should have felt wrong, it should have felt like she was crossing a line.

But it didn't.

That was going to have to be a problem for her future self to deal with though, Emily decided as she stuck her phone into her pocket and grabbed her jacket. First, she had to head to the hospital.

"Thanks for last night." She said again, as she headed to the door. "I uh... I'll see you later."

Meredith didn't move from her place on the sofa, but nodded slowly. "Sure. We can talk later."

Talk.

Yeah, Emily thought to herself as she left the apartment. *We've got quite a bit to talk about.*

THIRTEEN

Meredith watched Emily go, and when the door closed, she slumped back against the couch with an exhausted sigh.

"What the fuck was that?" she whispered. "What the *fuck*, Meredith?"

Since the accident, she had only told one person what had happened back in London, and that was Melanie. No one else knew anything about her personal life, or her family history, and that was the way Meredith liked things. She wasn't interested in cozying up to the rest of the staff and earning their sympathy, so she'd kept it to herself.

There were people she'd worked alongside for years who had no idea about the accident, but somehow, she'd spilled everything to Emily, who was still practically a stranger to her. And as she stared up at the ceiling, Meredith couldn't for the life of her figure out *why* she'd done that.

And then there was the other problem. The kiss.

Meredith wasn't blind. She knew that Emily was attractive, and had been able to see that since the day they'd first met. But she'd found plenty of people attractive in the past, and none of them had impacted her like this. None of them had managed to get this close to her, not since Jennifer.

She shifted uncomfortably on the sofa, and looked over at her bookcase. It was piled high with love stories that she'd read from cover to cover, over and over again until the pages were creased. That was where she'd buried herself for eight years, because it was a hell of a lot safer to just read about it from a distance.

There was no chance of getting hurt if she just read a book.

Meredith frowned, and touched her fingertips lightly against the swell of her lips, ghosting over the spot where Emily had kissed her. It had felt good to be kissed again. As confused and nervous as the thought made her, Meredith had to admit that it had felt nice.

"I should have just told her to go home last night." She murmured to herself, letting her head fall against the back of the couch with a groan.

———

Emily didn't come by the next night, or the night after that. In fact, three days went past without the two seeing each other again, even though Meredith found herself looking out for the younger woman every time she stepped out of the apartment.

She was coming home surprisingly early, three days after they had kissed in her apartment, when she bumped into Emily on the stairwell. Neither one was looking at where they were going, and they almost collided.

"Meredith!" Emily huffed out a nervous laugh. "How are you?"

"I'm fine." She tilted her head to one side, looking Emily up and down slowly. She was dressed in her normal running gear, with a water bottle in hand. "You're heading out?"

"I uh... yeah."

"I'm actually looking forward to a run myself, if you hang back I'll come with you."

"I actually—" Emily stumbled over her words. "I don't think that's such a good idea."

"Why not?" Meredith moved up so that she was standing on the same step as Emily again. She leaned in a little, until they were inches apart, and although Emily looked nervous, she didn't back up. "Are you worried you'll kiss me again?"

"I didn't!" Emily paused, and looked around the stairwell like she was worried someone would hear. "I didn't kiss you. You kissed *me*."

"That's not how I remember it."

"*Meredith*," she hissed. "I'm serious this isn't a good idea."

"Why not?"

"I'm *auditing* you, remember? What happened in your apartment was a mistake, and I'm sorry. We shouldn't... you know—do that again."

Meredith leaned in a little more. Emily still hadn't backed up, and now they were so close that the tip of her nose bumped against Emily's cheek when she whispered in her ear. "Was it really a mistake?"

"Meredith..."

She pulled back sharply, looking down at Emily properly for a few moments. If she was honest with herself, Meredith couldn't quite pinpoint exactly *why* she was so intent on chasing this. She hadn't even thought about pursuing anyone in a long time, but it was like Emily had flipped a switch on inside her, and she wanted more.

"If you honestly think that the kiss was wrong, that's fine. If you don't want it to happen again, if you want to just go back to playing doctor and patient, then I'm okay with that. *But...* if you *do* want it to happen again, then all you have to do is say so."

Emily swallowed nervously. "We aren't supposed to—"

"I'm not asking you if you think we *should*. I'm asking if you *want* to."

A long silence followed Meredith's words, and the stairwell was so quiet that they could hear people moving around on the floor above them. A door opened from one of the apartments, and they heard someone approaching the stairwell. The footsteps grew closer and closer, and as they began to descend the stairwell, Emily nodded.

"Good." Meredith smiled, taking a step back as one of their neighbors came into view. "I guess I'll see you around then."

"You aren't coming on the run?" Emily called after her, as she started to walk up towards her floor.

"No, I'm feeling pretty tired, I think I'll just see you later." She waved back, before disappearing around the corner. When she let herself into the apartment, it was with a self-satisfied smile.

I know she kissed me, she thought to herself, as she dropped onto the couch and kicked off her shoes.

FOURTEEN

I really shouldn't. I know I shouldn't. I won't. I'll just tell her it's a bad idea and I've changed my mind. Yeah, I've changed my mind. She'll understand.

For the entire duration of Emily's run she had been trying to convince herself that saying no to Meredith was the only option. Anything else was complete madness. A craziness she couldn't afford to be party to.

She was still allowing the same mantra to go through her head when she jumped in the shower an hour later; and again when she dressed twenty minutes after that, carefully picking out a top that she knew accentuated the color of her eyes. Even as she knocked on the door to Meredith's apartment she told herself this was just to put the record straight, about just how chronically bad the idea of pursuing anything between them would be... and then as the door opened, their eyes met and there was only one possible course of action.

Feeling Meredith's warm grasp on her hand, Emily allowed herself to be pulled gently forward, embracing the inevitability of their connection. The minute she crossed over the threshold, she knew there was no coming back, moving forward was the only choice.

As Meredith drew her into the kiss, pressing their bodies firmly together a surge of excitement travelled through her body. Her lips parted, allowing Meredith to tease her way along her bottom lip. She wanted this woman with every sinew of her body. Sinking deeper into the kiss the urgency of her desire tingled over her body. Hands weaved their way through each other's hair, drawing them ever closer. Teeth offered little biting teases to full swollen lips, as they lost themselves in the moment, in each other.

Breathless, they pulled back, eyes locked and then Meredith smiled and let out a quiet giggle, so soft and gentle it made Emily's heart sing. Under that harsh exterior was the most exquisite sexy, generous woman—a woman she wanted more of, in every way.

"Maybe you should take me to your bedroom? I mean I'm sure we could rock it on your rug, but your bed might be more comfortable?" Emily gave a small wink and smiled. But Meredith didn't answer. Instead she grasped the young woman's hand and, beaming, she led her through the apartment to her bedroom.

Keen, confident and cute... I could get too used to this.

The bedroom was a soothing combination of grays and muted mauves and the scent of lavender tickled Emily's nose as they entered the room. Relaxing as it might be, the way Meredith kicked the door closed with a casual flick of her foot suggested she had some less than restful activities in mind for them.

Meredith might have been a little older but as Emily ran her hands over the firm body pressed against her own she felt the corners of her mouth lift in anticipation. Every muscle was defined, taut and strong. Emily bit her bottom lip, her breath shuddering as she inhaled. God, she wanted Meredith to take her right now.

Clothes were strewn across the floor as the act of undressing yielded to more kissing, which in turn fueled the need to feel skin against skin. To feel each other's heat, their vulnerability meld together.

Naked, their hands explored, ghosting, almost frightened to unleash the raw primal need threatening to overwhelm them. Two fingers tilted Emily's chin upwards, until her eyes met the dark intensity of Meredith's gaze. Fingers ran over the soft smooth skin of her thighs... teasing with the lightest of touches.

"Oh god. Please Meredith."

Meredith accepted her pleas and walked her back towards the bed before laying her down with such tenderness it made Emily's heart melt just a little. Kisses landed on her neck, her collarbone, the tops of her breasts and the air filled with her light pleasure-filled moans. Lips sucked gently on her nipples, pulling and tugging with care. Emily allowed herself to open wider, her hips lifting with want. She felt the hot wet tip of a tongue, flick across her nipple and at the same time two long strong fingers slid down either side of her clit with exquisite precision it made her gasp and buck.

Fuck, if I had known surgeons were this good I'd have done this years ago.

The fingers squeezed her expertly and Emily's back arched. Panting and moaning she was giving everything she had to Meredith.

Oh, to feel that tongue thrash across my clit.

As if Meredith knew exactly what Emily wanted, what she needed, she moved down the younger woman's body kissing the tender skin on the inside of her thighs.

Emily felt the fingers explore through her folds and she pushed her centre towards their firmness, desperate to find friction. It was Meredith's strength, her power she wanted to feel her deep inside, driving into the most secret parts of her soul.

Her head rolled back with a loud groan and Meredith pushed inside, one finger, then two. The movement was tentative and tender but Emily's movements screamed her desire for more and Meredith obliged.

The softness of lips over her clit; the masterful flicks of the hard tip of a tongue; the purposeful movement of fingers, fostering and growing her need until she lost complete control.

"Oh god, Meredith, I'm going to..."

Emily's words were strangled by the low guttural wail that

erupted from her body. Everything was lost to the crashing orgasm which rolled through her body. All awareness of surroundings, all fear of crossing boundaries, all limitations of being were lost as she allowed herself to do nothing but feel. The tingling, the euphoria that filled her chest, her mind; her moans filled the room and each time the sensation began to ebb, Meredith allowed it to draw breath once more until she was being buffeted from wave to wave of sheer pleasure.

"Please, god, please. I need to—god. Fuck, no more. Please." Emily's body slowed then shuddered, then slowed again as she tried to settle back into her body. She tried to focus on Meredith's face but as tiny tremors of satisfaction spontaneously erupted across her body, she lost herself again and again.

A chuckle filled the room, and the weight of a warm body holding her tightly eventually brought her back into the moment.

"Well, it looks like I haven't lost my touch." The smug grin of Meredith's face made Emily burst into laughter. This woman was utterly endearing and her confidence just damned hot. Thank god she had taken the time to dig deeper.

FIFTEEN

Over the next few days, Emily could feel her blood pressure spike whenever Meredith got close to her in the hospital. With people all around them, she was worried that maybe Meredith would say or do something to get them both in trouble, but thankfully, she never did. She was the picture of professionalism in the workplace. When they passed each other in the hall, Meredith didn't even spare her a glance.

Emily didn't know what was hotter, the attention the surgeon lavished on her when they were alone or the haughty, indifference she treated her with in the hospital. What she did know is that she couldn't get Meredith out of her head.

When Angela checked out the hospital she'd returned home to Childress to recuperate, it had left Emily alone in the apartment and she found herself spending more and more time next door with Meredith, often leafing through her collection of books to find new reading material. They'd stay up late into the night talking about anything and everything, before making love until they fell asleep in each other's arms.

There was an uneasiness that hung over them though, even with all the time they were spending together. For Emily, it was the concern that this was a relationship that could get her fired, and if anyone were to ever find out about them, she would be in serious trouble. The more time they spent together, the worse the nerves got, until even Meredith noticed it.

They were watching TV together on the sofa one evening when Meredith brought it up, tapping her on the shoulder to get her attention.

"What's wrong?" Meredith asked, cocking her head. "You seem a little distracted."

"I..." Emily paused. She was about to just lie to Meredith and act like everything was fine, but she knew that wasn't fair. She'd been so adamant about pulling the truth from Meredith since they'd met, it wouldn't be fair of her to be evasive. "There's... Something is bothering me."

Meredith turned off the TV, and tossed the remote down on the coffee table. "Do you want to talk about it?"

"It's about us."

"Okay..." Meredith raised an eyebrow slowly. "Should I be worried?"

"I'm just..." Emily sighed, gesturing between the two of them while she searched for the right words. She wasn't sure how to talk to Meredith about this – the last thing she wanted to do was to offend her, but this was a conversation that needed to be had. "Is *this* really a good idea? I'm supposed to be evaluating you, I'm supposed to be writing up a report on you. How am I supposed to do that with everything that's happened between us? How can I know that the things I'm writing haven't been distorted by our relationship?"

Meredith didn't seem to share her concern. She didn't look worried as she listened to Emily ramble, and when she was finished, the only thing the older woman could do was smile gently. "So what?"

"What do you mean 'what'?"

"What do you want to do about it?" Meredith draped an arm

over the back of the sofa, and let her hand hang down, so that her fingertips danced over Emily's shoulder. "Do you want to end this?"

No.

Ending things was the *last* thing on Emily's mind. As much as she was worried about the consequences of their relationship, she was enjoying spending time together. Meredith was surprisingly easy going outside of work, although she did have a few hang ups.

That was the other contributing factor to the uneasiness. It was obvious that Meredith was a little rusty at allowing another person into her space platonically, let alone romantically. Her life was very much that of a chronically single person, and she seemed to live her life by a rigid routine that didn't leave space for anyone else to fit in. She didn't have restaurants that she loved going to, or friends she wanted to introduce Emily to. Her life only really stretched across the four walls of her apartment, and that was it.

She also didn't seem to cook for herself much, as Emily realized after a few weeks. At first she figured it was just Meredith's busy schedule that meant ordering takeout was just an easy option, but after a while she wasn't so sure that was the whole truth. One morning, as the two were getting ready for work, she realized that there was literally *nothing* in Meredith's fridge.

"What time do you finish tonight?" she asked, skirting around Meredith to open the fridge. "We could have dinner together, if you want."

"That sounds nice. I finish at six, if it goes according to plan."

Emily pulled the fridge door open and peered inside, frowning. Inside, there was a tub of butter, a carton of milk, three unopened beers and a block of cheese, but nothing else. There were no fresh ingredients, no Tupperware filled with leftovers that she could live off for half the week, like in Emily's fridge back home. It was just... bare. It looked more like a college student's fridge than that of a doctor.

"Well, one of us needs to go grocery shopping before that." She gestured inside. "I could make us grilled cheese, if you've got some bread, but that's about it"

"I don't." Meredith admitted, glancing at the bread bin on the countertop. "It expired on Monday. I think it may have a slight blue haze over it but I haven't checked yet."

"I take it you don't cook much?" She closed the fridge door and leaned against the breakfast bar. It would have made sense if Meredith didn't – her shifts were long and often unpredictable, so it didn't come as a huge shock that she didn't have the energy to cook for herself most evenings.

"Not really." Meredith puffed out her cheeks for a moment, and managed a small smile. "I used to."

"You did?"

"Back home, before the accident. I used to cook a lot. Jennifer wasn't exactly a culinary genius, so it fell to me most of the time. But then... after everything that happened..."

Emily swallowed nervously. She already regretted asking about it. "Sorry, I shouldn't—"

"It's alright." Meredith sipped her coffee and looked around the kitchen slowly. Her eyes flickered across the kitchen cabinets, the tiny cooker, the empty fridge, and then finally, she met Emily's gaze again. "We had this big open kitchen, with doors that opened right out into our garden. We had a little bar in the back corner, this huge stove so we could cook for the whole family during the holidays... I used to love spending time there."

Her voice was soft as she spoke about her home, and she smiled like she was talking about an old friend. But when she carried on, her expression clouded over, and she frowned down at her coffee cup.

"The day I got back from the hospital, I remember going back to that house, and realizing how big it was. I'd never noticed before, but that day, I could hear my footsteps echoing around me because there was just nothing else to hear. Normally the TV would be on, or I'd be able to hear Jennifer typing on her computer. She used to type really aggressively, so you could hear it wherever you were." A fleeting chuckle seemed to glance over her lips at the memory. "Megan would usually have music on in her room, so there was always just a..." She trailed off into silence, uncertain of how to describe it for a moment. "Buzz. I never noticed it until it was gone. But that day when I got back and I was alone for the first time, I couldn't stop thinking about it. The house was too quiet, it was too big. It was too much for one person, too much for me."

"What did you do?"

"I sold most of our things, and listed the house as semi-furnished. There were a few things that I just couldn't part with; some clothes, some books of Megan's, our family photographs. Those things I had boxed up and put into storage, but everything else I just got rid of, and threw at someone else to deal with. Then I sold the house off and got as far away from it as I could."

A long silence followed that. Emily wasn't sure of what to say, so instead, she reached over and laid her hand over Meredith's gently, rubbing her thumb over her knuckles. Meredith's hand clenched a little under her touch like she was about to pull away quickly, but she didn't.

"After what happened, I couldn't do any of the things I used to. I couldn't sleep in that big bed, I couldn't watch TV on that big flatscreen. I couldn't cook a full meal in that big kitchen. Even after I came here and started fresh with all new things, that didn't change. It just felt so pathetic to cook a whole meal to eat it alone. It just made me feel..." She grimaced, unable to find the words. She didn't need to though; her expression said it all.

"It made you feel lonely." Emily finished for her. She knew the feeling, to some extent. Of course she'd never gone through anything nearly as traumatic as what Meredith had experienced, but she knew it was tough to live alone and *not* feel lonely. When she'd first moved out of her parents' place she'd dealt with it, and she'd gone through it again once her roommate had moved out. Then last year when her ex had broken up with her, she'd been left looking around an apartment that had felt just a little too big for one person.

"That's exactly how I feel."

"Living alone isn't so bad, you know." She said gently, smiling up at Meredith. "I do it. It takes a while to readjust to living alone after you're used to having company – even if it's just having another presence in the house. You miss it."

"You sure do."

Emily frowned. They hadn't really spoken about Meredith's family since she'd told her all about the accident, and if she was honest, Emily was more than happy to leave it alone. In her mind, even just the small amount that she knew about the accident was enough to explain Meredith's behavior, so she had no reason to pry any more than she already had done. She figured that if Meredith wanted her to know anything more about the accident, she would tell her sooner or later. As far as Emily's report was concerned though, she had everything she needed.

Since their relationship had started, Emily had tried to put up a boundary between their professional relationship and their personal one. It was the best option, not only for her job, but for Meredith too. The only problem was, right now she wasn't sure of how to react.

Professional or personal? Was she supposed to be Emily the psychologist or Emily the friend or Emily the lover?

It was getting harder and harder to differentiate where one ended and the other began, and the line in the sand that she'd drawn was starting to blur and smudge out. When she set her coffee cup down on the countertop and wound her arms around Meredith's neck, Emily couldn't help but feel like at some point, the line would get washed away with the tide, but she pushed the worry out of her head.

"Thank you for telling me that," she whispered, hugging Meredith close. There was a pause while Meredith set her own cup down, and then she hugged back tightly, burying her face into the crook of Emily's neck. "I know it must have been difficult."

Meredith just hummed in agreement rather than respond, so Emily rested her hand at the back of her head, and buried her fingers into the older woman's sandy blonde hair. "What was your favorite meal to cook?"

"Hm?"

"You know, if you had a nice relaxing evening, maybe the day off... what would you cook?"

Meredith thought about it for a moment. "Chicken with a red wine sauce, and mushrooms. It was kind of like *Coq Au Vin*. I'd slow cook it if I had the time, so that it melted in the mouth, but most of the time I couldn't. I'd make it on my own, but I guess back then I didn't mind cooking alone – I knew I'd be eating it with someone else."

"That makes sense."

Meredith let out a long, slow sigh, and then pulled away from the hug. When she did, Emily saw a faint smile on her lips. It wasn't one of the grim smirks that she sometimes saw when the topic got a little too personal or uncomfortable—it was real, if a little sad.

"It's nice to talk about them." Meredith admitted. "I haven't done it for a long time."

"Not to anyone?"

She shrugged, stuffing her hands into her pockets. "No one else knows, except for Melanie. And we don't exactly have all that many personal chats over coffee and cake, you know?"

"I guess so..."

"To most people at the hospital I'm just a bitter, lonely woman who's never been married. They make no secret of it, I know that's what everyone thinks. They don't know the truth, and to be honest, that suits me just fine."

"You don't want to talk about your family? Not at all?"

"It's a part of my life that doesn't exist anymore." Meredith shrugged. "What's the point of dwelling on it?"

Emily opened her mouth to respond, but before she could, Meredith had turned on her heel and was heading for the door, waving goodbye. "I'll see you tonight, okay?"

"Yeah, see you."

She watched as Meredith stepped out into the hallway before the door swung shut behind her, and then she slowly walked around the kitchen counter and slumped onto one of the stools, frowning to herself.

Everyone handles grief differently. Everyone handles *everything* differently, but grief was one of the most difficult things a person could go through. It pushed a person to their limits emotionally, and brought out the best—and the worst—of people. Emily knew this; it was one of the first lessons she was taught when she was training. There was no step-by-step manual to follow when it came to dealing with something as traumatic and terrible as losing a loved one.

Even though she knew that, Emily also knew that this was by no means a healthy way of handling grief. After the accident, Meredith had locked herself into a bubble to try and cope, but eight years later, she still hadn't popped it and come back out into the real world.

This is the first time she's even come close to a real relationship since her wife died, Emily realized with a start. Her relationship with Meredith was the first—maybe the only time—since her wife's death that she'd allowed a person to get close to her. That was an awful lot of pressure to put on her shoulders.

But as she looked around the kitchen, Emily realized there was one way that she might be able to get a *little* closer to Meredith. She only hoped that it worked.

———

When Meredith made her way through the door to her apartment that night, she already had her phone in hand, and was scrolling through a delivery app in search of food. It wasn't until she'd dumped her bag on the floor and kicked her shoes off that she stopped and realized that something smelled *good*. Mouth waveringly good.

Something about it smelled familiar too, but she couldn't put her finger on what it was until she made her way into the kitchen. Emily was standing there waiting for her, wearing an apron with her nose in a cookbook.

"You're cooking?" Meredith asked, sniffing the air. God, that smelled good. It smelled like garlic and... red wine?

As she joined Emily in the kitchen, Meredith realized what she was looking at. It had been a long time since she'd seen the ingredients laid out like this, but it was definitely what would be used if she wanted to make something like Coq-Au-Vin. "Is this what I think it is?"

"Yes." Emily smiled shyly, biting her lip. "I went out and bought everything this afternoon. I... I know it's been a long time since you've had this, and maybe given everything that's happened you might not want to eat this, but I thought perhaps—"

"This is really sweet, Emily," she whispered, looking around the kitchen. It had been years since she'd walked home to the smell of dinner cooking, years since she'd had someone do something like this for her. She'd resigned herself to the idea that she would never experience it again, and she'd be doomed to a life of takeaway for one forever. "Thank you."

"You're welcome." She beamed across the kitchen at Meredith, and poured her a glass of wine. "The chicken is marinating, and I've made the sauce to go on top already. I was just waiting until you got home until I actually made it all. I didn't want it to dry out or anything before you got home."

Meredith's chest ached as she met Emily's gaze, and instead of taking the wine that was offered to her, she leaned in and captured her lips in a kiss, cupping both her cheeks. Emily was surprised by the sudden kiss, and put the glass down blindly on the counter before she sank into it, pressing herself against Meredith.

She pulled back for a moment, just enough to talk. She wasn't even sure what she was feeling, and she had no idea of what she wanted to say, but she knew that she wanted to say *something* to her. She wanted to thank her for doing something so meaningful, she wanted to show her how much she appreciated it. But she didn't have the words.

"Thank you," she whispered again, kissing her once more. It was all she could do, even though it didn't really feel like enough. "Thank you."

She kissed Emily again, trying to push everything she was feeling into the kiss. Her hands found Emily's waist, and Emily's hands sank into her hair as they fell back against the counter. There was a need, an urgency to Meredith's kisses, a fire burned deep inside her, a passionate heat that Emily had reawakened. She wanted more. She needed more.

Hands moved quickly and nimbly undoing buttons and zippers, but Emily was no match for Meredith's dexterity. The younger woman was naked, with the exception of the apron which hung loosely around her neck. Losing the last of her clothing, Meredith reached out and slipped the apron over Emily's neck. The younger woman's tanned skin, and soft, almost velvet curves were breathtaking and Meredith was overcome with something more than raw desire; she wanted to give Emily everything she had; everything she was, in the name of pleasure. In the name of... Emily's hand reached around the back of her neck pulling her into a kiss, her other hand clasped Meredith's guiding into down to the wetness between her legs.

"I want you, Meredith."

In one swift decisive movement, Meredith spun Emily around and bent her over the kitchen counter. Long fingers dipped into glistening folds. Emily was sodden with desire and Meredith let out a long groan appreciating her readiness.

"God, yes," Emily whimpered, widening her legs, as the evening sun shone across her golden body, from the window in front of them. Anyone could have seen them, in theory, but being six floors up, that only added to the sheer excitement of the moment.

Emily released a long moan as Meredith's fingers pushed deep inside. The contrast between the smooth flawless touch of the skin on her back to the hot, wetness of her desire sent Meredith's mind reeling. Pushing their thighs close together, Meredith ground against the firmness of her own hand, widening her stance. Emily met each thrust with equal measure until they were in perfect rhythm, the tempo unrelenting. Meredith closed her eyes relishing the undulating pulse of Emily surrounding her fingers. There is nothing she wouldn't do for this woman. Nothing.

Quickening the pace, Meredith reached around and slid her fingers over Emily's clit and the younger woman screamed, "Yes!" The shadow of her breasts as they moved in time with their bodies added to the excitement.

"Don't stop, please don't stop," Emily begged, arching her back and lifting her breast up to the light from the evening sun.

With deft precision, Meredith focused her exacting attention to her lover's G-Spot. The merciless, exacting movement had Emily's legs trembling, as she climbed towards climax.

"Come for me Emily," she whispered.

And Emily did. As if the words triggered her final undoing she came hard, squeezing and pulsing around Meredith's fingers, her pleasure oozing satisfaction.

"That's built up my appetite." Meredith let out a small laugh and then kissed Emily's back and wrapped her arms tight around her. "I feel so very lucky," her words which told the clear truth of her heart, were barely a whisper.

"What are you murmuring?" Emily asked, turning around to face her. Placing her hands on Meredith's cheeks she pulled her in for a kiss. Then with a laugh she nodded to the window and said "I think the guy in the block opposite got a little bit more entertainment than he was expecting for a week night."

"Just as well I know you are teasing." Meredith tickled her sides causing an eruption of giggles. "I want to grab a quick shower before dinner so shall we get the Coq-Au-Vin in the oven, so you can join me?" Then peering over Emily's shoulder she just did a quick scan to make sure they hadn't been overlooked.

"Mm, I could do with an appetizer." Emily grabbed the apron sliding it over her head and swiftly put everything into the Le Creuset casserole before popping it into the oven. Meredith leaned against the counter sipping her glass of wine, enjoying the view from behind...

She would never have enough of Emily.

SIXTEEN

Although Doctor Asquith has a shining record and history with her patients and operations, she does appear to struggle with interpersonal relations. While there are many examples of doctors in the medical industry who hold themselves in particularly high regard due to their successes in the OR, Doctor Asquith seems to take this to the extreme. It seems as though this attitude may be the core factor driving the obvious tensions between her and the other members of the medical staff, which could result in consequences in the future.

Doctor Asquith is quick to judge others for their mistakes, and will hurry to point out the flaws others make, but rarely sees any problems with her own work. She shows signs of narcissism when talking about her own achievements, and is unwilling to point out any of her own flaws.

Emily stared at the paper in front of her, drumming her fingers against the desk slowly. That had been the first assessment of Meredith she had made, weeks earlier, and she'd written it up not that long after their first meeting. It was pretty much just a very verbose and elegant way of saying what everyone else seemed to have already managed to agree on; Meredith could behave like an ass.

When she'd first written up the report, it had been accurate. Emily had pretty much taken everyone at face value, and when she paired it with her own meetings with Meredith, it was pretty easy to draw a conclusion—she didn't work or play well with others, and she had an obvious god Complex. But now, after everything that had happened between the two of them... was that really fair to say?

Emily set down her red pen with a sigh, taking the document she threw it into the trashcan by her desk. She had printed it off her initial report on Meredith to edit it, but it just didn't feel like there was much point. She would probably just be better off starting all over again from scratch. The woman she had gotten to know, who had let her see inside and that she had... she had developed feelings for... wasn't the person others wrongly judged her to be.

She opened up her laptop again, back to the same screen as before, where Meredith's report was waiting for her. For a few moments, Emily just stared at the blinking cursor in silence, frowning to herself. She knew that she didn't want to hand this report in any longer–it didn't reflect Meredith, not really. It was just a regurgitated script of what other people had told her, rather than the person Meredith was.

It would be unfair to hand this report in. It painted Meredith as some self-obsessed narcissist, who'd be better suited to writing a book of her own surgical prowess than operating on other people. And while that might have been the outward appearance that Meredith managed to give off round the hospital, it didn't even come close to explaining who she was, or why she acted the way she did.

There was a lot more to Meredith than she'd first assumed, although it had taken her a long time to dig deep enough to find it. She'd buried it under layers of sarcasm and an aloof, untouchable façade, and most other people didn't seem to know that it was there. Perhaps Meredith herself had even forgotten until recently that she still had the capacity to be warm and inviting, given how long it had been since she had let someone in.

Emily sighed, and pulled out her laptop to search through the files she had made on the hospital. She found Meredith's and opened it up again, before scrolling down to the bottom. It wasn't fair of her to hand in a report that critical, not now. She *knew* there was more to Meredith than met the eye, and she should make sure the hospital administration knew it too.

But her fingers hovered over the keys, and Emily found herself hesitating, nervous for the first time. Was this a good idea? She wasn't exactly the most impartial judge of character now, after everything that had happened between the two of them.

I could hand Meredith's case file over to someone else, she thought. But then people would start asking questions, they'd wonder why she couldn't take Meredith's evaluation anymore, and then she would have to tell them everything. Once that came out, it wouldn't matter that she'd tried to hand off the case file, she'd be reprimanded for unprofessionalism, maybe even fired. She'd definitely have to fly back home, and she wouldn't be able to see Meredith any more.

So she was stuck with the case, and with the dilemma. What if her judgement was clouded by rose-tinted glasses, and she was looking at Meredith as a lover, not as her patient?

"Shit..." She groaned, dropping her head into her hands. She'd never been in this position before. She'd *always* prided herself on being a professional in every aspect of her work, but something had flipped in her when it came to Meredith. She didn't care about keeping that professional distance between them anymore, and she didn't give a damn about whatever conflict of interest may have arisen because of what they'd started.

As she sat there, Emily's phone buzzed with a message. She picked up her phone to see she had a text from Meredith—a photograph of the package she'd ordered.

The sender lives in Palmdale apparently. Her message read. *Who do I know who hails from California?*

Despite how stressed she was from work, Emily couldn't help but smile at the message. As a thank you gift for everything Meredith had done for her, Emily had bought a copy of *Desert of the Heart*. It was her favorite book, and she only hoped Meredith enjoyed it too.

I wonder who sent that! She replied, just as the door to the office opened behind her. Two of her colleagues walked in, both with grim expressions. At the sight of Emily at her desk, they held up their hands to wave to her, before going back to their conversation.

"Everything alright?" she called to them. One of the men turned to look at her, and grimaced.

"Not really," he admitted. "Looks like we've got someone screwing with their prescription pad."

"Seriously?"

"Yeah." He threw himself down into the chair. "There are prescriptions that don't match up, you know? Prescriptions for patients that aren't his, medications that people don't need. Patients on the brink of death going through huge amounts of medication that they shouldn't have."

"You think someone's fueling a habit?" Emily frowned. Meredith had never mentioned suspecting any of her colleagues of anything like that but it wouldn't be the first time the team had uncovered something similar and given the size of the hospital it could be anyone of a number of doctors on staff.

"Either that or they're selling it on. Whatever the reason, this guy's going to get fired, if not worse."

Thank god I haven't come across anything like that. Emily thought to herself as she turned back to her desk. She wasn't looking at any drug pushing doctors when it came to her job, just surgeons who didn't like opening up to anyone about their problems.

She turned back to her laptop and stretched out, ready to start the report again.

SEVENTEEN

When Meredith left for work that morning, Emily had cryptically warned her that she was going to be in for a busy day. She refused to say anything more than that, so when Meredith walked into the hospital, she half expected to see the remnants of a bomb going off. The lobby was still intact though, and it took her a little while to realize just what was going on.

It started with hushed whispers that she couldn't quite make sense of when she passed the nurses. None of them told her anything though, and one even shot her a dirty look as she walked past them, so she figured it was better to ask someone else. None of the junior doctors on her team seemed to know what was going on either, and it wasn't until she went to the dispensary to check on some medication for a patient that she found out.

"Do you have any idea what's going on today?" she asked George, the middle-aged and perpetually annoyed Pharmacist.

"Wait, you don't know?"

"Would I be asking you if I didn't?"

"Good point." He leaned in, glancing around conspiratorially before he whispered to her. "It's just I figured you would, what with it being your department and all."

"Well clearly I don't." Meredith mimicked his whispering. "So get to the point."

"It's Phil!" he hissed. "He's been writing fake prescriptions, apparently."

"Phil?" Meredith pulled back in surprise. Of all of the people at the hospital to be pulled up for drugs, she wouldn't have assumed it would be him. "What do you mean, fake prescriptions?"

"Well, he's been writing out prescriptions for bedbound patients, coma patients. The kinds of people who won't need narcotics. Only no one ever noticed, not until the audit happened."

"Shit..." she breathed out, shaking her head slowly. No wonder everyone was so on edge. "But how did he... I mean we don't pick up patients' prescriptions?"

"Apparently he has charmed a couple of the nurses to do some dirty work for him and they admitted everything when they were confronted first thing this morning." George's eyebrows were raised to the very top of his forehead as he nodded sagely.

"So what's happening now?"

"Well, now they're going through *all* of our files to look for more problems, which means I have to go and look for—"

"Not with *you*, George. What's happening to Phil?"

"Oh!" George shrugged. "I don't know. I think they're requesting permission for a full investigation starting tomorrow, and he'll have to be put on administrative leave when that happens. Hey, that'll leave you as the top dog in the surgery world, right?"

"I was already, George." Meredith drummed her fingers against the counter for a moment, before pulling away. "All right, thanks George."

As she made her way to her office, Meredith heard more whispers about Phil. It seemed like everyone had now heard the news, and it would only be a matter of time before Phil was escorted out of the hospital by security.

Meredith made her way into the sanctuary of her office, away from all of the gossip, and tried to get a headstart on some of her work. She barely had the chance to open a file before the door to her office burst open, and Phil walked in.

"Meredith!" He closed the door behind him and rushed over. "Have you heard what they're doing?"

He looked frantic. Sweat was beading on his brow, his hands were trembling, and his speech was garbled. In his left hand, he was clutching a crumpled file.

"Phil, do you think you should be here?" she asked. "Given what I believe is happening?"

"That's exactly *why* I came here, Meredith. This company? This audit that they're doing, you know it's all bullshit, right? They don't give a shit about the job we do in the OR, they're just looking for screw ups, minor screw ups, so they can tarnish our reputations."

He sounded like one of the insane conspiracy theorists who paid for time on Public Access. Meredith let out a low sigh, and pinched the bridge of her nose. "Phil, this is all really interesting, but I've got to be honest, I don't think you should be here. There's going to be an investigation into you, and I don't want that kind of headache in my life."

"I came here to show you what they're doing to us." Phil hissed.

"What do you mean *us?*"

"Take a look at it." Phil tossed the file down on Meredith's desk. "It's their file on you. This is bullshit, right? I mean, look at the crap they're saying about you."

"How did you get this?" Meredith asked, looking up at him for a moment. Phil brushed that aside, as if it was nothing.

"Don't worry about that. Just read it. It's bullshit, I can't believe Melanie's letting them get away with this. What are they trying to do, ruin the department? You're impossible to work with and I'm forging my prescriptions? Who *are* these people?"

Meredith scanned the page quickly. It looked like a psych evaluation of her, and as she read through it, a few words jumped out at her. *Narcissist. Difficult to work with. Tensions. Future consequences.*

There was no way Emily would have written a report like this on her. It seemed like the kind of thing she would expect from any of the other doctors or nurses on staff, the people who didn't really know her, but Emily?

No. Meredith refused to believe that. When she looked to the bottom of the page though, there was Emily's name as the footnote.

All of a sudden, her heart felt like it was beating far too quickly in her chest. A wave of nausea came over her, and as she stared at the page in front of her, Meredith felt the sting of tears prick her eyes. She tried to swallow down the emotion but it lodged in her throat making it difficult for her to breathe.

After everything she had told Emily about herself, after she'd let her into her life and opened herself up, this was what she got? She dropped the file back on her desk with trembling hands, shaking her head. "No. She didn't write that."

"She *did*, Meredith," Phil insisted. "I found it in her office."

Tears blurred her eyes, but Meredith blinked them away furiously, determined not to let Phil see her cry. She couldn't believe she had let Emily get so close to her, only to have her stab her in the back and betray her like this. The file would end up on her permanent record, and she'd be screwed if she ever went for another position, or moved to a different hospital.

"Get out," she ordered Phil, without looking up. In her peripheral vision, she saw him standing there by her desk, not making a move for the door. "I said get *out*, Phil!"

"Why are you yelling at me?" he snapped. "I'm the victim here, just like you!"

"Jesus Christ." She snatched the report up from her desk and pushed past him, out into the hallway. Phil tried to follow her, but Meredith was faster, and managed to weave through the crowd of doctors and patients far more easily. She disappeared down the hallway, and made her way straight to the office where she knew she'd find Emily.

She pushed the door to the office open with so much force that it bounced off the wall, and the staff members inside all jumped to their feet in surprise. Emily was among them, working at the back of the room, and at the sight of Meredith in the doorway, she stood up with a start.

"Meredith... What are you do—"

"What the fuck is this?" She held up the file. "What the hell is this, Emily?"

A few of the other members of the audit team exchanged nervous glances with each other, and then looked at Emily, but she nodded to them. "It's alright. Could you guys give us the room, please?"

Meredith waited as the rest of the team shuffled out, before she approached Emily's desk and slammed the file down. "I'm a narcissist who doesn't work well with others? I don't care about other people, and I lack *empathy?*"

"Meredith, what are you talking about?" Emily asked. She seemed genuinely confused, until Meredith picked up the file again and pushed it into her hands.

"Your report on me. You know, I'd have expected anyone else from your team to write something like that, but not you. *Not you,* Emily. I told you everything. About the accident, I told you all about what it was like to lose my family, and you throw it back in my face like this? You write up a report like this? A report that's going to follow me for the rest of my career, and makes me look like some kind of sociopath?"

Emily shook her head in disbelief as she looked down at the file, scanning through it. "How did you get this?"

"Does that matter?"

"How?"

"Phil gave it to me, what the fuck do you care?" she snapped. "It doesn't matter how I got it, it matters what it *says.*"

"Meredith." Emily dropped the file, and reached out a hand. "Let me explain."

She jerked her hand away, and took a step back. "There's nothing to explain, Emily. I'm pretty sure *that* does all the explaining for you, doesn't it? Is that really how you feel about me? You think I'm some heartless monster?"

"*No!*" Emily protested. "Meredith, please just listen to me."

"No, you listen to *me*. I don't give a shit what your team finds on anyone else in this hospital. If Phil was really sneaking drugs for himself, then he *should* get fired. If someone was forcing other doctors to do their work for them, they *should* be punished, but how can you write something like this when you know exactly what I've been through? You know who I am, why I'm the way that I am. And you still wrote this?"

She drew in a deep breath, shaking her head in disgust. "If you hand that report in, Emily, I'll... I'll tell your bosses about us. I'll tell them everything that's been happening over the past few months, and I'll tell them your report can't be trusted."

Emily physically recoiled at that. Where she had been reaching out to Meredith only moments earlier, now it was her turn to look disgusted. "You... would do that?"

"Damn straight I would. You write something that's going to wreck my career, and I'll do the same."

"This report isn't going to be submitted to your boss, Meredith," she whispered. "I.. I can't believe you think I would ever *do* that to you, after everything."

"Well how do you think I feel? I can't believe you would even *write* something like that about me." Meredith's hands shook as she took a step away from Emily, and turned on her heel. It felt like she'd just run a marathon, and as she made her way out of the office, she had a vague notion that people were watching her walk off. She couldn't focus on them though, she couldn't focus on anything at all. All she wanted to do was go home, curl up in a ball, and pretend none of this was happening.

This whole thing had been a huge mistake. She should have known better. She had lowered her defenses, shared her most private pain, made herself vulnerable and now she was paying the price. Her trust had been misplaced.

EIGHTEEN

Emily stared at the finished report on Meredith. It had been two days since Meredith had threatened to report her, and while there was no email in her inbox requesting that she pack up her things and leave the company, she still didn't feel good. Perhaps Meredith had just been bluffing, and she never really intended to report her for what had happened, but that didn't matter any more.

What mattered to Emily now was that she'd done something that *could* get her fired if anyone found out. Acting the way she had done, did she really think she could stay on at the company? Even if no one else knew what had happened, she would always know.

On every level she had failed to put boundaries in place, failed to think about the impacts of her actions, taken advantage of people's vulnerability and broken trust. Trust that her employer had placed in her, that the hospital had placed in her and now the trust Meredith had placed in her.

She'd fucked up. She should have handed the job over to someone else and carried on with a clear conscience, but she'd let things go too far, and now she was having to live with the consequences, just like she'd feared.

She had tried to contact Meredith, to explain, but her calls and messages went unanswered and trying to speak to her at work given her recent threat just wasn't an option. Things were bad enough and the only thing that could possibly do was make a bad situation worse. The damage that had been done with Meredith was irreparable. In the cold light of day there was only one decent thing to do, finish the report and leave the company.

How the hell did Phil manage to get hold of that report? She wondered, looking down at it. The report, which had been screwed up and unfolded a few times over the past couple of days, sat beside her laptop. It served as a reminder of exactly why she needed to finish her work and get the hell out of town.

"Where did he even find this?" she wondered out loud, picking it up to get a closer look at it. It was only then that she saw a dot of red ink in the corner, and realized exactly what the print out was. It was from the day she'd begun rewriting Meredith's report. She'd gone to edit her old report by circling the bits that needed changing, before just starting fresh. Phil must have dug it from her trash. Shit. She had always been so careful about confidential reports and now to screw up on something so simple but so important. All because she hadn't emptied her trash in the confidential waste that night. That alone was a terminable offense.

"Bastard," she muttered, screwing the report up in anger. It sounded like he was going to lose his job—the investigation into his prescription pad had some grounds to it—and Emily couldn't help but be a little bit glad about it.

She emailed off the report to the head of the audit team, and as the email notification sounded, she closed the lid of her laptop and walked over to the locked confidential waste can, depositing the offending report. What an unholy shit show she had made of this. At least the pain of losing Meredith, of having broken her trust and screwing herself over professionally might seem a little less piqued, with 3,000 miles distance between them. Once she was back in California, maybe then she would be able to leave all of this behind her.

No matter how tightly she tried to hold her heart, there was no way to stop it from breaking.

NINETEEN

It had been four days.

Meredith had gone four days without talking to Emily, and that was the longest it had been in weeks, almost months. Every time she left her apartment she found herself looking at the door down the hallway. The heavy pain in her chest seemed to deepen everytime she pictured Emily's smile; or the way she'd tuck a loose strand of her hair behind her ear. Part of her wanted to knock on the door and apologize, but she couldn't bring herself to do it.

She missed Emily. She missed hearing her laugh, or watching her screw up her face as she concentrated on her laptop. Most of all, Meredith missed waking up next to her. There had been message after message, text after text, the day she had confronted Emily. Emily was begging to explain. To be given the opportunity to be heard. That night she had even knocked on the door to the apartment but Meredith had been so hurt, the mere thought of opening the door to her was out of the question. And then it had gone quiet.

Now after everything that had happened between them though, she figured she should give Emily at least a little bit of time before she approached her. Sure she'd been hurt. The fact that she'd allowed

Emily to get close to her and yet she still saw her in the same way as everyone else, was a knife in her heart.

"Let me explain... I can't believe you think I would ever *do* that to you, after everything." Emily's words kept repeating, at the forefront on her thoughts. She had never given her a chance. What if she had allowed her to explain? What would she have said? Would they still have ended up here? Although for Meredith here was just "pain." Was Emily feeling this way too?

Before she'd even made it to her office, Meredith was accosted by Melanie's secretary, who ushered her towards administration. Apparently there was something they needed to discuss, and Melanie wanted to get it out of the way as soon as possible.

When Meredith walked in, her boss was holding a crisp file in one hand, and beckoning her with the other. She took her seat, peering at the folder curiously. "What's that?"

"This? This is *you*. Your evaluation's been handed in early, so I wanted to go through it with you."

Meredith's stomach tightened nervously at that, and she swallowed hard. "Okay."

"I must say..." Melanie looked down at the folder. "I'm impressed."

"Impressed?"

"It's glowing! I've never heard anyone talk about you like this before. You want to take a look?"

Meredith snatched it out of her hands without even responding. There had to be some kind of mistake, there was no way Melanie was holding the right report. But no, her name was at the top. Emily's name was at the bottom.

It wasn't the report she had read before. This one was nothing but complimentary.

Although on the surface Dr. Asquith seems abrasive and difficult to work with, she is a highly skilled surgeon, and an invaluable member of the team. Due to past traumas, Dr. Asquith struggles in social situations that require deep connections with others, but this does not mean that she lacks empathy. In fact, I suspect that she feels a great deal more empathy for her patients than even she realizes. Over the weeks of investigation, I have found that Dr. Asquith has great capacity for growth and change, although it is recommended that she seeks some sort of counseling to help mend her past traumas.

"I have to say, Meredith," Melanie said gently. "I'm very proud of you for coming out and telling her about what happened back in London."

She ignored the compliment, dropping the file on the desk. "Emily wrote this?"

"She handed it in a couple of days ago, yes."

"I want to go to talk to her. I'll be back in a bit, I've just got to—" Meredith stood up and turned to head for the door, but Melanie's voice called her back.

"I wouldn't bother, Meredith. She's not here."

"What do you mean?"

"I mean she's not here. She handed in her notice along with your report. Apparently it came out of the blue, and they were all very surprised. She headed back to California yesterday, I think. Thankfully she had completed her assessments before she made the decision. The idea of telling everyone they'd have to undergo another psych evaluation with someone new isn't something I'd relish."

Yesterday.

"Do they have any contact details for her?" Meredith asked. "Any way of reaching out to her?"

"They don't give out personal details of their employees." Melanie pointed out. "Why, you want to send her flowers for writing such a nice report on you?"

Meredith let out a low sigh. "No, not that. I just... Never mind."

As she left the office, Meredith pulled out her phone and called Emily, listening to the ring tone over and over again. It went through to voicemail, as did the next one. Meredith tried four times before eventually she just gave up, and tucked her phone away again. Now, she wanted more than anything to call Emily and talk.

Had she written that report because it was how she truly felt? Or was it just because she saw how hurt Meredith was by the first report?

Had she just destroyed the only thing that had made her happy in all these long years?

Now that Emily was gone though, it didn't look like she had any way of knowing.

TWENTY

The next few days passed by in a blur. Most of the members of staff were still buzzing about what had happened to Phil, and at every corner, Meredith seemed to bump into gossip about him. He'd been put on administrative leave while the investigation was ongoing, and judging by the way the guys at the dispensary were acting, it looked like he was going to be fired.

She couldn't find the energy to care about Phil though. The only thing she could think of was Emily. She had resigned. Was that out of fear that Meredith was going to expose their relationship? Was it a relationship or was it just relations? The confusion and pain seemed to fill her, constantly threatening to spill over. For so long she had contained all her emotions, locking them away so tightly inside she didn't have to feel anything and now... now she seemed to be feeling everything.

As if she was sitting on the top of a bulging suitcase, desperately trying to keep it all from bursting out. Panic rose in her chest. *God, if it starts to all come out, it'll never stop. I can't feel that much pain. Not on my own.* It was overwhelming.

Every day, she tried to call Emily to talk about what had

happened, and every day, the call went straight through to voicemail. The only space that wasn't filled with grief, had been occupied by guilt and the one person that she needed, wanted; the person who had worked so hard to reach her was no longer within her grasp.

It was towards the end of Meredith's shift when she passed through the Intensive Care Unit, ready to drop off a file on a patient she'd operated on. Jason, one of the young nurses, was sitting at the station filling out paperwork, and he looked surprised when she greeted him.

"Evening, Jason."

"I—Hi, doctor."

"I've got the Mendoza file for you, it's the report on the pre-op." She dropped the file off in front of him, and smiled gently at his look of shock. "What?"

"Nothing. It's just... Well most days you just throw the file at me and walk off. I didn't even realize you knew my name."

"I'm full of surprises. You need me to sign off on his folder?"

Jason passed it over, still looking at her suspiciously. Meredith filled in her name and details in the file, just in case they ever got audited again, and handed it back over. When she looked up, she realized Jason wasn't looking at her anymore, but over her shoulder into one of the private rooms.

"That poor woman," he sighed, shaking his head. The blinds to the room were mostly closed, but there was a slight gap through which she could see a woman leaning over the bed. It looked like she was holding the patient's hand.

"Who's in there?" she asked, turning back to Jason. He looked up at her in surprise, blinking rapidly.

"Did you... Just ask about a patient?" He tilted his head to one side. "Are you feeling alright?"

"Don't be an asshole."

The corner of Jason's mouth twitched at that, and he produced a file from his desk. "It's one of your patients actually, you're listed on his file. Mr. Cooke?"

"Oh god..." Meredith opened the file to flip through it, even though she already knew what she would find inside. She remembered him, mainly because of how young he was, and how unfair it had seemed when she'd looked at his scans. He was only in his late thirties, but the headaches he'd been complaining of had been the result of an inoperable brain tumor. Meredith had been the one to find it, but she'd handed it over to Oncology to handle. Someone from that department had given his wife the bad news. "I'm surprised he's still hanging in there."

"Well," Jason shot her a pointed look. "Define *hanging in there*. He's on life support, has been for a few weeks now."

"There's no brain function at all?"

"No, none. I think for a while she was in denial, didn't want to admit that he was already gone. She signed off on them turning off the life support this morning, I think they're doing it tonight. She hasn't left his room all day, as far as I can tell."

Meredith looked back at the room, frowning. It was a horrible thing to go through at any age, but to lose someone that young... Well, she didn't have to imagine how painful it was. She knew firsthand just how painful that grief was.

"Are you alright?" Jason asked, tilting his head to one side. "You look kind of... Upset."

"Why would I be?" She tossed the file back on his desk with a shrug. "I don't even know the man."

"Fair enough."

Jason turned around to put the Cooke patient file with the others, and as he did, Meredith slipped away from the nurse's station. She wasn't sure what made her go to Cooke's room, but the next thing she knew, she was sliding the door open to poke her head inside.

When she first slipped inside the room, Meredith wasn't even certain that it was the patient she had treated months earlier. He looked different now, of course; the cancer had turned him into a frail shell of himself, and with all the wires and tubes sticking out of him it was hard at first glance to make out his features.

She recognized the wife though. Her name was... Claudia. Maybe. Maybe it was something else, but Meredith was sure it began with a "C." She was hunched over the bed, clutching one of her husband's limp hands between her own, with her forehead pressed to them. At the sound of the door sliding open, she lifted her head slowly.

She'd encountered the families of patients who were dying or dead so many times over the years, but as she met this poor woman's gaze, it felt like it was the first time. It was certainly the first time she'd ever really taken a moment to *look* at a family member, to see the pain and the worry on their face.

Her skin was pale, her eyes were bloodshot and rimmed a dark shade of pink. Her hair looked greasy, and Meredith wondered when the woman had last gone home to shower. It had probably been longer than she'd be comfortable admitting.

Was that how I looked? Meredith wondered. *Was this how I was, all those years ago?*

"I'm sorry to interrupt," she said softly. "I don't know if you even remember me. My name's Meredith Asquith, I... I saw your husband, when he first came to the hospital."

"You did?" The woman blinked, narrowing her eyes as she tried to think back. It was hardly surprising that she didn't remember meeting Meredith before; she'd probably spent so much time in and out of hospital for various appointments that the staff had all begun to blend into one. "I'm sorry. I don't..."

"It's fine." She said quickly. "I... I just heard what's happening."

"Yes." She swallowed hard, looking down at her husband for a moment. "He's... He'll finally be..."

"It's alright, you don't have to say anything." Meredith assured her, watching as her shoulders shook. She was trying to hold back tears, probably trying to save face in front of a stranger, but it was no use. Even from across the room Meredith could see the tears rolling down her cheeks. "I can leave, if you'd rather—"

"No, no." She laid her husband's hand down on the bed gently before wiping her eyes. "I'm sorry, please stay."

Meredith hesitated before walking to the bedside. She'd never been in this position before; she normally avoided patients unless it was absolutely necessary. Explaining the surgery, and asking if they had any questions about the procedure was as far as she'd go; doing her best to minimize any meaningful interaction. The residual anxiety was something she left for junior doctors and nurses to deal with. But this woman was sitting on the brink of the most difficult moment of her life, and she was asking Meredith to share it with her, just for a few moments.

I'm the wrong person for this, she thought, looking from the patient's wife to the door. She wasn't even sure why she'd come into the room, how would she know what to say to make this any easier for the woman? Knowing her, she'd probably end up upsetting the woman and making the last hours harder not easier.

Despite that doubt, that fear, Meredith accepted the offer, and dragged a chair over to sit down opposite the woman. She was young like her husband, probably in her mid-thirties. That was far, *far* too young to be a widow.

"I uh," she cleared her throat. "I'm sorry, but I don't remember your names."

"Clara. My husband is Alex."

Well, I was close.

Meredith rubbed the back of her neck, looking around the room for a few moments to distract herself. She felt so uncomfortable in this room, with these two people she didn't know, yet she couldn't bring herself to make an excuse and leave them. There was this completely inexplicable urge within her to try and help Clara, even though it was too late for anything to be done.

"How... How are you doing?" she asked finally, immediately regretting her words. It was obvious how she was doing: *badly*. "I'm sorry, that's a stupid thing to ask."

"It's not," Clara said with a kind smile. "I... I'm handling it better than I was when he was first diagnosed, and when he was first brought in here. I remember that first night, all of the doctors were telling me over and over again that I should start to think about... removing the life support. I didn't want to hear it. I was convinced that he would wake up like nothing had happened, and everything would be okay. I was... I honestly believed that if I didn't shut off the machines, he would open his eyes and tell me that he loved me one last time."

She shook her head, wiping away fresh tears. "The doctors must have thought I was insane."

There was a lump forming in the back of Meredith's throat. She could remember waking up after the car crash, when they'd told her Jennifer was brain dead. She'd gone through the same process. "You'd be surprised."

"Hm?" Clara sniffled, reaching for one of the tissues on the nightstand. "Sorry?"

"When..." Meredith began, clearing her throat. Her eyes were starting to sting, threatening tears of her own, but she looked up at the ceiling for a few moments, steadying herself before she continued. "I was married. My wife and daughter.... We were in a car accident one night. The roads were wet, my wife swerved to avoid something on the road, and we ended up wrapped around a tree. I woke up the next morning, and they told me my daughter was gone, and my wife may as well have been."

"I'm so sorry..." Clara whispered, but Meredith shook her head tersely.

"Don't, it's alright. I... I'm telling you this because I went through the same thing when I woke up. I was convinced... I'm a *doctor* and I was convinced that my wife would wake up. She was on life support but... " Meredith shook her head, glancing down at the floor as memories threatened to flood the moment. *This isn't my grief.* She cleared her throat and looked at Clara. "You're grieving, you're going through something more difficult than most people could ever come up with in their worst nightmares. Right now, you get to be as irrational as you want, no one is going to hold it against you."

Clara's lower lip quivered as tears brimmed in her eyes again, and she brought her hand to her mouth to try and muffle a sob. "I'm sorry, I just..."

"You've got nothing to apologize for."

"I just... I'm not ready to say goodbye," she whispered, covering her face with her hands. "I thought that I could let him go, but I can't. I'm not ready. We were supposed... to spend the r-rest of our—"

The rest of her sentence was drowned out with another sob that wracked her body. The sound cut straight through Meredith like a knife, and she winced. *Oh god, I'm definitely the wrong person to be here right now.*

She wanted to get up and find a nurse. Jason was always good at handling grieving relatives, he had that gentle and calming presence that people gravitated towards. He was the *perfect* person to be there for Clara in this moment, not Meredith.

But Jason wasn't there, and she was. And as uncomfortable as all of this made her, Meredith knew that she couldn't just leave the poor woman like this, sobbing at her husband's bedside with no support. So, after taking a deep breath to try and prepare herself, Meredith pushed her chair out, walked around the bed, and crouched beside Clara.

"There's... there's so much that I wanted to tell him." She whimpered, her voice barely intelligible through her hands. "S-so much and now I ca-an't."

"You can." Meredith rested her hand on Clara's knee gently. "There's still time for you to tell him everything that you want to. I... I did. I talked to my wife for—I don't even know how long for. You can still tell Alex everything you want."

Clara was sobbing so loudly that she didn't notice the door slide open. Two doctors walked in, but when they spotted Meredith by the bedside they both froze, a little confused. She shook her head quickly and mouthed "get out," pointing back to the doorway, and thankfully they left before Clara was calm enough to raise her head again.

Meredith plucked another tissue from the box and handed it to her so she could wipe her eyes. "If you aren't ready to say goodbye, I'll tell them to wait for a while to turn off the life support machines. But if you want to spend some time now just making sure he knows you love him, then that's fine too. It's up to you."

"I—" She hiccuped while trying to suck in a deep breath. "I don't want to let him go yet."

"I know it's hard. It feels worse, making the choice to turn off the life support than just—letting things happen passively. But it's for the best, to say goodbye, tell him everything that you want him to know, and then... Let go."

Clara drew in a deep, shaky breath through her nose, and then nodded. "Okay. Okay, I know you're right. Can I... Have some time with him please?"

"Of course." Meredith stood up and dusted herself off. "Take as long as you need."

She left the room quickly, sliding the door closed behind her to come face to face with Jason, who looked surprised to see her. "What are you doing in there? I thought you left."

"I just... checked in on her. Were those guys here to turn off the machines?"

"Yeah, they wanted to see if she was ready, but they said there was already a doctor in there with her, so they're coming back in a while." He peered at her suspiciously. "Why were you in there with her?"

"I was just talking to her." Meredith shooed him away from the door, and back over to the nurse's station. "She's just taking some time to say goodbye, and then she'll be ready for them to come in and... You know."

"Pull the plug," he finished. Meredith grimaced, and shook her head slowly.

"Yeah. *That*. Just be gentle with her, she's... fragile."

"I never would have guessed, what with her husband dying and all." Jason cocked his head to one side. "Are you sure you're not sick? I swear, I've never seen you in a patient's room before, especially not when they're *dying*."

"Well what do you want me to say, Jason? I'm turning over a new leaf," Meredith snapped. The young nurse held up his hand in mock surrender before walking back around to his side of the nurse's station.

"Alright, alright…" he murmured. "Excuse me for asking."

TWENTY-ONE

In the years she had been working at City General, very few patients had ever really stuck with Meredith. Most of the time, when she went home after a long day, she couldn't remember their names, or their faces. But that night as she made her way back to her apartment, Meredith couldn't stop thinking about that poor woman.

She wanted to talk to someone about it. She wanted to tell someone else how crappy she felt, she wanted someone to pat her on the back and assure her she'd done everything she could. But when she got home, the apartment was silent.

The only sound that greeted Meredith as she came through the door was the low hum of the refrigerator in the kitchen, and the steady drip of the faucet she'd never got around to fixing. There was no one waiting for her on the couch, there was no sleeping figure in her bed.

She had always prided herself on being sure of her own actions. While everyone around her second guessed their own decisions and ran for another opinion, Meredith was never shy about her confidence in herself. She never found herself lying awake in bed at night, staring up at the ceiling and going over an operation again and again, trying to point out any flaws in her work or any areas for improvement, because she knew she didn't need them.

It had been a long time since she'd had to admit to a mistake. But now that she was alone, staring at the walls with nothing to distract her from her thoughts, she realized that she had screwed up, badly. She'd been happy with Emily, in a way that she thought she'd never be again. She'd been lucky to find someone who was that good to her, and like an idiot she'd thrown it all away.

With a heavy sigh, Meredith pulled her phone out and scrolled to Emily's contact. She'd already done this so many times before, and each time she'd ended up going through to voicemail. Logically, it was a stupid move, but that didn't stop her from clicking on Emily's name and praying that *this time* she would pick up the phone.

It rang over and over again, taunting Meredith as she waited, before she finally heard the now familiar tone of her voicemail. *The person you have called is unavailable. Please leave a message after the tone.*

She hung up before she had the chance to leave a message. If she was honest, Meredith wasn't totally sure of what she wanted to say to Emily, other than that she was sorry for how things had turned out between the two of them. Perhaps even ask for an opportunity to repair the damage. She certainly didn't want to leave that on an answering machine.

Emily was avoiding her calls, she was certain of that now. Meredith couldn't exactly blame her for that; given the way their last conversation had gone, it wasn't exactly surprising that Emily wasn't jumping at the chance to talk to her again. Emily probably thought if she picked up the phone it would just end in another argument, given that fact she'd never once heard Meredith admit she was wrong.

That wasn't what Meredith wanted though. She didn't want to fight, she wanted to apologize, to try and fix things. How was she supposed to do that now though, given that she had no way of contacting Emily? Her desk was clear, her company refused to give out an address, and she refused to pick up the phone.

"When in doubt," she told herself with a sigh. "Drink."

It probably wasn't the healthiest way to handle what was happening, and she had no doubt that if Emily could see her reaching for a bottle of gin she would *tsk* and roll her eyes, but Meredith didn't really care. She poured herself a decent measure of alcohol, far more than was reasonable with the small amount of tonic that joined it, before slumping back on the couch.

If only she had some way of finding Emily's address, that way maybe she could see her and talk to her about all of this. If Emily hadn't resigned she'd have appeared at her office in California... but she couldn't even do that.

She sat upright, almost spilling the last of her drink in the process. *Of course.* She did have a way of getting Emily's address; it had been on the billing information of the book she had sent. The paperwork had gone in the recycling bin, but she couldn't remember taking it down to the garbage disposal in the basement. There was a chance—a big chance— that the slip was still in her apartment.

Meredith downed the last of her drink and rushed into the kitchen, tugging the waste basket she used for recycling out of the cupboard. It was overflowing with scraps of paper and cardboard, and when she pulled it out she left a trail of trash across her kitchen floor.

It has to be somewhere in here, she thought to herself, picking through the bits and pieces that already fallen onto the floor, before tipping the rest out. Junk mail, flyers, memos from work and bank statements that she'd ripped into little squares all skidded across the tiles, leaving her kitchen floor a mess. Meredith started to sort through it, tossing junk over her shoulder as she hunted for the one piece of paper that would actually be useful to her.

"Come on..." she said quietly, screwing up a note she had made for herself earlier in the week. "You've got to be in here. You've *got* to... Oh!"

There it was, the bill that had been slipped inside the cover of her present. It was a consignment from Barnes and Noble, addressed to her but with a billing address listed as Palmdale, California.

TWENTY-TWO

California... It was a long way to go, and it sure wasn't going to be just a day trip. But Meredith did have all of those vacation days that she never used; she could take advantage of them, slip away from work for a long weekend and book a flight to see Emily. She knew if she could just see her face to face, she'd be able to explain everything to her, and apologize.

Without bothering to clean the mess she'd made on her kitchen floor, Meredith headed back into the front room to grab her laptop. There were available flights to California on Friday, so as long as she could get the time away from the hospital, she'd be able to see Emily again.

"Dear Melanie..." she murmured, opening her email. "Please, please, please, give me a vacation..."

Flights to California were more expensive than Meredith had initially thought.

Well, technically they weren't that expensive, unless you were planning on making a big show of love to your significant other at a moment's notice. Then, they turned out to be very expensive. But the cost of not grabbing this opportunity was far more than she could afford.

———

It was a pretty long flight across the country, so Meredith threw a couple of books in her bag to read on the journey. Almost as soon as they took off though, she opened the first page and realized she couldn't focus. She read the same paragraph three or four times without taking any of the information in before figuring it was probably pretty futile to try and concentrate on anything other than what was waiting for her when she landed.

She closed her eyes as the city melted into the clouds and disappeared from view, leaning back in her chair as she tried to get comfortable. At least she could use the flight to try and figure out what she wanted to say when she saw Emily again; in all of her frantic last minute planning, she hadn't actually thought that far ahead. She had no idea of what she actually wanted to say, she only knew that she had to say *something*. If she didn't, she would regret it.

Her mind was blank though. For hours she just sat there, trying to come up with the right words for how she felt, but as hard as she tried, she couldn't find them. When she checked how far through the flight they were on the screen in front of her, to see that they were somewhere over the Midwest, she let out a heavy sigh. She was over halfway there, and had nothing.

What good is it, reading all those romance books, if I've learned nothing from them? She thought to herself bitterly, shaking her head. She'd spent *years* reading about heartfelt confessions of love, watching characters overcome their own personal demons to be with the one they loved, and now when she needed that experience the most, it was nowhere to be found.

Fuck.

When they landed in California, she still didn't know what she was going to say to Emily, but she had more pressing concerns to take her mind off it for a little while. She needed to hire a car, find her way to Palmdale, and then get to Emily's house.

She'd never been to California before, so at least on the drive from the airport, Meredith could distract herself a little by looking out over the great expanse of desert into the horizon. It was different to what she was used to back out east, from the crystal clear sky above to the big empty *nothing* that stretched out either side of the highway.

She'd moved from England to New England, always living in cities where everything and everyone was squeezed into the smallest possible spaces. The buildings were tall and the streets were narrow, and you'd usually have to travel pretty far to be able to look out around you and not see a skyscraper. Whenever she set foot on the street and heard the buzz of the city around her, Meredith felt like she was a part of something. It felt a little stupid, but there was so much constant noise and movement around her in the city that she never really felt like she was completely alone.

Out here though, with nothing but the road, it was hard *not* to feel alone. She switched the radio on for a little company as she saw the sign for Palmdale up ahead, just so that she had *something* to take her mind off how little there was around her, and even that didn't help much. She'd go crazy living out here, staring into the expanse with only her thoughts for company.

When Meredith drove into Palmdale, it didn't take her long to find Emily's place with the GPS. She lived in a nice cul-de-sac with a view of the mountains in the distance, a well-manicured lawn, and a shiny SUV in the driveway. It was a fairly standard semi-modern build that looked almost exactly like all the other houses in the area, and it wasn't really what Meredith had pictured her living in. She'd figured Emily would have gone for a place with a little more charac-ter, a little more charm.

But then, as she got out of the car and straightened her clothes, Meredith realized that she had no idea what kind of a house Emily would want to live in. She'd never thought to ask.

A car was parked in the driveway, but when Meredith knocked

on the door she got no answer. She pressed her ear to the door to try and listen in, but there was no sound from inside either. Emily wasn't home.

"Shit..." Meredith hissed, turning on her heel to look around the cul-de-sac. She could see kids playing on bikes, parents chatting over their fences, and a mother walking with a stroller, but no sign of Emily.

Surely she can't have gone far. Meredith reasoned. *Her car's still in the driveway, and you can't get anywhere in California on foot. Maybe she took her dog for a walk?*

She hoped that was the reason Emily wasn't home, and that she hadn't gone out with friends or something like that. If she'd only gone for a walk, she would be back soon.

At least, that was what Meredith told herself when she dropped down onto the front step of Emily's place. She told herself that Emily wouldn't be long, that she would be right around the corner with a big smile on her face when she realized Meredith had come all this way for her.

She wasn't sure how long she sat there on the front step, tapping her feet against the ground as she waited for Emily, but it was long enough for several delivery trucks to turn into the cul-de-sac, drop their packages and leave again. Meredith watched families gathered in front yards, some older kids shot hoops while others rode their bikes. She could hear laughter and idle chatter and felt a familiar nauseating pain in her stomach. She knew that laughter of a happy child so well, and she missed it *so* much.

Meredith waited for her here for so long that she'd started to think perhaps Emily wasn't going to show at all, but then finally, after what felt like an age, she saw a familiar figure walking down the street, with a dog in tow. Her hands suddenly felt clammy when she stood up, and she wiped them down on her leggings anxiously, suddenly wishing that she'd at least planned *something* to say.

In all the time she'd spent traveling and waiting around though, she still hadn't managed to come up with the heart-wrenching declaration of love. She wanted so badly to be able to find the words, she wanted to say exactly the right thing so that she could fix all of this, but when she saw Emily approaching, there was just nothing.

Meredith stood up slowly, and held one hand up in a wave as Emily approached. Emily had reached the end of the driveway before she seemed to realize who was on her doorstep, and at the sight of Meredith all the way out in California, Emily froze.

"Meredith?"

"Hi, Emily." She walked towards her slowly, smiling. "How've you been?"

"What are you doing here?" Emily asked, looking around as if she was worried someone else was going to jump out and catch all of this on camera. "Why aren't you at the hospital?"

"I took a few vacation days. I wanted to come see you." Meredith swallowed hard. She could feel her throat starting to close up with nerves, and she knew that if she didn't start saying *something* soon, she wouldn't be able to get the words out at all. "I wanted to talk to you."

"Meredith..." Emily began slowly. "I don't think—"

"I miss you," she blurted out. "I didn't think I could ever miss anyone so badly that it hurt, I didn't think it was possible after the crash. But as soon as you were gone, I just... I missed seeing you. I missed being around you. I missed *you*."

"You came all the way here to tell me that?"

She didn't sound very happy at Meredith's sudden appearance, but that was probably to be expected. The last time they'd seen each other, things hadn't exactly gone well. Even so, the frostiness in her voice made Meredith wince just a little.

"Yes," she whispered. "Because I don't think I ever told you how much you meant to me when I had the chance. I didn't treat you the way I should have, given everything you did for me. I didn't show you how much you meant to me, I didn't tell you how much I cared. And I'm sorry for that, I really am. I came here because I want to try and make up for that, at least a little bit. I want to tell you everything I didn't when I had the chance."

Emily still didn't look like she was being swayed by the speech. With a sigh, she dragged one hand through her hair. "Meredith, so much has happened... With everything that happened back at the hospital, what you said to me the last time we met—"

"I know," she said quickly, reaching out to take her hand. "I know I screwed up, and I said some awful things. But you've changed me, Emily. Don't you get that? That's why I came here, I wanted to tell you, I *had* to tell you just how much you've changed me since I met you. Even you saw it, you said so yourself. In my first report you said that I was an asshole, that I was closed off from everyone around me, but that's not how you saw me when you got to know me. You... You made me open up in ways I never thought I would be able to again, you made me *better*. It took me too long to realize that, and I'm sorry. I truly am, and I know I should have believed you when you told me that Phil was screwing with you, but... I came here for you. I can't lose you, Emily."

A silence followed her rambling, and while Meredith caught her breath Emily just blinked in confusion, still surprised by her sudden appearance.

Maybe she doesn't get it, Meredith wondered. *Maybe I just haven't been clear enough.*

"Emily," she whispered, squeezing her hand gently. "Emily, I'm in love with you. I thought after everything that had happened to me, losing Jennifer the way I did... I never imagined I would feel like this again. But then I met you, and it's like you... opened up something inside of me. I *love* you, Emily."

She'd had several hours during the flight over to think about what she was going to say to Emily when she arrived, and she'd gone over a few different scenarios for how things might go down. Perhaps Emily would tear up and hug her. Maybe she'd slap her on the shoulder and call her an ass for everything that had happened before she kissed her.

Every scenario Meredith had come up with had ended the same way though. Every time she thought about her confession, things always went *well*. Emily was always happy to see her, she always welcomed her back with open arms.

She never once thought that Emily would turn her away. In all those hours in her cramped economy seat, Meredith had never even entertained the thought that she would turn her down. So when Emily frowned and tugged her hand away, she was lost for words.

"I'm sorry," Emily said quietly, slipping her hand into her pocket. "I'm sorry you came all the way out here for me."

"Why are *you* apologizing?" She laughed, shaking her head. "I... I'm apologizing for everything that happened. I'm telling you that I've changed."

"Have you?" Emily's tone was surprisingly sharp, and when she met Meredith's gaze, she could see a flash of anger in those hazel eyes she'd missed so much. "Have you really?"

"What do you mean?" Meredith asked, shaking her head. "Why would you—"

"Do you remember our last conversation at *all*?" Emily asked coldly. "Do you remember what you said to me?"

Heat rose to Meredith's cheeks. The threat she'd made wasn't exactly one of her finest moments, but she'd been emotional. It had been a heat of the moment accusation, and she'd let her temper get the best of her, that was all. "I... I said some things I didn't mean."

"You threatened to ruin my career." Emily said slowly, enunciating every word so she could drive her point home. "You threatened my livelihood, my future. Just because things weren't going the way you wanted them to, you changed like *that*."

She reached out and snapped her fingers in front of Meredith's face. "You told me you could destroy me, and you said it like it was *nothing*. Because I think... I think to you, it really would have been nothing. I think if you'd wanted to, if you'd *really* wanted, you could have done exactly that."

"I wouldn't though. I was angry, upset, I—" Meredith tried to explain, but before she could get anything else out, Emily interrupted her.

"Jesus Christ..." She shook her head slowly, and let out a cold laugh. "You really don't get it do you? Whether or not you followed through doesn't really make a difference here, Meredith. The point is that when *you* freaked out, you thought the best thing to do would be to fuck up my life, and now you expect me to forget all of that just because you flew all the way out here and made a speech about love? What kind of toxic fairytale are you living in?"

"I'm not... That's not..." Meredith stuttered for a few moments, but the words just wouldn't come to her. This wasn't how it was supposed to happen, it wasn't the reunion she had planned on. "Emily, please, just listen to me."

"*No,*" she snapped. "*You* listen, Meredith. Your whole life revolves around that hospital and that OR, and in there you get to play god. When the scrubs go on and the patient is under, your word is law, and you get off on that shit. But you've spent so much time in that hospital, you've got no idea how things work in the real world. You've been treating this relationship like you'd treat a patient and expecting things to work out the way you want. But that's not how this goes. You don't get to treat me like I'm some secondary character in the movie of your life. You don't get to toss me aside like that and then expect me to come running back to you when it all falls to shit, okay?"

As she spoke, Emily's voice grew steadily louder until she was almost shouting at Meredith. The older woman felt her eyes grow wet as she saw Emily's cheeks flush pink with anger. The outburst caused her chest to rise and fall with heavy breaths, and when she was done with her speech, she almost seemed surprised by herself. A heavy silence fell between the two of them, and after a few uncomfortable moments while they avoided eye contact with one another, Emily finally spoke again.

"I wasn't wrong, Meredith," she said gently, with all of the anger that had been in her voice now long gone. Now she just sounded tired, almost defeated. "I said you had a god complex in my report, and I wasn't wrong. I thought maybe... Maybe it wouldn't matter when it came to us. I told myself that you wouldn't treat me the same way that you treat everyone else."

"I didn't," as she spoke, Meredith heard her voice crack. "I didn't treat you like everyone else. I *never* did."

"When things were good, sure." Emily's voice shook, and she looked down for a moment. She took a deep breath in, and then exhaled slowly, before looking back up at Meredith, her eyes shining a little brighter than they had done before. "But as soon as things were bad you turned on me. And then you started treating me the same way you treat everyone else. I was nothing but collateral to you. And I—I deserve better than that. I'm worth more than that."

"That's not true. Not that you are worth more than that, you are but I didn't treat you like everyone else." Meredith reached out to try and take Emily's hand again, desperate to try and mend things. "Emily, *please.*"

She jerked her hand away quickly, shaking her head. "No. I think... I think you need to go home."

No.

This wasn't the way it was supposed to happen. They were supposed to hug, laugh, maybe even shed a few tears together. This was supposed to be the part where Emily forgave her for all of those mistakes she'd made, and things went back to the way they'd been.

She wasn't supposed to walk away from Meredith, and head back inside without another word. Meredith wasn't supposed to be left on the pavement, with hot tears choking her throat. She wasn't supposed to be alone.

But that was how it was happening. Emily walked past her, tugging her dog, Reno, along on the leash as she went, and then the door closed behind her. The rest of the world kept turning, the kids on the cul-de-sac kept playing and laughing, but Meredith just stood there, frozen in horror.

She'd been so sure that she would be able to fix this. It wasn't often that she made mistakes in her life, but whenever she did, Meredith always managed to fix them somehow. But maybe Emily was right; this wasn't a problem that could be fixed the same way she would in a surgery. How did she manage to destroy everything they had, so completely?

Fuck.

TWENTY-THREE

When she returned to the hospital a couple of days earlier than expected, everyone was surprised to see her. She made up an excuse about her plans falling through, and was vague enough about it that nobody questioned her too much, after all where else would you expect a workaholic with a god complex and no private life to be.

It was better to be at the hospital, she decided. The overwhelming feeling of confusion, or being so completely lost after her encounter with Emily had left her reeling. She couldn't stay a moment longer than she had to. Returning on the first available flight she'd driven straight home but being alone in her apartment with such a feeling of loss was unbearable. It took only a day before she fled back to work, to the hospital.

Work wasn't exactly fun, but at least it was a distraction. Through most of the day, Meredith was busy enough that she couldn't think about what Emily had said to her, and at night she was too tired to think about anything at all. It didn't take long for her to fall back into her usual routine, long hours, daily running, pushing her body to the limits to avoid her own thoughts.

Even though she was punishing herself to exhaustion, there were still some evenings that she couldn't sleep properly. On those nights she'd pour herself a drink or two, curl up by the window, and watch the city go by.

It was on one of those sleepless nights that her phone started to ring. Her first reaction was to snatch it up, hoping that maybe, just *maybe* it was Emily, calling to try and patch things up. Of course, it wasn't a call from Emily though. It was a call from Phil.

Meredith frowned, and hesitated before answering it. She hadn't spoken to Phil since he'd left the hospital in disgrace, and for good reason. No one wanted anything to do with him after what had happened, and it wasn't like the two had been close friends *before* everything that had happened.

Against her better judgement though, Meredith hit "answer," and brought her phone to her ear. "Hi, Phil."

"Meredith!" he called, stretching out the vowels of her name. "How've you been? It's been a while, hasn't it?"

"Yeah, it has," she murmured, tapping her index finger against the rim of the glass. "How are you?"

"Me? Oooh... You know, pretty fucking awful. Getting fired ain't exactly a walk in the park, is it?"

"I can't imagine that it would be, no." Meredith tried to keep her answers as clipped and cold as possible. She didn't really want to be having this conversation with Phil, especially given the way he was slurring his words. He was probably drunk, and had phoned to rant.

As it turned out, she was right. "How's the place doing, huh? Has it fallen apart without me? They've got to be putting my surgeries on your timetable now, surely?"

"I've had a few more patients than normal," she admitted. "It's a little tough, but we're managing."

"Managing, yeah. *Managing* isn't really good enough though is it? I mean think about it, you're working with amateurs out there now, aren't you? Who else have you got that you can rely on during surgery?"

Meredith paused before answering. If she was honest, Phil's presence hadn't really been missed around the hospital since he'd been fired. The nurses all seemed a little more relaxed now that he was gone, and with the exception of some of his paperwork ending up on Meredith' desk, her workload hadn't changed all that much. She didn't have anyone else in the department at her level of seniority, but the junior doctors weren't bad at their jobs. They were managing just fine without him, but she knew that wasn't what he wanted to hear.

"We haven't lost anyone," she said diplomatically. "I think we're doing well."

There was a long silence at the end of the line, and then she heard an aggravated sigh. "Meredith, listen to me. I know that you think you can pull the rest of the department along, and carry the rest of the doctors. I know you're a great doctor, I really do. But let's be honest here, you need someone like me there with you, don't you? How is it fair that someone like *me* gets thrown out of the hospital, and you're left babysitting those kids who've just joined the department, huh?"

"What are you asking me, Phil?" Meredith snapped. She knew that this conversation wasn't just a catch up. Phil wanted something from her, she knew that.

"I... I'm just saying, I'm a valuable asset, right? I'm sure if you put in a good word for me, Melanie would change her mind about this whole thing, and I'll be back on the team in no time. That's what you want, right? I mean, how much longer is that place going to keep running without me? I've had a slap on my wrist and if they thought they might lose you because I wasn't there..."

"I actually think we're doing just fine," Meredith told him coldly. "The rest of the team is picking up some of your responsibilities, and this has given some of the younger doctors a chance to learn a little more. If you're just calling me to try and weasel your way back into a job, then you're calling the wrong person. I'm not helping you."

"Why the hell not?" he spat. Meredith winced, and pulled the phone away from her ear a little.

"Don't misunderstand me, Phil. You're a good surgeon, a very good surgeon. But you're not... It's not like you're the glue that was holding the whole hospital together. We're doing just fine without you. And if you're really as good as you think you are, then you'll be able to get another job somewhere else easily."

"Meredith—"

"Please don't call me about this again," she said quietly, before hanging up the phone. The line went dead, and Phil's protests were cut off in an instant.

In the silence that followed, Meredith stared out of the window, frowning to herself. She and Phil had always had a mutual begrudging respect for each other, largely out of their shared skill, expertise, and ego. They were two of the best surgeons in the hospital, and their arrogance had made them uneasy allies. Now that she'd seen him at his lowest, Meredith couldn't help but wonder if that's how *she* would have reacted, if she was in the same position.

Am I that person? She thought to herself. *Am I that wrapped up in my own brilliance that I'd call someone else to demand they help me get my job back?*

She didn't want to admit that she would do the same thing as Phil if she found herself backed into a corner, but the more she thought about it, the harder it was to deny. She'd threatened to have Emily fired because of the report, because she valued her own career more than Emily's. If she'd been fired, the chances were she would have made the same phone call Phil had done, demanding her position back.

I don't want to be this person anymore. I don't want to be this miserable and lonely.

Meredith pressed her forehead against the cool glass of the window, taking a deep breath in through her nose. She hated feeling like this. Was this how she had felt for all those years after she'd first come to the States? Had she been this miserable, without even having the awareness to realize it?

The worst part was, she had no one to talk about it with. She'd never had anyone to lean on, not since she'd left England, and for a long time that hadn't bothered her at all. Back then. She hadn't wanted to talk to anyone about what was going on with her. She'd spent all that time building up walls around her, making that painstaking effort to not have anyone close enough to hurt her, but in doing that, she'd never let anyone get close enough to become a friend.

And now, when she needed one the most, there was no one. Emily was the first person in all that time to get close to her, and now she was gone, and there was no one she could talk to about it. The one person she *wanted* to tell all about how she was feeling wanted nothing to do with her.

There was a cold, cruel irony about the whole thing, Meredith realized. She'd been so careful about making sure she could never be hurt again, but then she'd slowly let her guard down enough that Emily could get close, little by little. Then, somewhere along the way, Meredith had gotten a little too relaxed, and she'd let Emily get too close, and she'd gotten hurt all over again.

She'd never imagined she would be open to another relationship after what she'd been through. The idea of falling in love again just seemed so foreign and terrifying to her, and she never in a million years imagined that she would meet someone who would change her mind about that. But then Emily had come into her life, and she'd touched parts of Meredith that she'd almost forgotten even existed, the parts of her that were still scarred. Now that she was gone, it was like those same wounds had reopened all over again, and they were just as raw and painful as they had been before.

"There are people out there who actively go out looking for this kind of shit..." she murmured, pulling her forehead away from the window. The glass was a little fogged up from where she'd breathed on it, blurring the city lights behind a murky off-white veil. "Unbelievable."

She turned her head and looked across the front room, at the rows and rows of romance fiction that lined the shelving unit on the far wall. In a way, even *she* chased after all of this heartache and bullshit, but she at least did it from a safe distance. She couldn't get hurt from reading a couple break up in a book.

"Maybe I should've just stuck to reading," she said quietly, sighing. There was always a part in one of those stories where the main character sat in the same place she was, and then after a few chapters of moping around feeling sorry for themselves, things got better. They'd pick themselves up, dust themselves off, and then they'd go and declare their love for the other person in a grand romantic gesture, and everything would work out perfectly. They would live the Happily Ever After.

But she'd done all of that, and it hadn't worked out. She'd done everything that she was supposed to in one of those stories, and she was still in the same situation she had been before, feeling no better about herself. In fact, in all honesty, she probably felt *worse*. Books were nothing like real life.

So now, what was she supposed to do? Now that she knew there was no future with Emily, how was she supposed to reach that final chapter of her own story? She wanted it, she wanted the ending that was so syrupy sweet she'd need to brush her teeth when it was over.

"Well, you've been here once before..." Meredith reminded herself, breathing on the window to fog up the glass again. She pressed her index finger against it and drew two dots, then a downward curve. It was a sad, pathetic little face. "Could always just do that again."

She could shut down again, just like she did when she left London. She could find something to devote her time to, something that would take up so much of her energy outside of work that she wouldn't be able to even think about Emily any more. That was always a possibility.

But did she really want to put herself through all of that again? Did she really want to throw herself into her work so deeply that she shut off the rest of the world, so that the only thing she could see was the desk in front of her? The idea of going back to the robot that she had been before, with her world no bigger than her little two bedroom apartment was a depressing one for sure, and it wasn't one that she wanted to entertain for long.

Meredith sighed and pulled herself away from the window, wandering back through the empty apartment to her bedroom. As she walked, she couldn't help but be acutely aware of every footstep she took, because it was the only noise in the apartment. It was so quiet that she could even hear the soft sounds of her feet against the floorboards.

She didn't want to go back to being the person she was before she'd met Emily. For eight years, she'd been stuck inside that bubble she'd made for herself, and now that she was finally out, she didn't want to go back in again. So, drowning her sorrows and locking herself up again wasn't really an option.

"What do normal people do with their time after work?" she mused out loud. Of course, she knew the answer. At one point in her life, she had actually *been* a normal person, not the shut in that she'd become over the years. Normal people went out with friends, they hung out in bars or at home. They had people they could connect with when they were lonely, people they cared about, and people who cared about them.

It had been a long time since Meredith had had that.

She didn't have friends. She didn't have hobbies either, well apart from running and she enjoyed the solitary aspects to that so there was no way to *make* friends, and she'd spent eight years burning every possible bridge at the hospital, so there was no way she could befriend anyone there either. The only things she liked to do were run, and read.

Her gaze fell on the bookcase that lined the back wall of her room, and she sighed. Reading wasn't exactly a team sport, which was exactly why it had become such a sanctuary of peace for her since she'd left London.

But then again...

I don't have to be completely alone, do I?

Book clubs were still a thing, right? It's not like she was the only person in the world who read, so surely she'd be able to find a few people with similar interests who she could turn to, as long as she looked hard enough.

Meredith hurried to grab her laptop, and curled up on the couch to start her search. It turned out, after trawling through a few dubious posts on Craigslist, that there were quite a few book clubs in her area. Most were women only, some were dedicated to specific genres, and one was even within walking distance.

She clicked on the contact details, and brought up the profile of a friendly looking woman named Sophia, with her contact details attached. Meredith's fingers hovered over the keyboard for a few moments, while she thought about what to say. It had been a long time since she'd been a member of a club, and she wasn't really sure how to introduce herself.

The last club she'd been in was back in University, and even then, it had been less of a "club" and more of a group of medical students who enjoyed tequila a little too much. They'd all collectively gathered at the cheapest place in town, had too many shots, and stumbled into their morning lecture still half-drunk. They'd been drinking buddies, and there had never been an application process.

Hi there! She began typing, gnawing on her lower lip. She didn't want to sound too eager, but at the same time, she wanted to be *just* eager enough that they'd want her in the group. *My name's Meredith, I was hoping I could talk to you about joining your club.*

She typed out an introductory message, invited Sophia to message her back if she was interested in having a new member, and then sent the email. When she closed the lid of her laptop, there was a small smile on her face. Perhaps this would be something she could do to fill her time, and maybe even make a few friends along the way.

It took a few days for her to get an email back from Sophia. The two talked about their favorite romance books, a few of the tropes they enjoyed seeing the most, and some of the worst books they'd ever come across. She told Meredith that the group met every Thursday night, and that she was welcome to come along if she liked.

The following Thursday, when Meredith's shift ended, she didn't hang around in her office like she usually did, reading or catching up on paperwork. When she headed home, she didn't immediately change into running gear and headed out towards the park either. Instead, she changed into the only pair of jeans she owned, pulled on a shirt, and drove to Sophia's house for the first meeting.

TWENTY-FOUR

Easing into the group took Meredith a little while. Always so confident at work, she just couldn't exude that same confidence in this social setting. The mastery and precision of her incision into neurons and glia meant nothing here and that made it a little daunting.

At first she went along and just listened, nodding sagely but not adding anything to the fierce debates. There were discussions on how hot should the sex be for for the novel to be considered a romance, and even though her answer was the more emotional and steamier the better, she simply listened with active interest.

What if they don't agree with me? Meredith always wondered, drumming her fingers against the cover of whatever she'd read that week. *What if I'm wrong and they all just roll their eyes at me? Christ, how did I lose my confidence with people?*

When Sophia approached her at the end of a meeting she realized she wasn't the only one aware of her lack of interaction.

"Hey Meredith," Sophia said quietly, touching her elbow to get her attention. "Have you got a minute?"

Meredith's mouth went dry. Was her inability to join in making others feel uncomfortable? After all that's what happened at work. Her heart dropped. Why couldn't she just fit in like a normal person?

"I'm sorry I've been quiet over the past few weeks." Meredith decided to come out with her apology before Sophia had the chance to say anything. "I'm a little self-conscious and everyone knows each other and I just…"

"Meredith," Sophia interrupted her with a small smile, leaning against the kitchen counter as she spoke. "It's okay. I understand it can be hard to start giving your own input for the first time. And the longer you leave it, the worse it gets. Right?"

"Yeah," she admitted, a little embarrassed. "That's basically how I feel." The irony of the contrast between her profession and how she came across in the group wasn't lost on her.

"Well, the good news is you're not alone. Everyone feels like that at first, but it gets easier once you get over that first hurdle." Sophia smiled kindly. "The girls are just… Well, they're worried you don't feel comfortable and we just wanted to make sure you knew whether you're quiet or talk at a hundred miles an hour, you are always welcome. None of us bite."

"I didn't think that—" Meredith stopped herself, and managed a wry smile. "Thanks. I'm not really… used to things like this," she admitted. "I've never been part of a group like this, and to tell you the truth, I'm just a little rusty at this sort of thing in general."

"This sort of thing?"

"You know…" Meredith gestured between the two of them with an awkward smile. "The people thing."

"Rusty with people?"

"Yeah. It's been a while since I've tried to even… make new friends, I guess." She paused, chuckling. "Wow, that sounds pathetic."

"Not as pathetic as you'd think," Sophia assured her. "And besides, we're a pretty good group to be friends with, not to blow my own horn or anything."

The two women shared a smile, before Meredith decided it was probably time to leave. "I appreciate that. Thank you for checking up on me. It's... it's nice to know that you care."

As she gathered her things and said her goodbyes, Meredith felt like a weight had lifted off her shoulders. These women were happy for her to spend time with them, without expectation. The smile of happiness that came from being accepted just for being her, didn't leave her face the entire drive home. Maybe she could do this.

———

Sophia was right, after you took that first plunge and started talking in the group, it got a whole lot easier. It started with a few light comments, then some more ideas about what the author might have done with a character to make the book even better until she found herself cracking jokes and being rewarded with laughter and smiles. It felt good. Really good.

Thursday night rapidly became her favorite nights but the more she gained by the interaction the more she craved. But it wasn't just for more Thursday nights, no it was for something more, something deeper.

It was the empty apartment, she realized one evening, when she came back from work and stood alone in her kitchen. It was just after seven, and for the first time in months she had managed to leave the hospital on time, but it felt like less of an achievement when there was no one for her to come back to.

The idea of cooking a whole meal for just one person was depressing, so she just ordered takeout from the Mexican place down the street, and resigned herself to eating it alone while she watched some bad TV. It was a normal night, the same one she'd lived through for eight years, but where she used to crave the quiet solitude of her apartment before, now it felt suffocating.

She tapped on her phone to light up her screen, but there were no messages waiting for her, no missed calls or conversations on the group chat for her to join in with. No one was reaching out to talk to her. For the first time in a long, *long* time, Meredith realized she was craving human interaction and intimacy.

She missed simple things, like coming home and talking about her day, or cooking dinner with another person. Even just sitting on the couch watching TV with another person rather than doing it alone sounded like a good idea at that moment. She missed having a *partner*.

"Why not join a dating site?" Sophia suggested as she and Meredith laid out snacks, for the rest of the group who were due to arrive any minute.

"A dating site?" She pulled a face. "Sophia, I'm 46. I'm not joining a dating site."

"Why not?"

"It'll be full of twenty-year-olds looking for a quick fling. What the hell do I have in common with a twenty-year-old?"

"There are a few things that transcend age, Meredith." Sophia reminded her with a grin. "Anyone who's ever had a boytoy will tell you that."

"I'm old enough to be their mother."

"That doesn't stop some people."

"Well, it's stopping *me*."

Sophia laughed, "You've not even given it a chance. You can't dismiss something without trying." Sophia grinned, placing her hands on her hips as she surveyed the abundant table of food. "Seriously, give it a try. What's the worst that could happen?"

———

First there was the angst of what profile photo to use. Her hospital profile image was a little... stuffy. But she didn't have lots of smiling images surrounded by friends to choose from either so she resorted to a little selfie indulgence, something which was certainly not in her comfort zone. Finally picking one that didn't make her look as though she was about to deliver a devastating prognosis, she moved onto the wonders of "How would you describe yourself?" *God, this is painful, surely there has to be an easier way?* Gritting her teeth she ploughed on and after several hours of writing and deleting and rewriting she had a completed profile.

Scrolling through the abundance of women on the app was a little overwhelming, until she found the filters. From there, it was more a matter of her personal taste, whittling down women who seemed to be boring, or weren't acting their age. Anyone over the age of thirty-five who had a photo of themselves in a miniskirt at a night-club was immediately pushed aside.

Then, of course, it came down to a matter of whether the women she *did* like actually liked her too, which made the pool of potential women she could date... well, very small indeed, even across the four apps she had downloaded.

It was several weeks later, with no real success that she decided to call in help. Bribing Sophia with chocolate cake she explained her predicament.

"It's got so many users," she complained, pushing her phone into Sophia's face. "But look, look at how many matches I've got!"

"Maybe you're just too picky," Sophia suggested, smiling at Meredith over the top of her latte. "Perhaps you need to just... lower your standards."

"At this point they can't get *much* lower."

"Give me the phone," Sophia held out her hand, wiggling her fingers. "Come on, hand it over. I'm a seasoned professional user of Tinder."

With a sigh, Meredith slapped her phone into Sophia's hand. "Go ahead. Find me a date."

For a few moments she was silent, swiping back and forth across the screen. Faces came and went, flashing away before Meredith herself could even judge them. "Jesus, you move fast. You can't even tell anything about them if you're looking that quickly."

"I can tell enough," Sophia murmured, swiping another woman away.

"And you called *me* picky."

Sophia ignored her, pausing on a profile. "Ooh, what about her?"

She held up the phone so Meredith could see the face of a young woman – Carla, 32, only three miles away. She was a pretty brunette with a pixie cut and deep bronzed skin, and the photo looked like it had been taken somewhere tropical, judging by the background. "No, not her."

"What's wrong with Carla?"

"She travels. Look at that, she's somewhere in South America."

"So? You can travel. Doctors still get vacation time don't they?" Sophia pursed her lips, shooting Meredith a pointed look. "See? This is what I meant. It's okay to be picky, as long as you're picky about the right things. Carla stays."

They went through the random selection of women on each app for a little while longer, before Sophia turned her attention to the ones who wanted to talk to Meredith. "You've got loads of requests sitting here, you know."

"Mm."

"Jade says she's originally from Michigan... She's wearing a cowboy hat in her picture though, for some reason," Sophia grimaced. "Ooh, and she's listed her hobbies as 'anything you want' with a winky emoji. You know, the one with its tongue out?"

"Yeah, I'll pass."

"Good choice. What about... Irina? She looks pretty, and oh! She's a veterinarian, she's forty, and she likes watersports." Sophia's eyebrows raised suggestively, although Meredith had no idea why. "Okay, perhaps not. Who else looks promising? We've got Joanna, who works in PR, she's *stunning*. You should message her too."

Sophia fiddled with her phone before Meredith snatched it back. "Don't send anything!" But before she could get out another word of complaint her phone pinged. She had received a message from Joanna, the one from PR.

Hey, how's it going?

"Oh god, she messaged me. What have you done?"

"Oh, which one?"

"Which one? How many did you... " The ping signaling the arrival of more messages left her lost for words.

"Just talk to them... it's really that simple. I promise." Sophie offered her an encouraging smile.

————

Over the next few weeks, Meredith did as she was told, and gave dating apps a fair chance at finding her love. Perhaps she was putting too much faith in an algorithm and a few photographs, but with every date she went on, she found herself beginning to despair more and more. Not one of them could hold a candle to Emily.

Each time she tried to tell herself, *this one will be better,* but then they'd meet, talk, swap a few stories, and then the conversation would fizzle out, only to be replaced by an uncomfortable silence. A couple of women looked wildly different from the photographs Meredith had seen on the app; one was much older than she'd thought, and one seemed to have either photoshopped every one of her features or had undergone drastic plastic surgery. Meredith had kept sneaking glances looking for stitch marks.

Of all the crappy dates she went on, Meredith actually met with someone she liked; the veterinarian, Irina. She was pretty, she was funny, and their first date was at a restaurant rather than a bar. They had fun together, and even ended up going on a second date, but it just didn't feel *right* to Meredith, for some reason that she couldn't quite put her finger on. When Irina invited her on a third date all she could do was apologize and tell her she'd rather they just stayed friends.

Meredith wanted that chemistry, that spark she'd found with Emily. She was searching for a woman that could engage her mind, her emotions, her senses and—her clit. But none of them were Emily.

Just as she was about to abandon hope, and delete the profiles a new notification appeared on her phone. It was from Joanna in PR.

They had chatted but it had never gone beyond that simply because their busy work schedules had meant they'd struggled to find a day they were both free.

'Hey, I was wondering if you wanted to be my date to a work event at the end of next week?'

This Meredith decided would be her last roll of the dating dice...

'Sure, I'd love to.' She sent back quickly. *'Send me the details!'*

Meredith caught herself momentarily and let out a light chuckle. Here she was sitting in her car, after spending an evening with friends, spontaneously agreeing to a date with a woman she had never met before... she had come so far.

Even at work people were treating her differently. They were asking her questions, taking time to find out how she was. Meredith wasn't sure when things had altered, or how, but it was real. There had been layer upon layer of tiny almost imperceptible changes until she found herself cracking a bad joke with several nurses who were standing around the water cooler. The shocking realization meant she nearly forgot the punchline.

The one clear thought that occurred then, occurred to her now... *I wonder what Emily would think if she could see me now?* With a bittersweet sigh, she let the moment melt away. After all wasn't it Emily who had shown her that being stuck in the past and closed off to the moment wasn't living. Maybe an evening with Joanna was just what she needed.

TWENTY-FIVE

The date turned out to be a medical fundraiser for Doctors Beyond Borders, which was why Joanna had invited her. With tensions growing in Myanmar and Yemen, more teams were being deployed, and that meant more money needed to be spent. A few rich businessmen who wanted to look charitable were prepared to host a fundraiser for the group, and Joanna had helped to organize it.

Meredith had high hopes for the evening. Joanna was smart, accomplished, funny... Everything she was looking for in a partner. She was even thoughtful enough to invite Meredith to a fundraiser she thought would be really interesting. They clicked instantly when they messaged each other, so there was nothing that could go wrong, surely.

There was one thing that could go wrong. Of course there was one thing.

In all of the messages they had sent each other, it had seemed as thought they'd had so much in common. They clicked on every level, they made each other laugh. But when the taxi pulled up and Meredith hopped inside to meet Joanna face to face for the first time, it was like she was a different person.

There was none of the charisma or charm that she'd seen when they were messaging. In fact, there was almost no personality at all, and as hard as she tried, Meredith couldn't seem to draw anything out of Joanna. *Is this the same person I've been messaging?* Meredith wondered, sinking back against her seat as Joanna pulled out her phone. *She seems so... lifeless.*

She watched as Joanna pulled out her phone and began texting someone, her fingers tapping away furiously at the keys, and cocked an eyebrow, a little confused. It seemed as though Joanna had no problem when it came to text conversations, but had no idea of what to do when it came to the real thing. The fact she had a career in PR was edging on the ridiculous.

Almost as soon as they made their way into the hall and introduced themselves to a few people, Meredith saw Joanna pulling away a little. She had to talk to a few people, she explained, and then she would be right back. It was just a little networking that needed to be done, to make sure the event was going smoothly.

A little networking turned into Joanna disappearing into the crowd of people. Meredith lost sight of her date, and when she didn't return after a few minutes, she resigned herself to the fact that she'd been ditched.

What's the point of inviting someone on a date and then not talking to them at all? She wondered, taking a drink from a nearby waiter. *Maybe she just didn't want to turn up to an event like this on her own.*

Of course, that left Meredith on her lonesome. With a sigh, Meredith drifted across the ballroom, nursing her champagne flute. Another date, another wasted evening. It was a shame, she'd really thought Joanna would be the most promising date out of all of them. What hope was there for everyone else on the app?

Maybe I'm the problem, Meredith thought to herself as she wandered around the room, eavesdropping on snippets of conversation as she passed by. *Maybe all of these dates would have been fine*

with someone else. Maybe I'm the one that keeps screwing them up. It
wouldn't be the first time I'd messed up a relationship, after all.

She picked up another glass of champagne—if she was going to
stay, she was at least going to get a drink. As she wandered around,
Meredith heard little snippets of conversation from groups of people,
most were businessmen or venture capitalists, people who made more
money in a day than some earned in a year.

Just as she was starting to wonder if there were *any* other doctors in
the room though, Meredith stumbled on the table of people from Doctors
Beyond Borders, and overheard them talking about their experiences.

"Hi." She stopped by their table, smiling gently. "Do you mind if
I join you?"

Someone pulled a chair out for her, and she dropped into it gratefully. There were four others there, and as it turned out, three of
them were doctors who'd already spent time working abroad. The
other was an operations manager, who spent half her time in the field,
and the rest of the time in an office trying to make sure they could
keep sending people out there.

"I'm Meredith, I work at City General," she introduced herself,
and shook hands with each of them. The operations manager was
Dominique, a French woman who'd spent most of her time with the
group in Haiti. The doctors had come from all over the place, wherever they were needed most.

"I'm afraid I don't have a lot of money to donate," she admitted
with a small smile. "Not like the rest of the people here."

"Well, donations aren't everything." Dominique laughed. "What
do you do at St Michael's?"

"I'm a—surgeon." It stuck Meredith that this was the first time in
a while she'd introduced herself as anything other than a doctor. It
hadn't taken her long to realize that the title "surgeon" tended to
bring conversations either to an abrupt end or would have them
whipping out every minor (or major) ailment afflicting them. Either
which way she realized it was a barrier to her creating the real

exchanges she now so desperately craved. Here however, it was a safe admission to make.

"Oh, a surgeon? General or do you have a speciality?" Dominique seemed very interested in Meredith's reply.

"Neurosurgeon, board accredited in Neurotrauma." She felt her cheeks blush a little.

"Neurotrauma," Dominique repeated. "You'd be worth your weight in gold out in the field."

"Are you making me a job offer?"

"I make a job offer to every doctor I meet. We need all the hands we can get, as you can probably tell."

Meredith paused, looking around the room for a moment. She spotted Joanna in the crowd, schmoozing with some of the richer potential donors, laughing along at one of their jokes like they were the funniest men on the planet. Most of the other crowds she could see were doing the same thing; laughing along at jokes, talking about things that didn't matter.

She turned back to the table, and set her glass down. "What's it like, working out there?"

"With the DBB?" Neil, a middle-aged anesthesiologist who'd just come back from a stint in Thailand. "It's hard work. I worked in downtown Atlanta, and I thought I'd pretty much seen some of the worst shifts possible, and then I signed up. You get no sleep, half the time someone's shooting at you. You see a lot of horrible things, kids who are sick from things we haven't dealt with in years, or that shouldn't still be happening, mothers who don't have access to food..."

"Mothers who are using baby formula with filthy water, because they haven't got anything else to use..." Dominique added, shaking her head in disgust. Meredith winced at that. She knew about formula companies pushing their products on young mothers who were too malnourished to produce enough milk for their baby, when they didn't have the access to clean water that they needed for it to be safe. "So it's fun," she quipped, trying to ease the tension. The doctors around the table let out soft, half hearted laughs.

"Fun isn't exactly the word I'd use." Neil admitted. "But... rewarding."

"Definitely rewarding." Kathleen, a woman who looked a little younger than Meredith nodded. "I used to work in a neonatal unit in upstate New York. It was a private hospital, very uh... "exclusive." Going from helping trust fund kids to women who didn't have access to clean water was something of an eye-opener. I was supposed to go back after my first year with the DBB, but after seeing what I had... I couldn't go back to that. It just felt wrong. I figured if I was going to be exhausted and overworked, I may as well be exhausted and over-worked doing something that really matters."

Something that matters.

Meredith thought about that for a moment, savoring the words. She'd always wanted to do something that mattered, it was the reason she became certified as a neurosurgeon. She wanted to make sure that she could save people where others might have failed, just like these doctors were doing.

"You said I'd be worth my weight in gold," she turned back to Dominique. "Is that true?"

She blinked in surprise, looking from Meredith to the other doctors, and then back again quickly. "I... Of course. We're always in need of specialists."

"Assignments last for a year, right?"

"Are you thinking of putting your name forward?" Dominique leaned in. "Just like that?"

"It's a serious decision, you know," Neil piped up. "With the things you end up seeing, it's not the kind of decision you want to make on a whim and once you are in you can't just change your mind."

"I know," Meredith said, without looking away from Dominique. "Assignments. They're a year?"

"Yes. Generally they are, but some stay on for longer periods afterwards." Dominique eyed Meredith carefully. "It's a big decision to leave the comforts and friends of home."

Meredith shrugged. "I don't have much to stay here for. Why not go somewhere I can really make a difference?"

"Other than all of the things we've just told you?"

"Other than that. How about you get me a business card or something, and I'll talk to someone about how I might be able to help?"

There was a card in her hand before she had the chance to second guess her decision. They spent the rest of the evening chatting amongst themselves, every so often stopping to talk with one of the donors. Meredith couldn't remember the last time she had been at an event she had enjoyed quite so much and the entire evening flew by faster than she would have liked.

It was until the night ended that Meredith's thoughts turned back to Joanna. Some date she had been. *That's a positive of working with DBB, I've the best excuse for ducking out of dating apps.*

Chuckling to herself she picked up her phone and messaged Joanna.

Thanks for the evening, I'm sorry things didn't work out for us, but I ended up having a good evening. I met some of the doctors from DBB, and I'm even thinking about working with them. Hope the evening was a success for you too.

As Meredith climbed into her Uber, she couldn't help but revel in the utterly crazy decision she was about to make. Maybe that's why she felt like her heart was racing at a hundred miles an hour. For the first time in a long time, she really felt excited about something. She didn't feel like she was just drifting, letting life pass her by. She was actively *choosing* what she wanted to do, and who she wanted to help. *The decision has already been made.*

TWENTY-SIX

Signing up to work with the DBB wasn't as difficult as she had imagined, in fact it was far easier than anticipated. There was an interview process that she had to go through in order to show that she was a suitable candidate, then she had to have a few physical checkups, and then they formally offered her a job. She'd decided to wait until the offer came through before she requested a sabbatical from Melanie, but on the morning that the email came through, she began drafting her request.

The whole process hadn't taken very long, only a few weeks from when she'd first phoned about a position, and Meredith hadn't really had much time to think about what she was doing. It all just seemed like a ridiculous joke until the email, and that was when reality finally sank in for her.

This was *happening*. It seemed so surreal and so crazy, and at the same time, when the letter was finished and printed, she just looked at it and nodded. This was the right choice. This was her choice.

Even though it was Friday and she had the day off she didn't want to spend the whole weekend waiting to hand her letter in, so she headed to the hospital to catch Melanie. With the letter clutched in her hand and a fizz of excitement in her stomach, Meredith made her way to the administrative wing. A slow smile edged across her lips as the now familiar thought crossed her mind. *I wonder what Emily would think if she could see me now.*

The pain she once associated with that thought, had all but gone, now it was replaced with something much softer.

"What can I do for you?"

"I've got something for you." Meredith tossed the letter down, and it skidded across Melanie's desk, almost falling into her lap.

"What's this?" Melanie asked, looking down at it. "You aren't resigning, are you?"

"It's not a resignation. It's a request for a sabbatical." Meredith grunted, stuffing her hands into her pockets. A line appeared between Melanie's brows as she picked the envelope up, turning it over in her hands a couple of times. "It's not rigged, you can open it."

"Has something happened that I should know about? You seemed to be happier."

Where do you want me to start? Meredith thought bitterly. A *lot* had happened to her, but she didn't really want to discuss most of it. And there were other parts of it she *couldn't* talk about, in case Emily ever planned on returning to her company. "Why?"

"What are you planning to do with your sabbatical? You're not just taking a year out to go backpacking or something, are you?"

"I cleverly wrote all the details in the letter." Meredith pointed to it. "You know, the one in your hand?"

Melanie dropped the letter on her desk, and motioned to the chair across from her. "Sit."

"Why?"

"Because I had to fire one of the best doctors in my hospital, and now another is asking for a year out of work. I'm starting to worry there might be something in the water, so take a seat." Melanie paused, and smiled gently. "It's not rigged, you know."

Meredith dropped into the spare chair, crossing one leg over the other. Melanie rested her chin on one hand, peering at her. "First you come to me pouting about the audit like a spoilt child and I have to tell you to behave, then I tell you how glowing your audit evaluation was, and now the audit's over, and you want to leave anyway?"

"I'm not *quitting*. I'm asking for a sabbatical. I just want a year off to—"

"To what, Meredith?" she asked.

"I'm joining Doctors Beyond Borders. They want me in the field for a year, but I can't do that unless I take a year out from here. It's got nothing to do with the audit. This is something I want," Meredith hesitated for a beat, "Something I need to do."

"Doctors Beyond Borders?" Melanie echoed, arching an eyebrow. "Really? Well... I guess I never saw that coming."

"Yeah, well—" Meredith paused and offered up a lame shrug in response. "I guess neither did I, until it did."

"Why now?"

Meredith sighed and looked down at her hands, trying to avoid making eye contact with Melanie.

"I..." Meredith paused for a moment, struggling to find the right words to summarize everything that had happened to her over the last couple of weeks. "I'm not happy here anymore." She looked up to see Melanie frowning, her head cocked to one side.

"Don't take this the wrong way," she said eventually. "But have you ever really been happy here?"

Meredith looked confused. She shook her head imperceptibly in question.

"Have you though?" Melanie pressed gently. "I'm only asking because... I mean, in the eight years since I've known you, I don't think I've ever been able to tell. Since you left England, have you been happy?"

Meredith's throat went dry, just as it always did whenever someone brought up England, and she felt her chest tighten a little. If she was honest with herself, Melanie had a good point; for a long time, she hadn't been happy. Not really.

Before she had met Emily, Meredith hadn't felt the real need to chase anything, or push herself. She'd just shut herself into her little two bedroom apartment with her books and her running gear, and she'd told herself over and over again that her isolated comfort zone was where she was happy. After a while, she had started to believe it.

But now she knew it wasn't a life. She had just been existing, drifting through each day as it came, but she hadn't really been *living*. She'd made it through eight years at the hospital without forming any relationships with her co-workers, she'd walled herself off so much that no one was able to break through, and she would have fought them tooth and nail if they had tried.

Then Emily had come along, and everything had changed. She might not have been happy, but she had contented herself with what she had in America, until someone had begun poking holes in the fabric of her life. When she'd finally let Emily in, it was like she had been holding a flashlight, and she'd illuminated all of the parts of herself Meredith would have rather kept hidden, and now she was gone, and she'd taken that light with her.

She missed that light.

"I guess not." Meredith said finally, sighing as she looked up at Melanie again. "I need to ask... Why are you nice to me?"

"What do you mean?"

"You've been looking out for me since I started. I always thought it was a pain in the ass, to be honest, but you've just been looking out to make sure I'm okay, haven't you? Even with the audit you wanted to give me a heads up. Why?"

The corner of Melanie's mouth twitched, and she looked down at the desk for a few moments, shaking her head slowly. "You're—a good doctor. You're one of the best in the hospital, if not *the* best, and I knew that whatever came up in the audit would have to go in your employee file permanently. If you ever chose to stop working here, I knew that report would end up following you to your next hospital, and I didn't want that to happen."

Meredith shifted uncomfortably in her seat. "Why?"

"What do you mean *why*?"

"Why do you care? It's not like anyone else does."

Melanie leaned back in her chair, folding her hands in her lap. Her gaze flickered from Meredith to the photograph that sat on her desk beside her computer monitor, and her expression changed, just for a second. Melanie picked up the photograph from her desk and handed it over so Meredith could see. It was an old picture, maybe ten or fifteen years old judging by the quality, but Meredith recognized Melanie straight away. She was hugging a young boy who shared her strawberry blonde locks, and they were both laughing into the camera.

"Harry." Melanie's voice was thick and heavy as she spoke, and Meredith heard her take in a shaky breath. "His name was Harry."

Was. Meredith looked up at Melanie again, and when she met the other woman's gaze, she realized with a start that she recognized her expression. She had seen it enough times in the mirror to know it anywhere.

"What happened?" she whispered, placing the photograph back down on the desk. It took Melanie a moment to answer, and when she did, her voice trembled.

"He was born with a hole in his heart, and after I delivered him, we thought we might never be able to take him out of the hospital. After a few surgeries we did, but he was in and out for the next few years with all sorts of problems. After one visit he just..." She looked off to the side for a moment, brushing away a stray tear that slipped down her cheek. "He didn't come home again."

"I'm sorry." Meredith frowned, looking down. It wasn't a lie, she felt the woman's pain—after all, she knew from experience just how hard it was to bury your own child. "That's not something a parent should ever have to go through."

"No, it's not." Melanie cleared her throat and looked back over at Meredith, smiling sadly. "After we buried Harry, my husband and I both changed. When you become parents, no one really thinks to warn you what it might be like to go through that, and everyone ends up taking it differently. I suppose some people become stronger because of what they go through, and they end up moving on from it together. Most people don't, of course."

"What happened?"

"Well, we both found comfort in other things, to try and deal with what had happened. My husband found god, and I suppose that must have helped him."

"You didn't?"

"No, I didn't. I threw myself into my work. For a few years after Harry..." She trailed off, unable to finish the sentence. "Ironically, it's probably the reason I have this job, I probably wouldn't have put in the hours necessary to get here if that hadn't happened. For a long time, I would work any shift that was needed, sometimes staying here for two or three days at a time, just showering in the locker rooms and sleeping in my office. I didn't want to go home, and it was easier not to think about Harry when I was busy at work."

Meredith looked down at her lap, frowning. That definitely sounded familiar.

"It wasn't healthy though," Melanie pointed out. "One morning I woke up, looked around me and realized three years had gone by. I had hardly any friends, I'd lost about twenty pounds because I was barely eating, and I was a wreck. I'd just fallen into a life where the only thing I did was work or sleep, and I was miserable. It took me a while, and a lot of very expensive therapy, but things are better now."

"When did this happen?"

"A few years before you came to work here. I think I'd probably been in therapy for about a year when I hired you, so the wounds still hadn't healed."

"Is that why you hired me?" Meredith asked, frowning.

"No." Melanie laughed. "I hired you because you're a good doctor, Meredith. But when I found out why you'd left London, I was worried about you. I knew first-hand what that kind of grief does to a person."

Meredith sighed, looking down at the photograph on the desk for a few moments. "I feel like an ass."

Melanie laughed properly this time, throwing her hands up in the air. "Well, my work here is done then."

"I'm sorry."

"I believe you," Melanie said gently. "I think that's the first time I've ever actually heard you apologize for something."

"It's the first time I've felt like I've got something to apologize for, honestly."

"I also believe *that*."

A silence fell between the two women while Melanie took her photograph back and put it on her desk again, propping it upright by her computer screen so she could see it while she worked. Her gaze then fell on Meredith's letter again. "So do you think working with DBB will make you happy?"

Meredith shrugged. "I don't know. I *won't* know until I try, will I?"

"I mean that's certainly true." Melanie nodded. "Given your track record at the hospital... And given how little time you've taken off work in the past eight years... I really can't say no. Besides, I'd rather it was a sabbatical than a resignation. I'll read through this and approve it, and then I'll tell your department to cover you. You won't even have to say goodbye to anyone before you leave."

"Thanks." Meredith stood up and flashed Melanie a tight-lipped smile, before turning to leave. Before she could make it to the door though, Melanie called her name and she turned to look back at her boss one last time.

"I don't know what happened to you over the past couple of months to make you realize what the past eight years have been like... and I'm not going to ask again. You don't want to talk about it, I get that. But can I give you a little advice, if you promise not to snap at me?"

"Go ahead."

"You came here from London because you were running away from what happened. That's understandable, I think a lot of other people in your situation probably would have done the same thing.

Now you're running away from something *else* to join the DBB. At some point, you're going to have to stop running. At some point you need to tackle it."

Meredith simply nodded. There was nothing else to do, she knew she was right.

TWENTY-SEVEN

Within a month, Meredith found herself on her first assignment with Doctors Beyond Borders. Myanmar, was her new location, where the civil unrest was escalating, and doctors were a scarce commodity.

Before she left, Meredith had been given advice on what to expect. She was reminded again and again that this would be a huge culture shock, and it would take time to adjust to her new working conditions. Nothing anyone could have told her would ever have really been able to prepare her for the things that she came across though.

When people had gone over the basics of what to expect, it was hard to imagine just how different life would be from the comfort of the DBB offices. They showed her pictures, gave her testimony from other doctors who'd been out there, but that paled in comparison to the real thing.

At City General, if there was something that Meredith needed, she would have it in her hands without question. Every so often there would be an alert about the shortage of a certain blood type, but there was always a solution. Medicine flowed freely—maybe a little too freely— from the dispensary, they had supplies that they *had* to use in order to justify the hospital expenditure, and they were working with state of the art equipment.

In Myanmar, it couldn't have been more different. She was working in a military style compound most days, except for the time she was shuttled off to smaller hospitals with a few other members of the team. The equipment they were using was always *good*, and got the job done, but it was a far cry from the tech she was used to.

Any kind of sleep schedule that she might have managed to develop over the years was trashed almost as soon as she landed. As the only neurosurgeon, and one of the most experienced doctors in the camp, she was often on call for emergencies, and found herself waking up in the middle of the night with a flashlight in her face.

The background music that a nurse might play over the speakers and the gentle hum of machines was replaced by the distant noise of civil unrest. As Meredith worked, she tried to block out the noise of gunfire, the sound of explosions outside the compound, maybe a few screams. Forgetting where you were was never an option.

Her job as a surgeon back in the U.S. might have been stressful, but it was nothing compared to her current situation. The emotional strain that came with seeing the effects of the unrest, was far worse than what she would have come across in her normal job. Even worse, she didn't have access to her usual ways of relieving stress.

Back home, if she'd had a rough day, Meredith would go for a run. She'd take the long path that snaked through the park, up along the river before coming back on herself and arriving at her building again. Then, after a quick shower, she'd flop down onto her couch with a book, and lose herself in the pages. That wasn't an option now.

The compound wasn't really big enough for her to run around, and she was lucky if she could find enough peace and quiet to read more than a few pages of her book without being disturbed. As the weeks went on, with no outlet for her stress and frustration, Meredith began to feel a lot like she had done back in the U.S.. She felt like she was climbing the walls, slowly going insane without a way out.

One evening though, as she headed back from the mess tent to her own bunk, Meredith passed by a makeshift game of basketball. A few of the doctors had managed to erect a hoop, and they'd found a ball somewhere, and as she made her way past them, Meredith paused for a moment to watch. It looked like they were having fun, just passing the ball amongst themselves and taking (admittedly terrible) shots.

Sharif, one of the other doctors on the team, spotted her watching from the side lines. "Hey, you want to join in?"

"I'm not a very good player," Meredith called, watching as one of the nurses took a shot. The ball hit the rim and bounced off, narrowly missing Sharif's face.

"Neither are we," he pointed out, tossing the ball in her direction. "Don't worry, it's not like we're playing for money."

Meredith bounced the ball against the ground once, and smiled gently. It had been a long time since she'd played any kind of team sport, let alone basketball, but she figured it would be a fairly good way of getting out some of the pent up energy she hadn't been able to shift.

"Sure." She approached the group. "I'll play a few rounds."

A few rounds turned into a full game of basketball, which turned into a mini-competition between the group. After four games it ended in a tie, and as the sun began to set behind them, they agreed that they would finish up the next evening to see who was the real winner.

The next morning, for the first time in a long time, Meredith found herself looking for Sharif and the others when she walked into the mess tent for breakfast. That morning, she didn't eat alone, and she found herself in the middle of a conversation about the lives they'd all led back home. It felt a little strange, sharing her life with people she hardly knew, but it was... nice. It was nice to just sit there and talk aimlessly for a while.

Weeks passed and Meredith found herself settling into life with the rest of the doctors. On some quiet evenings she'd manage to tuck herself away with a book to read, but she didn't find herself running to it as a crutch the way she used to anymore. It wasn't something that she needed, the way it had been in the past, it was just something that she *wanted* to do.

Of course, just as she found herself starting to relax into her new life, something came up, because it always did. She'd been working in Myanmar for three months when news came that a small team was needed in Yemen—they were short of doctors there, and the situation seemed to be getting worse rather than better. They needed volunteers, and quickly.

A few hands around the room shot up, and Meredith's was among them. She didn't even have to think about it for long before she volunteered, offering to go wherever she was needed, and a couple of days later, she found herself on a plane for Yemen, along with a couple of other doctors.

———

Almost as soon as they landed in Yemen, the small team of doctors were flanked by armed guards who brought them to their vehicle. Meredith rode with Carlos, a veteran trauma surgeon from Argentina, and Mees, a male nurse from the Netherlands. Their driver was a young Yemeni boy, he couldn't have been much older than twenty or twenty-one. His name was Fakhir, and once they were on the road, he informed them that he was happy to answer any questions they had about Yemen.

Meredith had plenty. She wanted to know exactly what she was going to be heading into before she was dropped right into it, but there had been very little time for a full briefing before she'd had to fly out. Everything had happened so quickly that she didn't even know what the compound they were working in would look like.

"What's waiting for us when we get there?" Meredith asked. Carlos turned in his seat to look back at her out of the corner of his eye for a moment, before turning back to look out at the road ahead.

"What do you mean? What kind of conflict are we going to see, or what kind of place are we going to be working out of?"

"Either. Both." Meredith looked out of the window as they flew down a barren side road in Sanaa. She couldn't see much – some destroyed buildings, a few kids sitting on the side of the street, staring off into the distance. "What kind of care will we be providing out here?"

"The water here is not clean." Fakhir piped up from the front seat. "Many people get sick from drinking it, and they come to the doctors for help. Sometimes though, they are too sick to be helped."

"Cholera and dysentery?" she asked, looking at Carlos, who nodded.

"They're the big killers, as well as malnutrition, especially among children. Then there's the issue of women who die during pregnancy, or childbirth. Infant mortality rates are skyrocketing, and this is all without factoring in the conflict."

Meredith sucked in air through her teeth, gazing out of the window again as they headed to the outskirts of the city, where the camp had been set up. "It looks bad. Worse than the last place I was stationed."

"Where were you before this?" Mees asked. He was glancing at their surroundings uneasily, swallowing nervously as he took in more and more of the devastation that seemed to be all around them.

"Myanmar. It's a similar situation over there, but this is..." Meredith trailed off after a moment, struck dumb by the sheer weight of the situation. "This is a lot."

"It is," Carlos agreed, his tone grim. "That's why we've got a psych team out here with us at this camp."

"A psych team?" Meredith looked over at him sharply, and felt her heart begin to pound at the mere mention of it. For a moment, She saw Emily in front of her, dressed in her neat suit with her recorder on the table between them. She blinked, and Emily disappeared, but the nerves were still there, swirling in the pit of Meredith's stomach.

"Yeah, it's a team of four. They're anticipating there's going to be a lot of demand for them out here, and with the operation out here as large as it is, they figured they'd need a few people, rather than just sending one out here to accompany us."

"Makes sense," she murmured quietly, turning her head away again as they pulled into the compound. It was bigger than the Myanmar camp she'd been stationed in, with heavy metal gates and high walls that the locals had already spray painted. Things looked bad.

They were greeted by a couple of doctors on their arrival, but the majority of the crew were in the mess hall together, so that was where they headed. Leaving their trunks in the truck to be collected later, Meredith followed Carlos to the mess hall, where they could hear voices and laughter.

The tent was crowded with people, all hunched over their plates in little groups, swapping stories and telling jokes to try and ease the tensions of their work.

"I need to find whoever's in charge at the moment," Carlos said quietly, before excusing himself and leaving Meredith with Mees at the doorway. The two looked around the sea of unfamiliar faces, and exchanged grim smiles.

"Do you want to try and make some friends?" She offered, gesturing out towards the room. Mees opened his mouth to respond, but as he did, the door opened behind them again, and someone walked in, almost colliding with them. Meredith's back was to the door, so she didn't see who it was, but over the chatter and noise of the room, she could have sworn she recognized the voice.

"Oh, sorry. I didn't see you there."

I know that voice.

For a split second, the room seemed to freeze around her while Meredith's mind whirred. No, it couldn't be possible for her to know that voice. She was thousands of miles from home, miles from where anyone could possibly know her. And there was no way, after everything that had happened, that it could possibly be—

Emily.

Meredith turned on the spot and came face to face with the woman she thought she would never see again. She'd come halfway across the world to escape everything that had happened, everything she had managed to screw up for herself, and yet against all odds, there was the ghost of her past.

Emily stood in front of her.

In fairness, Emily seemed just as shocked to see her. For a few moments, they just stared at each other in silence, neither one able to form so much as a quiet "hello."

Am I living in the fucking Truman Show? Meredith thought to herself. *How is this possible?*

"Hi, Emily," she said quietly. "It's been a while."

"Meredith, what are you *doing* here?"

"That's becoming a familiar question from you. I could ask you the same thing."

"I'm... I'm working. I got a job here, I told you I was applying."

"No, you didn't," Meredith pointed out. The last time they'd spoken, Emily hadn't mentioned anything about applying to work with Doctors Beyond Borders. "Trust me, if you had done, I'd have remembered it."

Emily cleared her throat, as Mees looked between them, frowning. "Do you two know each other?"

"Quite well, actually," Meredith glanced at Emily out of the corner of her eye. "Right, Emily?"

"Right," she said quietly.

TWENTY-EIGHT

How was it possible that she had come so far, and Meredith Asquith had managed to find her yet again? Emily had changed jobs, left no forwarding address, and had come across the globe, and yet somehow, Meredith was in front of her yet again.

The worst part was, Emily wasn't angry about it. She was shocked, of course, but when she saw Meredith for the first time, she couldn't be angry. If anything, she was excited. And *that* made her angry.

She wished she wasn't happy to see Meredith after all these months apart. She wished that she was able to just smile, welcome her, and move on with her day, but Emily couldn't.

Meredith looked good. There was something different about her that Emily couldn't quite put her finger on. She'd nodded to her colleagues when she joined the table with the rest of the psych team but her mind was elsewhere.

Meredith didn't necessarily *look* different—she seemed to weigh the same, her hair was the same, and other than a fresh tan that she hadn't had before, nothing had changed.

It wasn't her appearance that was different, Emily realized, but it was everything else. It was the way Meredith carried herself, with her head high. That was what was different about her. She looked happier now, more confident in herself, and that suited her. She didn't look like the cold, arrogant ice queen she'd first met at City General.

Meredith walked off with the younger man she'd been talking to, and the two found another table at the back of the hall. Emily watched at a distance as Meredith introduced herself, shaking hands and exchanging details. She laughed along with jokes and stories, and generally seemed happy to be a part of the group.

What had happened to her?

Emily got her answer a couple of days later, when Meredith knocked on the door to her tent, and stuck her head inside. "Hi there."

"Hey." She'd been laying in bed rereading *Desert of the Heart*, but at the sight of Meredith, she sat up quickly, swinging her feet to the outside of her mosquito netting.

"Do you mind if I come in?"

She smiled gently, and beckoned Meredith closer. "Come on."

Meredith wandered into the tent, with her hands shoved deep into the pockets of her trousers. She looked around Emily's tent with a rueful smile. "It's nice to see your digs are as good as mine."

"I think olive drab suits me."

"I'm inclined to agree." Meredith grinned, and perched on Emily's trunk. As their gaze met from across the tent, her expression turned a little more serious. "How have you been?"

"I got a new job." She motioned around the tent. "So I'm not doing too badly for myself. What about you?"

"I..." Meredith stretched out her legs. "Am doing better than I have been in a long time. And that is, in no small part, due to you."

"Me?"

"I realized something, when you left. I looked around me and realized that I hated what I saw. I didn't want to be the person that I was anymore, I wanted to be the person I felt like when I was with you. I wanted to be happy. I was sick of wallowing in my own misery and grief all the time." Meredith paused. "I was sick of being lonely."

Emily swallowed nervously. If she was honest with herself, she'd imagined Meredith might have just gone back to her old ways once she left, but it didn't seem like that was the case at all. "And are you lonely?"

"No. I joined a book club, and made some friends through that. I've made a few friends here at camp already too."

"What about—I mean, are you seeing anyone?" Emily hesitated as she asked the question. She wasn't completely sure she wanted to know the answer.

"No. I tried dating a few times, but it didn't work out. None of them were what I was looking for. Some of them were just downright awful, of course. But then there were others... I guess I should have liked them more than I did, but they weren't—"

Meredith trailed off into silence, and glanced up to meet Emily's gaze. She shook her head quickly, as if trying to correct a mistake, and then cleared her throat. "Anyway. How about you?"

"Me?"

"Are you seeing anyone?"

"Jesus, no." She laughed, shaking her head. "I went on a couple of blind dates, friends of friends... but it didn't amount to much."

"That's a shame."

"Mm." Emily hummed in agreement, looking up at Meredith. If she was honest, she knew exactly why none of those dates had worked out. As angry and hurt as she had been with Meredith after everything that had happened between them, there was a little part of Emily that had always wanted to see her again, to see if things could be better between the two of them. On every date she'd been on, she'd found herself comparing them to Meredith, and none had. They weren't as smart, or as funny, or as interesting, or as attractive. Ultimately, they just fizzled out.

The two sat in silence for a few moments, before Meredith cleared her throat again. "I missed you."

"You did?"

"God, yes." She laughed mirthlessly, shaking her head. "I missed you so much that it hurt sometimes. I don't think I ever managed to get over you, to be honest. You changed me so much that... I don't think I could ever forget about you."

Emily's stomach turned to knots at that, and her mouth went dry. She wanted to cross the gap between them, rush to the other side of the tent, and tell Meredith that she felt the same way. She wanted to kiss her, to feel her again. She wanted that desperately.

But at the same time, there was a part of her that was still hesitant. When she looked at Meredith, she didn't just see the ghosts of all of their good memories together, she saw the bad too. She saw Meredith accusing her of betraying her trust, she saw a woman who had been prepared to destroy her career in an instant. Even if Meredith had changed, that memory would still be there.

"I didn't forget about you either," she admitted. "Not at all. And I'm sorry."

"Sorry, for what?"

"The last time we met I was harsh with you. You travelled so far to..." her voice trailed away as she looked into Meredith's eyes. "I was unkind. I'm sorry for that. But I never forgot about you. Not once."

Meredith smiled gently, and nodded before standing up and dusting herself off her cargo shorts. "Well I suppose it's good that I made a lasting impression. I won't ask if it was a good or bad one."

Emily stood up too, and joined her by the door. For a few moments they stood there in silence, stood only inches apart. She could have reached out and kissed Meredith right there and then, she could have shown her just how much she had missed her, but she didn't. Something stopped her, something made her hesitate.

"It's good to see you again, Emily," Meredith said softly, before stepping out into the night air. All Emily could do was watch her go, melting into the darkness.

———

The next few days were almost unbearable.

Meredith didn't mind the workload. She could handle the sound of gunfire overhead, and the long hours that stretched into the middle of the night. She could even grit her teeth and bear the stress of working in such cramped conditions, but the one thing that got to her was Emily.

Every time she caught a glimpse of her out of the corner of her eye, it felt like everything was back to the way it had been when they were at City General, just after they'd started their relationship. Meredith found herself watching Emily as she crossed the compound, smiling at her from across the mess hall. And Emily was smiling back.

Given how badly things had gone the last time they had met, Meredith wouldn't have blamed Emily if she'd been angry at her surprise arrival, but she wasn't. Even though she was a little hesitant at first, she genuinely seemed glad to see Meredith, and over the days, began to warm to her.

She was starting to hope that maybe, over time, she would be able to build up that trust and intimacy that they'd once had, and get back to where they were. It was a slow process, given how hesitant Emily seemed, but she was willing to wait. Emily was worth it.

TWENTY-NINE

"This *civil war* has so many sides to it, so many perspectives. Just when I think I am getting a handle on what to expect, I'm blindsided by something new, something different." Meredith ran her hand through her hair. "I had to operate on a twelve-year-old boy yesterday. He had blast fragments embedded in his spine, we did the best we could, but it'll be a few days, weeks maybe, until we know the full impact of the nerve damage. His life will be infinitely harder going forward though." She sighed. "As if it wasn't hard enough. Twelve years old." She shook her head. Nothing prepared you for the on-the-ground experience, until you lived it you couldn't know. Not even vaguely.

"When we cut off his clothes we saw a bulge in his pocket. For a moment I thought I was seeing things but when I reached out and grabbed it before it fell from the table, I knew I wasn't. It was a grenade. We all just stopped and looked at each other. Then, Adil lifted it out of my hand and walked it out of the operating tent and we carried on as if it had never happened. And the doctors here, the local doctors I mean, are amongst the most skilled surgeons I've ever worked with. I sometimes wonder if they really need me here. They do for numbers but not really for expertise. I'm learning from them, Emily." Meredith looked at Emily earnestly.

Emily's hand cupped her cheek, "I'm a little in awe of you, never mind them." She leaned forward and placed a kiss on Meredith's lips, barely grazing them. "Your capacity and willingness to change is just..." Emily shook her head and let out a small sigh.

"Is what?" Meredith cocked her head in curiosity. *Have I really changed that much? Or am I finding myself again? The old me?* Everything happened so fast here there was no time to reflect on how things were impacting you. You were so insignificant here.

"I was going to say sexy... but I don't want to distract you from sharing."

"I think I might like to be distracted." A small devilish smile played across her lips. They had taken to spending any shared free time together, more often than not in the privacy of one or the other's tent. Discretion was everything.

This wasn't their culture, and while they were there to help, respecting local laws and customs had to be done whether you agreed with them or not. Who in their right mind could ever agree with imprisonment, stoning or vigilante death sentences for just being who you are; for loving someone who happens to be the same gender as you. But they were there to heal and their own agendas had to be left at home.

Meredith glanced over her shoulder to the door of the tent and made sure it was tied in place. "You'll need to be very quiet..."

"No, you'll need to be very quiet." Emily let out a small laugh and pushed Meredith back onto the lumpy mattress. "I'm here to help you unload and relax, right?"

She put a finger to her lips and hushed Meredith's response away and then teased up her tank to reveal a cotton bra. "I have a very specific type of therapy in mind for you, Dr. Asquith," she teased, pulling down the black cotton and releasing two beautifully erect nipples. Taking the puckered, hard nubs into her mouth she sucked gently then rolled her tongue over the tip, never breaking eye contact.

Meredith groaned, only to be immediately hushed again.

"You need to be completely quiet."

"You're not making it easy," Meredith muttered, wrinkling her forehead in protest.

"Then you need to try harder." Emily caught Meredith's glance towards the entrance again. "And stop looking at the door. Nobody is coming in and besides I'll hear them if they come near." She paused. "In fact... "

Grabbing her eye mask she leaned over Meredith's body and slid it into place. Meredith reached out to grasp Emily's hand but Emily caught it first and pulled her knuckles close to her lips, kissing them gently.

"Whoa, let me worry about keeping us safe. All I need you to do is lie back and let me indulge myself in your pleasure." Emily said half soothing, half teasing as she ran her fingertips around the edge of her exposed nipples. The delicate touch sent a shiver of anticipation through her body.

Meredith let her head fall back onto the pillow. She wanted to give control to Emily but it felt, well... a little alien. Her back arched as the warmth from Emily's mouth tugged at her nipple. There was nothing to do but surrender.

Less than a year ago, the idea of allowing herself to be surrounded by uncertainty and emotion would have scared her into running; the ice cold shield of arrogance and indifference would have been thrust in anger, to keep her safe. But safe was never how she felt, just a little more scared and lonely every time.

The final shred of resistance slid down her cheek in a single tear. If there was anyone in this world she would give herself to without question it would be Emily, and as the younger woman's tongue swirled in languorous torment Meredith did just that.

The terse tweaking of one nipple between thumb and forefinger, set against the hot, wet slow movements of Emily's mouth on the other was divine. The conflicting torment between the two equally hot yet opposing sensations escaped her body in a series of low slow moans which reverberated in the sticky, humid air of the tent.

Encouraged by Meredith's audible relinquishing of control Emily upped her game, moving from tongue to teeth, grazing them against Meredith's erect, puckered bud.

"Oh, Emily." Meredith's breath shuddered as the nerve connection between nipple and clit became electrified, with intense throbs of brazen want. Her sodden centre was begging for attention and her legs fell wider, encouraging Emily to take her.

She had gone from reserved to unabashed within minutes as she capitulated to the power of Emily's tongue.

"I'm going to *whip* you into shape, Dr. Asquith, with my tongue." Emily giggled.

Meredith swallowed, hard.

The potency of every stroke, every whisper of breath, was amplified tenfold under the darkness of the mask Meredith wore and it was all moving down. Down the muscles of her stomach, the purr of light kisses descended closer towards her now aching centre.

The caress of Emily's hair on her skin, ghosting the promise of what was to come, but the sound filling her ears came from the fast beat of her heart as she felt warm breath tease over her short trimmed hair. Her hips rose involuntarily, desperate for attention and she pressed her palms flat against the cotton sheet beneath her. *Oh, god, please touch me. Please.* Silently begging for more, Meredith's hand reached down searching to ground herself against the touch of Emily's brown hair. Long fingers teased through soft strands in the lightest of touches, stilling only when the first graze of a hot lazy tongue, languidly passed over her centre.

"Fuck. Yes. Please."

The puff of hot air that escaped from Emily's chuckle tickled against her sensitive wet lips causing her hips to buck in desperation.

"I love a woman that begs." Emily flicked her tongue over Meredith's labia, bringing each perfectly placed teasing movement ever closer to her swollen twitching clit. "All you have to do is ask nicely, Dr. Asquith."

"Oh, Emily please... "

"Want me to give some much needed aid to this little attention seeker?" Emily's tongue gave one rough dart from the smooth, slick wetness behind Meredith's clit, upwards.

Meredith gasped.

"Yes, please Em." Her breathing was coming in desperate gasps, which announced her arousal.

"How much do you want me to take care of you?"

In the darkness, every tiny sound of human breath held possibility, every sigh of skin against skin, potential. Meredith's body was shaking, exploding with the hunger to be consumed. She was completely vulnerable, utterly exposed as she took the final step off the ledge into the abyss that was Emily.

"Please, Em' I beg you. Take me. All of me." For the merest second she paused. "I'm yours." Her breath came out in shudders of hope. "Suck me. Fuck me. Do anything you want, but please god, take me." Meredith's voice rose with desperation, unable and unwilling to try and contain her all consuming need.

Without another word but one long inhalation of breath, Meredith could feel Emily's smile. The excitement of giving herself without condition was the ultimate exercise in trust. Meredith took every ounce of faith she had and placed it unapologetically with Emily.

In this moment, in this ravaged world in which they found each other, Emily was the custodian of her heart, her mind and right now her body.

She felt movement as Emily's weight lifted from the cot, then warm hands on her ass pulled her to the edge of the precarious bed. The same delicate touch lifted her into position, and with a wiggle she aided the movement. The brush of hair, the soft skin of Emily's shoulders supporting the backs of her thighs, arms hooking her in place, as fingers teased over her mound. Emily was at her very core;

facing Meredith's axis of vulnerability. Her hips bolted, surging forward; *Take me,* she screamed silently, into the darkness.

A gasp vibrated in the air as Emily's tongue slid up one side of her lips and down the other. The heat grazing against her ready clit sent convulsions of exquisite torment through Meredith's body. Another cry of anguish filled the small tent.

Passing from tip to base, Emily's tongue was sending her wild hips bucking. She felt encircled arms tighten around her thighs, pinning her in place. Emily was in control and as her tongue delved deep into her folds, slurping on her juices, she writhed against the torment of pleasure. As if sensing Meredith could take no more, Emily's lips sealed around her engorged nub. *God, she loved this woman.*

With an arched back, Meredith thrust forward engaging as much of herself with Emily as she could. She needed to be consumed, to be devoured so that Emily absorbed every fibre, every sinew, every cell, as they melded into one.

With the urgency of the sucking tugging her into complete submission, Meredith felt the tingling of an orgasm rise from the depths of her core. The low, light fizz started around her clit, rising to her stomach, but as Emily slid her fingers between Meredith's lips it grew faster. Again her hips kicked forward wanting more.

"You are so incredibly beautiful, Meredith." Emily's words were slow and heavy against her wetness. "You taste divine."

Emily was driving her crazy. Every part of Meredith's being was crying out for more and then in an instant, she felt fingers slide inside.

One, then two, then three, then... the rough, harsh dart of the tip of a tongue whipped her clit mercilessly, in a fast incessant rhythm. Fingers pushed harder against her G-Spot in an ever strident tempo; the tingle turned into a wave bursting out through every pore as her body exploded into spasms over which she was powerless to control. But Emily didn't stop.

Slowing her efforts Emily allowed Meredith to come back to

earth momentarily before licking the abundance of juice from just behind her still swollen clit. Her tongue was soft, yet rough, the movements imperceptibly light, yet abating. Meredith squirmed and thrashed against Emily's firm grasp.

"Oh god!" Meredith exclaimed, "Fuck, I'm going to co—"

Her body screamed louder and clearer than any words she would ever be able to form, orgasming yet again in a series of violent, audacious quakes. A guttural groan strangled within her throat as her body lost its ability to breathe and, unable to take anymore, she pushed the top of Emily's head away.

"Please, god, stop. I can't take anymore." Her voice shook echoing the reverberations erupting through her body, before a sob ensued, heaving itself from her chest.

"Are you all right?" Emily's voice was filled with alarm as she extricated herself from between Meredith's legs to join her on the narrow mattress. "Baby, are you okay? Talk to me."

A light kiss whispered against Meredith's cheek and, as Emily pushed back the dark mask revealing tear-soaked eyes, she kissed away the first small saline drop that broke the tension into the darkness of the night.

"I've got you, babe. I've got you." Emily's arms held her in a tight embrace and Meredith knew one thing for certain; *You really do have me. All of me.*

THIRTY

The concept of time at the compound was something that seemed beyond grasp. In hours of high tension everything moved so quickly you barely had the chance to take a breath. Days rolled from one into the other, darkness offering no lull in the constant tide of heightened tension. There had been what felt like weeks of gunfire, lost limbs, death and the miracle of life being born into a world unready for their purity. The constant juxtaposition of terror and toil was taking its toll.

Meredith lay on the makeshift wooden cot that passed for a bed. Tiredness seeped into every pore of her being from a grueling and grisly night-long surgical session. There had been extensive bombing in the area, and the casualties kept rolling in. The irony of being in a place that resembled hell in so many ways, but not being unhappy made her eyes roll. *You are twisted Meredith, very twisted.*

But the truth was she was more than not just unhappy, she was happier than she had been in a very long time. In three days time she would be turning 47 years old, and unlike the last number of birthdays that went uncelebrated, unnoticed, this time she would be surrounded by a team of people she loved and respected, doing a job that allowed her to make a very real difference in the world. That sense of purpose, of being part of something so much bigger than herself was the best present she could have ever have hoped for. And to be able to share that with Emily, the woman who had won her heart not just once, but twice over... she sighed as a slow smile relaxed her face. Closing her eyes she drifted closer towards much needed rest.

"Meredith... Meredith..." The voice called again, accompanied by the rattle of knock on the frame of her tent.

"Yeah," her voice was thick with sleep and her hands grasped the side of the wooden cot in an attempt to orient herself. Grasping the scarf she had placed over her eyes, she pulled it down. It was still bright, she can't have been asleep for long.

"Meredith." Carlos called. "Can I have a word?"

"Now?" Meredith swung her legs around allowing her feet to hit the cool of the plastic groundsheet. "Can you give me a minute?"

"Yeah."

Grabbing her T-shirt, she pulled it over her head and reached for her cargo pants. She hadn't heard any more artillery but that didn't mean there weren't still casualties coming in. With her boots on she stepped out of her tent and immediately brought her hand up to block out the harsh daylight. Her body winced at the sudden blast of arid hot air. There was no amount of time in Yemen that would help her to adjust to *that*.

"Come on, we should talk in my office." Carlos's voice was quiet as he beckoned her over to the tents that had been set up as adminis-trative offices, and let her inside. Meredith followed, a little nervously – it was the first time she'd seen Carlos ask *anyone* to talk in his office, so she figured it must have been serious, or confidential at the very least. Normally he just pulled people to one side and talked to them in hushed tones, and his voice was so naturally gentle that no one ever stood a chance of overhearing him.

"Is something wrong?" she asked, sliding herself into a chair.

Carlos didn't walk around the desk to sit on his own, instead choosing to just lean on the desk itself, crossing his ankles.

"Well, yes, as it turns out."

"Have... I done something wrong?" she asked, a little uncertain. For a moment, she wondered if he had somehow managed to find out about her relationship with Emily, and her heart began to speed up. There was no way though, surely not. They'd both been so discreet so there was no possible way, was there?

Unless Emily told him... Meredith thought to herself. That was always a possibility; albeit it didn't seem logical given the recent time they had spent together. Emily had talked about how inappropriate their relationship was while she had been investigating the hospital, surely this wasn't coming up again?

But Carlos waived those fears away quickly. "No, no. Of course you haven't. Someone else did. In the scramble to make sure doctors could be sent out here to Yemen, we've become a little... oversaturated is probably the best way to describe it. What's the saying? Too many cooks spoil the broth?"

"That's right..." Although Meredith was off the hook, she still didn't like the direction this conversation was heading in. "What happened?"

"An administrative issue, or a problem with the system. They aren't sure which it is, but to be honest, the why doesn't matter all that much, especially not to me. What *does* matter is that we've got too many doctors here, possibly for the first time ever, and I don't know what to do with everyone. In some areas, it doesn't matter that much; if we take on a few extra midwives, no one's going to be complaining, especially not the pregnant women in the city. But, when I have two neurosurgeons..."

He trailed off, shooting Meredith a pointed look.

"We... have a second neurosurgeon?"

"Mm. Turns out, it's the one I was *supposed* to be getting, fresh from France. He arrives tomorrow morning."

"Well... What does that have to do with me? I mean, I'm already here. Why not just send him somewhere else?"

Carlos smiled gently at that, rubbing his heavily stubbled chin. "We could. But when it comes to the places that need doctors most desperately, it doesn't make sense to send him there—but it *does* make sense to send you."

Meredith swallowed nervously. "Myanmar?"

"Myanmar," he confirmed with a grim smile. "We had a briefing this morning. It's getting worse, and as you've already worked out there, it makes more sense to send you back."

"Yeah... yeah, it does." Meredith dragged a hand through her hair with a sigh. She didn't want to agree with Carlos, she didn't want to make him think that she was completely fine with the idea of heading back to Myanmar, but she knew he was right. She'd already built up a rapport with the other doctors out there, and that kind of relationship could take weeks to forge. It didn't make sense to keep her in Yemen, while she still wasn't all that familiar with the situation, the staff, and send a new doctor out to Myanmar.

She didn't want to go though. Carlos could see from her reaction that she didn't like the idea of heading back to her original posting, but he had no idea why. "I know that it's got to be nerve-racking, sending you back out there when things are starting to get worse again, but I don't want you to think of this as... you're not being treated as though you're expendable. No one is trying to get rid of you, or anything like that. This is just the course of action that makes the most sense, logistically."

"I know."

"But you still don't want to go."

"No, I don't want to go." Meredith looked up at him slowly. "But it's got nothing to do with how dangerous it's going to be out there. I don't care about that at all."

"You don't?" He raised an eyebrow. "Then what?"

Meredith opened her mouth, about to tell him everything. For a split second, she thought that maybe if she just came clean to him and told him everything about the relationship, Carlos would take pity on the two of them, and he'd send the other doctor out to Myanmar.

But she knew that wouldn't work. Carlos was too committed to the charity, the medical needs of those they served to entertain reservations because of some romantic notion. And then there was the conflict because of their differing roles. Perhaps if they were both working in Human Resources, or they were both surgeons or both psychologists things wouldn't be as bad. With their jobs as they were though, she knew he wouldn't let her stay. It would be inappropriate.

Inappropriate. That word seemed to follow her around like some kind of sword of Damocles, but it had already fallen once already, and Meredith knew the consequences all too well. She didn't want to face them all over again, and she certainly couldn't put Emily through it once more.

So rather than trying to explain to him that she had very good reasons for wanting to stay, Meredith just accepted it. "When do you want me to fly out?"

"There's a plane taking you, a few nurses and an anesthesiologist out to Myanmar tomorrow morning at 7 a.m. You'll need to leave here by six."

It felt like someone had slammed a fist into her stomach, like the wind had been knocked out of her completely. 7 a.m.... That only gave her fourteen hours with Emily before she'd be flying out of the country. It was a lot less after she factored in transport and packing.

"Seven..." she echoed. "Wow."

"I know it's short notice. I'm sorry, it's got to feel like you're being pulled around quite a lot."

"Yeah," she murmured, sighing. "It does feel exactly like that, to be honest."

"At least you have tonight to say goodbye to everyone."

There was only one person she wanted to say goodbye to. There was only one person in the camp who she cared about enough to even tell them that she was going, but she was also the person Meredith dreaded talking to about this. Things seemed to be going so well between the two of them, to rip her away from that all over again and keep them so far apart just felt cruel.

Meredith stood up, and thanked Carlos. He said something else, maybe an apology for how fast everything was happening, but whatever it was, Meredith hardly heard it. She wasn't paying attention to him as she pushed her chair out and headed for the door. Whatever he had to say to her now didn't matter, but there was one thing that did.

She had to find Emily.

THIRTY-ONE

When she knocked on the door to Emily's makeshift office, Meredith didn't get a response. It was the middle of the afternoon, so there was nowhere else she could be but there.

She's probably with a patient, Meredith realized. Sure enough, when she peeked through the plastic window of the door, she saw Emily at her desk, and the back of a man's head.

She reached for the doorknob to let herself in uninvited, but stopped herself before she could actually open the door. How would she feel, if she was in the middle of a private meeting with a doctor, only to have some stranger burst in and demand she left?

A few months ago, that thought wouldn't have stopped her, at least not for long. Sure, she'd have known that it would have annoyed her, if it happened to her, just as she knew now. The difference was, a few months ago she wouldn't have cared. She would have just pushed the door open anyway, and insisted that *her* time was more important than anyone else's.

That wasn't who she was now, though, and as much as she *wanted* to push her way in there to get as much time as possible with

Emily, she stopped herself. It wasn't fair to pull Emily away from her work.

Meredith resigned herself to just pacing outside the door, back and forth over and over again, like a caged animal slowly going insane. Hopefully, if she spent enough time prowling around outside the door, no one else would be able to sneak in for another meeting. Sure, she wasn't going to interrupt a session that was already going on, but that didn't mean she had to let anyone else get in ahead of her.

It felt like they talked for hours. Meredith had no idea of how many times she walked the few meters outside the door, lifting her head up every so often to check that she hadn't somehow managed to miss the patient leaving. Up and down, again and again, over and over.

Then finally, the door swung open. She heard someone thanking Emily for her time, and then Meredith came face to face with the patient. It was a young nurse, someone she'd only met briefly and couldn't remember well. She flashed him a small smile, and then darted around him to get into Emily's office, as if she was afraid someone else might sneak in ahead of her if she wasn't careful.

Emily was still sitting behind her desk, looking through a file when Meredith made her way in, and slammed the door shut behind her. At the sound, Emily looked up in surprise, and then smiled at Meredith.

"You don't have an appointment," she teased, before the smile slipped from her face. She must have realized that something was really wrong; maybe from the way Meredith had burst in there, because she stood up, a frown creasing her face. "Are you alright?"

"No." Meredith wasn't going to sugar coat it. She didn't have time to break the news gently. "I'm not. I'm not okay, Emily."

"What happened, what's wrong?" Emily walked around the desk to join her, and grabbed Meredith's hand in her own. "Is it a patient?"

"No." Meredith stared down at their hands, and swallowed hard. This would be one of the last times she would be able to hold Emily's hand for a long time, and she knew it. Maybe it would be one of the last times *ever*. She wanted to savor it, to cling on tightly until the moment she stepped onto the plane.

"Meredith, you're scaring me." Emily whispered. "What happened?"

"I have to leave."

There was a beat of silence as Emily processed that information. "What do you mean, you have to leave?"

"They don't need me here anymore, but I'm needed back on the ground in Myanmar."

"Oh." Meredith looked up into Emily's eyes, to see her struggling to find the right words. It was a little comforting to know she wasn't the only one who wasn't sure what to say. There was so much that Meredith knew she wanted to get out, but there was so little time to say it. So they both just stood there in silence, staring at each other in mute horror.

"When do you leave?" Emily asked finally.

"Tomorrow at six."

"Six?"

"I know." Meredith shook her head. "It's not enough time. I came straight here when Carlos told me, but it's... It's just not enough time. It's not fair."

"Why can't they send someone else?" Emily wet her lips and gestured to the door, like she was about to march through it and find Carlos. "You're not the only surgeon. They could send someone else out there to Myanmar and keep you here, right? We can go and tell them that, right now!"

There was a panicked, almost frantic look in her eyes that Meredith had never seen before, and it made her own heart pound. Emily was desperate to keep her there, and she wanted nothing more than to stay, but she knew it couldn't happen. Deep down, behind her anxious, rambled planning, Emily probably knew that too.

"I've already worked with the team out there, Emily." She said gently, squeezing her hand. "I know what it's like out there, I know the people. It doesn't make sense to drop someone else in it."

"Well, then..." She swallowed hard, and her eyes darted around her office. "Why don't I come too? You'll need a psych team out there, right? I can ask to be transferred."

"You know they won't do that."

"They *might!*"

"Emily," Meredith whispered, reaching out with her free hand to cup the younger woman's cheek. "Stop."

"I can't... and your birthday. I was..." She faltered and swallowed hard. "I don't want you to go."

"I know. Ironic isn't it. I don't want to leave either. But it looks like this is how things are going to have to be. There are too many people here, not enough people out there. It's simple math, right?"

"But—" Emily began to protest, but Meredith shushed her with another smile.

"Please don't. We've only got one more night together before I leave, and I don't want to spend it trying to scheme and plot so I can find a way out of this. I know what I'm in for when I land in Myanmar, and I just want..." She paused, and let out a shaky sigh. As she was talking, the realization was beginning to truly settle in, and it was getting harder and harder to keep her composure. There was still a part of her that wanted to give into Emily's panicked plans and beg to stay, as selfish as it was. She wanted to stay there in that office forever, and just let everything else pass them by.

"I just want..." she continued, stoking the pad of her thumb against Emily's cheekbone. "One night with you. Just a nice, normal night where we can pretend that everything else isn't a shit show."

"That feels like we're just giving up though," Emily whispered. Tears were brimming in her eyes now, threatening to spill over and roll down her cheeks, and Meredith only hoped that they didn't. If she saw Emily break down into tears, she wasn't sure she would be able to keep calm and collected.

"There's nothing we can do. You know that. There's no point in arguing about it, so can we just make the most of the time we've got? Please?"

She let out a choked sound, somewhere between a laugh and a sob, and looked away for a moment, sniffling. "Why weren't you like this back at the hospital? I don't think I'd have gone back to California if you were."

"Really?"

"Yes. Or... Or maybe I would have. But I probably would have been won over by that speech of yours." Emily managed another shaky, tearful laugh, and shook her head. "Why weren't you *this* Meredith back then?"

"I thought it was obvious." She smiled, wiping the one stray tear that had managed to fall. "I met you, and you helped me. I told you that when I came to California."

"Yeah, well back then I thought it was bullshit. I thought you were just trying to... To force my hand or something. To manipulate me into coming back."

"I probably was," she admitted. "I think I really *was* a different person when I came to find you in California, but I still wasn't... I still wasn't good. I mean, I'm probably not even good *now*, but I'm better. I'm different. I'm more like the person I wanted to be when I found you in California."

Emily dropped her hand and wiped her nose on the back of her sleeve. "This is bullshit."

"It *is* bullshit and it feels unfair but look around us... life is unfair."

"I have a bottle of wine. It's not good, but it's alcohol," She laughed shakily, and dragged a hand through her hair. "You want to crack it open with me?"

"Sure." Meredith grinned. "Your place?"

"You know where I live. About seven?"

"I'll be there." Meredith dipped her head close and pressed a gentle kiss to Emily's lips. One of the last, she reminded herself. One of the last she'd be able to give.

It really wasn't fair.

THIRTY-TWO

Meredith headed back to her tent and managed to grab a couple of hours of fitful sleep. The dreams came thick and fast. She was in the makeshift OR and body after body was piling up all around her. They just kept coming; too many to handle and a man kept shouting "Don't stop, there are more coming." But try as she might she couldn't find her scalpel. There were other people around her dressed in the same blood-splattered light blue scrubs she was wearing. She shouted in desperation for someone to hand her a scalpel, but time after time they handed her her cloths and hammers but never a scalpel. *"How can I operate without a scalpel?"* she cried in frustration.

With a start she banged her arm on the edge of her cot. Grabbing it, she pulled it tight across her chest and held it. It took a moment for her to drag herself out of sleep. The sweat-drenched shirt was wet against her skin. Her arm would surely bruise. The clock balanced on her trunk told her she had about twenty minutes to grab a shower. A loud sigh heaved its way from her chest.

Picking up a towel she made her way to the makeshift shower block only to find the power was out again and it was bucket wash or bust. It'd do. It had to.

The same could be said for her choice of wardrobe as she looked down at her trunk, she wished she had something nice to wear. It had never occurred to her to bring anything other than comfortable clothes; she had a choice of t-shirts, loose shirts and khaki pants. Not exactly hot date material.

This would be the last night the two of them would be able to spend together, and in an ideal world, Meredith would have everything perfect. They'd be able to go somewhere nice and private, maybe to a restaurant. They'd be able to push everything else out of their minds and just focus on each other for the last few hours they would have.

But this wasn't a perfect world. They weren't back in the city, there were no nice restaurants to go to, no secluded spots they could hide away in. All they had was the privacy of a tent, and a bottle of booze. It wasn't much, but out here, it was a lot.

Meredith pulled on her cleanest pair of cargo pants, threw a loose cotton shirt over her vest, and splashed some water on her face. Before she left for Emily's tent, she caught sight of herself in the little mirror that sat on top of her clothing trunk, and grimaced at her reflection. Her hair was messy, thrown back in a ponytail that was already starting to fall out. There were dark circles under her eyes from the scattered sleep pattern she'd developed over the past few months, and her nose was sunburnt.

She looked about as good as she felt, which was *not very*. There wasn't time to try and tidy herself up any more than she already had done though; Meredith was acutely and uncomfortably aware that every moment she spent in her tent was a minute less she'd have to spend with Emily. So even though she looked like a wreck and felt even worse, Meredith left her tent and crossed the compound.

With every step she took, a sense of dread mixed with the swell of excitement in the pit of her stomach. There was a completely irrational part of her that just wanted to turn away and head back to her tent, to bury her head in the sand until she had to get on her flight. At least that way, if they didn't have their one last night together, it wouldn't feel like it was so *real*.

Meredith didn't have that option though. Before she could even knock on the door to Emily's tent it swung open, like she'd been waiting on the other side for her. Emily stood there in the doorway, smiling nervously with a bottle of wine in one hand.

"Hi," she said quietly, stepping to one side. "You want to come in?"

Meredith stepped inside. A ridiculous nervousness fizzed in her stomach and she wiped her palms against her cargo pants.

"Have they told you anything about what's going to happen tomorrow?" Emily asked, sitting down on the cot. Meredith joined her, wincing as the bed dug into her. "Once you get to Myanmar, I mean. Do you know what it'll be like out there?"

"Not really. It'll probably be the same as here, a little worse perhaps."

"Probably." Emily agreed quietly. "What do you think they'll have you—"

"Emily," she interrupted quietly. "I don't... I'm sorry, I just don't want to talk about it."

"It's fine, I understand," Emily sighed. "It must be nerve-racking."

"Just for tonight, can we just... pretend like we aren't here?" Meredith asked tentatively. "Can we pretend that this isn't happening? It's just you and me, and nothing else?"

Emily smiled gently at that, and laid her hand over Meredith's, squeezing tightly. "Just you and me, and nothing else." Emily whispered. She leaned in close, and kissed Meredith slowly. It was relaxed and languid, and felt so familiar and foreign all at the same time. All Meredith could do was melt into her touch, and kiss her back.

They drank wine, wincing with each acidic mouthful, and chatted about the probability of finding each other again, as they had done. *What were the chances...*

Life felt more than a little cruel but the sweet bitterness of their predicament could be left for another day. Tonight all Meredith wanted to do was to feel close to Emily.

"Will you stay tonight? Please?" Emily took her hand, holding it tight between her own. "I just want to lie with you. To feel you next to me. I know it might sound a little soft but I want to hold onto that feeling so when you're not..." She swallowed and pressed her lips together and inhaled deeply, "you know. Then I can pretend you are with me." The shrug she offered didn't hide the pain.

Meredith gathered her in her arms, inhaling her scent. The last thing in the world she wanted to do was let her go. *How can this be happening?* She tilted her head up in an attempt to stem the tears and swallowed hard.

"Of course I will. I'm not going to leave you. Not tonight."

THIRTY-THREE

It was still dark when Meredith woke in Emily's tent, and for a few moments, she forgot everything. Waking up in Emily's arms again, able to smell the last lingering touch of her perfume, Meredith thought for a moment she was back in her apartment, and everything was just the way it had been months earlier.

But then she shifted around in the bunk, and the springs dug into her side, and it all came flooding back to her at once. She *wasn't* in her bed at home, waking up for an early shift in the OR. She wasn't about to go out on a leisurely run with Emily, and watch the sunrise over the river. She was miles and miles away, in the middle of a war zone.

And soon she would be leaving for *another* war zone.

Meredith checked her watch, and groaned gently. It was just after five, and she needed to be ready at six to head out. She was going to have to slip out of bed, no matter how nice it was to lay there with Emily, and pack up her things, which she hadn't bothered to do the night before.

She tried not to disturb Emily as she sat up in bed, but as she eased herself up, Emily's hand shot out and her fingers curled around her wrist. "What are you doing?"

Her voice was still thick with sleep, and she was probably only half aware of Meredith even moving around, judging by the way she was slurring. With a soft smile, Meredith pulled her hand away, and laid it down on the pillow by Emily's head.

"I need to pack up." She explained quietly. "I didn't mean to wake you."

"What time is it?"

"A little after five."

Emily curled her hand underneath her face to prop her head up, looking at Meredith through her lashes. "You're leaving at six, right?"

"That's right."

"So we've got less than an hour together."

"Yes."

"Then stay with me." Emily slid her hand back out, and knotted her fingers with Meredith's. "Just for a little while."

It was hard to say no. The bed was warm, Emily's skin was soft, and it felt good to be held by another person. But Meredith knew if she laid back down in the cot with her, it would only make it harder to leave when the time came.

"I'm sorry." She pulled away and stood up. "I have to go."

"Then I'll help." Emily sat up. "I can help you pack, and then I can see you off when you leave."

Meredith smiled gently at that, and picked up her clothes from the night before. "All right then, you can help me pack."

They got dressed in silence, and then slipped out into the compound together, walking hand in hand to Meredith's tent. It felt like they were a pair of teenagers sneaking around after curfew as they crept around, ducking inside before anyone could spot them, and if the situation was any different, it might have felt fun and exciting.

It was neither fun *or* exciting to pack up her things though.

There wasn't much either one of them could say while they

packed her trunk, tucking clothes and books away for safekeeping. Thinking too much about what was ahead of her made Meredith feel nervous, and Emily just seemed lost.

It wasn't until everything was packed away that either of them spoke. With nothing else to do while they waited for the car to be ready, Emily began pacing the tent, while Meredith locked her things away.

"I could come to the plane with you," she suggested, wringing her hands together anxiously. "To see you off?"

"You know that's not a good idea." Meredith frowned, closing the lock on her trunk. Drives through the city were dangerous enough, there was no way Carlos would allow anyone out of the compound unless it was completely necessary. "You can't do that."

"So I just have to say goodbye here? I've just got to sit here and..." She trailed off, shaking her head slowly. "That's not fair."

"I know it's not." Meredith sighed, running a hand through her hair as she looked around her tent. None of this was fair. "But it wouldn't be like you were seeing me off from LAX or something, even if you could come with me. You know that."

"It would feel more normal though. This just feels—I don't know how it feels." She dropped down onto the cot, leaning hunching over resting her elbows against her knees. "I just hate it."

Meredith crouched beside Emily, and took her hands. As she gave them a gentle squeeze, she pressed a kiss to Emily's forehead. "Look at me. Come on, look at me."

Emily looked up slowly, and when she did, Meredith could see how red her eyes were. Tears were welling, and when she blinked, one splashed down her cheek, leaving a trail that glistened in the overhead light. Meredith smeared it away with her thumb, drawing in a shaky breath. "Come on now, don't cry. If you start crying then *I'll* start crying, and where are we going to be?"

"I don't want you to go," Emily's voice cracked as she spoke. "We only just found each other again. I'm not ready."

"Neither am I," Meredith admitted, feeling her throat tighten.

She swallowed past the painful lump of tears that was building, and managed a small smile. "But this is the way it has to be."

"It's going to be dangerous out there, isn't it?"

If Meredith had said "no" to that, they both would have known she was lying. All she could do was nod silently, and brush away another stray tear.

"It's dangerous here too."

"I wish we'd had more time," Emily whispered, reaching out a hand to caress Meredith's cheek. "Just a little more time..."

Meredith leaned in her touch instinctively, and breathed out a low sigh. It felt so good, after so long without Emily, to just feel her. It was so good just to have her *there*. "Yeah."

They looked into each other's eyes silently as the moments ticked by. There was something Meredith knew she wanted to tell Emily, something that she already *had* told her, months earlier. If they'd had a little more time, she would have held back and waited until she knew how Emily would take it, but that wasn't an option for them any more. She wasn't sure whether Emily would want to hear what she had to say, but she had to take the risk, she decided. If she didn't, she would only regret it as soon as she got on the plane.

"Emily..." she whispered, swallowing nervously. "I—"

The sound of a horn outside made them spring apart suddenly. Meredith checked her watch, and sure enough, it was six. That was the truck, ready to take her to the airport.

They were out of time.

"Shit..." she whispered, looking back up at Emily. "I have to—"

"I know." Emily was still clinging to her hand though, too tightly to pull away, and when Meredith stood up, Emily came too. "I know you do. I just... I have to tell you something."

"You do?"

"When you came to me in California I didn't believe what you said. You told me that you loved me, and I just... I brushed it off. I shouldn't have done that, and I understand if you don't feel like that anymore, but I don't know when I'm going to see you again, and I know if you get on that plane without hearing thi—"

"Emily." Meredith interrupted her with a small smile. She must have been nervous, given how much she was rambling, and as endearing as it was to watch, they really didn't have any time left. The truck horn blasted once more, and Meredith knew if they waited much longer, someone would come looking for her. "In the nicest way possible, you're going to have to get to the point."

"I love you," she blurted out. "I love you, Meredith. I realized the moment I sent you away when you came to see me in California, but I was still so hurt and angry, and angry with *myself* and... fuck, none of that matters anymore. I just needed you to know."

Meredith let out something between a laugh and a sob, and her vision went blurry for a moment as tears sprang to her eyes. She blinked them back furiously, and shook her head in disbelief. "Really?"

"Really. I couldn't let you go without making sure you knew that."

"I love you too, Emily," she whispered, cupping both her cheeks so she was cradling her face. "And I'm sorry. Maybe if I hadn't been such an ass. Maybe if I'd listened, sooner."

"Maybe." Emily laid her hands over Meredith's, and smiled gently. "But as much as this sucks, I'm glad I met you again."

"So am I."

The horn was louder this time along with the growl of an engine. Meredith let out an exasperated groan. "Shit, we don't have time."

"I know, you have to go. I'm sorry, I know I should have told you this last night. But better late than never, right?

"Better late than never," Meredith agreed, closing the gap between them for one last kiss. She wished she could take her time and memorize every detail of the way it felt when she pressed her lips to Emily's. She wished she could just melt into her touch and stay there forever, but even as she sank her hands into Emily's soft locks, she could hear footsteps approaching the door.

She pulled back just far enough that they could whisper to each other, and pressed her forehead to Emily's. "You stay safe here, okay?"

"You too. I mean it, Meredith. I don't want to hear about something happening to you as soon as I let you out of my sight."

"I'll try my best," she promised, before pulling away. There was a knock at her door, and Emily flinched.

"Meredith?" They heard Carlos's voice. "Are you awake?"

"Yeah, Carlos," she called, taking a small step away from Emily.

As Emily's hand slid from her grasp she knew she had only seconds left. "I'm coming back for you. I promise." With one last smile, Meredith turned away from Emily and pulled the door open to see Carlos on the other side.

"Morning." He peeked inside to see Emily standing there. "Saying your last goodbyes?"

"Yeah." Meredith looked behind him to see the truck was already. The only thing that needed to go on it was her, and her trunk. "Last goodbyes."

"Well, we'll all miss you," he assured her, patting her shoulder a little awkwardly. "Go on, hop in the truck and I'll get some of the boys to grab your things."

"Sure, thanks," she let him steer her away from the tent, and glanced over her shoulder to see Emily trailing behind them. She was hugging her arms around herself, looking down at the ground as she walked, and at the sight of her looking so upset, it took all of Meredith's restraint not to walk over and gather her into her arms again.

She took her seat in the back of the truck, and when Carlos closed the door behind her, all she could do was look out into the compound, at Emily. It wasn't a proper goodbye, the tender confession she had hoped for. It wasn't the stuff of all of those romance books she'd read over the years. There was no beautiful music, grand gestures and running off into the sunset despite all the odds. Neither of them knew when—or if—she would be back. The only thing that lay ahead was uncertainty and unrest

The engine of the truck rumbled to life beneath her, and as it did, Meredith felt her throat close up all over again. The compound was too dark for her to see Emily's face clearly, but she had a feeling if the sun had risen, she would have been able to see tears.

All too soon, they set off, and Emily faded out into the darkness of the early morning. As they moved through the compound and out of the gates, Meredith slumped back in her seat. It was hard not to feel like this was all just some cruel joke the universe was playing on her; after eight years, she'd finally opened herself up to the chance of being with someone again, and just when she thought there was a chance for them, they were pulled apart all over again.

We met again though, she reminded herself, looking out of the window at the city as they whipped through cramped side streets. *Purely by chance, we met each other again, halfway across the world.*

What's stopping that from happening again?

THIRTY-FOUR

"Emily, are you all right?" There was a pause around the table as everyone waited for a reaction but nothing happened. "Ground Control to Emily. Do you read me?"

Everyone sitting around the table looked from Luis, the camp's Clinical Director, to Emily and back again. Finally, the surgeon sitting next to Emily elbowed her in the ribs.

"Ow." Emily turned to the man with a look of confusion and he simply nodded towards Luis.

Shit. Everyone is staring at me. What have I missed? "Sorry, what were you asking?"

"I was checking you were all set to ship out at the end of next week?" A smile played on Luis' lips, amused by Emily's obvious embarrassment.

"Yes, sorry. Miguel is arriving tomorrow so we'll have eight days to complete a handover. He's an experienced team leader so he should hit the ground running."

"So it'll be refreshments in the mess on Tuesday to say goodbye?" Luis raised his eyebrows and gave her a nod of encouragement.

"Yes, absolutely. Teas and coffees are on me," Emily said with a chuckle. "Sorry I've so much to think about before I go I've been a bit distracted."

Her colleagues waved it off with murmurs of "understandable."

But she had been distracted, more than distracted. It had been six months since Meredith had left and not once during that time had she had she stopped thinking about her. The first few weeks had been the worst. Things as simple as eating and sleeping became harder, as if someone had sucked all the air from her life.

The message to say that Meredith had arrived safely had boosted her spirits but equally it brought with it pangs of loneliness. It took a while to reconcile that was what was eating away at her but even surrounded by so many people, without Meredith, she felt lonely.

Sure they had called when they could but with patchy connections, a three-and-a-half-hour time difference, and heavy workloads the sessions were short and infrequent. The military had shut down all internet connections in Myanmar earlier in the year and Emily had cursed them everyday. As precious as every moment was, Emily found herself always wanting more and the irony that she had been the one to turn Meredith away hung heavy around her shoulders.

Days, and sometimes nights, were long and full and for that she was grateful. Losing herself in others problems was what she needed to do right now. But not for much longer. In eight days time she would be heading home to California, to her dog, Reno, and her family. But not to Meredith. Not yet.

There were a few pats on the back as they left the tent and promises of catching up before she left as they all filtered out the tent. There was an hour to spare before the team meeting, so she collected her mail from the admin tent. Her grandmother refused to use a computer insisting that letter writing was a dying art. Every so often Emily would receive a bundle of letters all at once and she'd have to try and place them in order before reading them. They were a blow-by-blow account of an octogenarian's daily activities; as Emily and her mother called them they were the golden diaries. Memoirs of golden years from the Golden State. But reading them brought her immense happiness.

The usual bundle of letters all bound in a brown elastic band awaited her but this time there was something else. A small thin brown box accompanied the bundle. Emily turned it over and looked at it. There were no U.S. postal service markings, instead this had come via DBB's internal logistics system. *Must be something to do with my contract,* she mused, tucking it into the side pocket of her cargo shorts along with the letters. Right now she had work to do. A team meeting followed by the first of a new series of workshops they had set up for local children helping them deal with the trauma they had witnessed. She was still making a difference, she reminded herself.

———

The trunk was almost half full and she had three days left before she had to leave to get her transport back to the U.S.. Packing each item away when she no longer needed it made her feel a step closer to leaving everyday. The camping lamp flickered, sending odd shaped shadows over the small space.

She lifted her grandmother's letters to slide them down into the side of the trunk. The thin box she'd picked up a few days earlier came with them. It was still unopened. Emily grabbed it and slumped down on her cot ready to tear it open. Inside was a letter and something small and hard wrapped in white tissue paper.

She looked at it curiously and popped it on her lap as she unfolded the letter.

Emily,

When you read this it won't be long until you leave. I know you'll be excited to see Reno, and everyone at home.

It feels odd knowing you are going even further away, when I wish you were coming towards me... but knowing you'll be safe and out of harm's way means everything. I have only ever wanted what is best for you because it is no less than you deserve.

Our conversations and messages have felt like home to me over the last six months. It would be too easy to say fate brought us back together and now we've found each other, we'll waltz off hand and hand into the sunset.

Life doesn't work like that, as the last nine months have taught us both.

I know you've always said that you'd understand If I chose to renew my assignment with DBB and lord knows they are desperate enough for good surgeons here...

But...

I've known for over the last year I have been in love with you. Not a day goes by when my thoughts don't turn to you. What you might be doing? What you'd think of something I've seen? I don't want to wonder any longer, instead I want to share every moment I have with you. Life is such a precious gift that can be taken in an instant and I don't want to squander a moment of it.

I know that we haven't talked about what comes next... not properly, but hear me out.

I have written to Melanie and the board and thanked them for their support and understanding but told them I won't return to City General. I have resigned. I have no home as such. No fixed abode. Everything I own is in storage.

For the first time I am choosing to stop running away. I no longer want to hide from life.

Now I am choosing to run towards my future, to embrace everything it holds. Emily, you are my future and I want to spend the rest of my life with you... if you will have me?

I arrive back in the U.S. in just over a month and until then I am offering you something I hope you will accept. My heart.

I will love you always.

Meredith x

. . .

Emily clutched the letter to her chest as tears ran down her cheeks. "Yes," she whispered, "yes, yes, yes." The white tissue slipped from her lap and she caught gently in her hand.

She glanced at her watch. It was ten o'clock, so that meant it would be one-thirty in the morning for Meredith. All she wanted to do was speak to her. To hear her voice. To say, yes.

With trembling fingers she unwrapped the crinkly white tissue and gasped as she saw the most beautiful silver carved locket. The heart shape was etched with such beautiful detail and inlaid with small pieces of red glass. Even in the dim light of the tent, it seemed to glisten and sparkle as she moved it. As if it had its own beat.

Inside the locket, words were etched and Emily had to get close to the light to read them.

Even in the depths of despair, have faith in love. It will lift us.

Fresh tears came in a rush and she grabbed the phone, selecting Meredith's name to call. The long beeps felt like they went on forever. *Answer please Meredith, just pick up your phone and answer.*

"Hello," the voice was drowsy with sleep but the British accent was unmistakable.

"Meredith, it's me. I know it's late and I'm sorry but I've just read your letter and... the locket and... " Emily tried and failed to hold back a sob.

"Emily? Are you all right?"

"Yes. Yes. Yes, I'm all right and yes I want you. All of you. All the time. And always."

"Good." Meredith let out a laugh and Emily could feel the warmth in her smile. "We've still got stuff to work out, I know that, but Emily, I love you. And this is just the start."

This is our start, and we have everything ahead of us. The adventure is just beginning.

EPILOGUE

Meredith padded around the large open-plan living area, the marble tiles giving a pleasant cooling sensation under her feet. It was almost eight o'clock and if she didn't get her run in now, she'd have to forego it for the day. Tapping her watch it announced it was already in the mid-seventies, pleasant enough to warm her muscles but still cool enough to breathe. Plus, it meant Reno could come too and so they could both run off some pent up energy.

Sneaking silently through to the bedroom door, which she had left purposely ajar, Meredith peered into the dark room, resting against the door frame. She inhaled deeply, taking in the scent of the room, her face lifting in an endless smile.

The long, sleek bumps under the comforter moved slightly but didn't rouse. Meredith stilled, fighting the urge to climb back into the warmth and wrap her body around the beautiful young woman who lay there.

A small whimper came from the hall behind her; Reno, unable to contain his impatience. "C'mon, boy," she whispered walking towards the door and grabbing his running lead. Reno's eyes brightened with excitement as he realized he'd be coming too.

Quietly she clicked the door closed and snapped Reno's lead onto the belt around her waist. The Lab bounced on his front paws eager to get underway. The sunlight caught the white almost golden color of the flat coat, making him shine.

They headed farther up the hill passing through the quiet neighborhood. The Sunday morning chill meant they were the only people up and about, well apart from an older man who lived at the end of their street. Meredith waved, smiling, as she watched him potter about through the open garage door.

Within minutes asphalt turned to scrub, and the flat undulating landscape and vast blue skies opened up to them, inviting them in. Pushing herself harder and faster than she would normally do, Meredith pressed on, still unable to suppress her smile.

It had been three weeks since she had flown to the U.S. To LAX. The sight of Emily waiting behind the barrier, beaming in excitement, had been so overwhelming she hadn't been able to hold back the tears. The younger woman had been a vision. The reality of a dream that had kept her going through long grueling days. The blue summer dress, with brown hair falling gently onto her shoulders and that perfect smile was a sight that had made Meredith's heart sing.

The plan had been for her to stay a few days with Emily then look for a place of her own. Somewhere close to the Chung Mercy Hospital, where she'd be starting her new position as Physician in Chief. Ironically, she'd secured the role because of her "warm disposition," according to the board trustees. It was a new teaching hospital foundation with a particular focus on the physical and mental well-being of women and children, although it would cater to the community as a whole.

But the few days had turned into a few weeks already and every time she took Emily to look at apartments, the younger woman always found fault. Location was the first issue, it was too far from Palmdale, or so close to the hospital it would feel like she was never leaving work, or too small for her and Reno to visit... Meredith had the distinct impression Emily just didn't want her to leave.

They had seamlessly slid their lives together and without even trying they had found their rhythm. In fairness, for Meredith, the thought of being on her own again wasn't something she was eager to return to, but she didn't want to jeopardize what she and Emily had by rushing things.

Her watch beeped, indicating she and Reno had completed five miles, at a pace of six minutes and fifty-nine seconds per mile. She nodded to Reno, "That's not too shabby for a couple of forty-seven-year olds."

There was just one mile left to go on the circuit for today's run which would take her to the end of Paintbrush Drive and minutes from home... Meredith caught herself. It wasn't her home it was Emily's home, albeit Emily had gone out of her way to help Meredith settle in. She'd even suggested that Meredith get the storage container with all her belongings placed into the huge backyard. She hadn't responded when that suggestion had landed over dinner. It had caught her off guard and she needed time to think about it all. Reno had an extra surge running up the last hill. He knew his breakfast was in range.

As the pair of them unceremoniously crashed through the gate and into the backyard, Meredith clicked her watch.   Forty-four minutes and three seconds to cover just over 6.2 miles. Damn. It was always that last hill that got them.

Unclipping Reno from his lead and removing the waistband, her attention was grabbed to the smell of grilled ham wafting over the air.

Kicking off her sneakers, she entered the kitchen to see Emily in panties and a tank, cooking breakfast. Meredith's eyes wandered up the young woman's tanned limbs. She almost had to pinch herself to remember this was her current reality and that Emily had chosen her. Just over a year ago she'd have thought she'd walked into someone else's life... she sort of had, because she wasn't the same person anymore. The person that was striding towards her young lover, grabbing her playfully around the waist and kissing her neck was a better, happier version of Dr. Meredith Asquith; a woman she liked very much.

Nothing would bring back Jennifer or her daughter and whilst she would never forget the joy they had brought to her life, it was time to start living again. It is what they would have wanted and she knew that because it is what she would have wanted for them, if the cards had fallen differently.

"I'm making your favorite breakfast stack," Emily murmured, her words getting lost in the distraction of having her earlobe expertly nibbled. "Go jump in the shower and be quick and I'll plate it up." She pulled her ear away from Meredith's mouth and smiled. "You are such a tease."

"You don't want to join me?" Meredith raised her eyebrows, "In the shower?"

"I'm beautifully clean, not all sweaty like you."

Reno barked in agreement, eager to be rewarded with a tiny sliver of ham. Emily rubbed his ears and continued with a wicked smile, "Let me build up your stamina a little and then we can get dirty again... together."

Meredith didn't have to be told twice and she scooted through to the shower stripping off her running gear as she went.

"And don't drop your clothes on the floor," Emily's voice followed her as she skipped through the house.

One ice cold shower later and Meredith was standing in front of the eight-drawer dresser that contained all her worldly belongings, deciding what to wear. She pulled on a cotton sports bra, and lifted a pair of panties and then hesitated. A slow smile crept over her face. Discarding the pants she pulled out the new pair of boxers complete with an O ring fitting, that she and Emily had painstakingly picked from the aptly named *sowetforher* website, the previous week.

Why the hell not. Life had been a little hectic since the package had arrived and they hadn't had a chance to experiment with the new toys. But today was Sunday and neither of them had plans so... what else were Sundays for...

Meredith wiggled the boxers up her thighs shimmying her ass into place, they were a beautiful fit. Opting for the new dildo with the more pliable memory core, in a beautiful shade of vibrant sky blue, Meredith pulled the boxers away from her skin and slipped the new toy into place. Looking down she felt a slight thrill go through her body. It had been years since she'd worn a strap-on and an odd combination of nervousness and exhilaration shot through her body. Standing looking at her reflection in the mirror, she let out a small gasp. It looked good.

"Are you dressed yet? I want to plate up."

Meredith gazed at the woman mirrored in front of her, watching her chest puff out. "I'm just coming. Give me a minute." She reached into the drawer again and pulled out the small silver bullet vibrator. Nodding to herself she placed it in the neat little pocket below her entrance and shimmied again, feeling the slight pressure it offered.

The last piece of the outfit was a pair of baggy gray cargo shorts she'd worn in the field. They had fitted her when she'd left Boston but she'd dropped a good twelve pounds in weight since then. Pulling them up her legs she tucked in the dildo and pulled up the zip. Turning back to the mirror she admired herself front on and then turned to each side. The heavy cotton hid the shape of the toy well. They were so baggy they hid everything well.

"What are you doing?" Emily asked as she swung into the bedroom giving Meredith a start.

"Nothing. I was just getting dressed," her reply came out as a meek stutter and Emily looked at her quizzically. "They look huge." She nodded down to the shorts and Meredith felt herself blush. The redness in her cheeks caught Emily's attention and she narrowed her gaze, cocking her head to one side. "What are you doing?"

As Emily took one then two steps further into the room, Meredith took one, then two steps backwards.

"Stand still," Emily's tone took a stricter tone but one that seemed to be driven by curiosity rather than annoyance.

Meredith did as she was told but her cheeks burned, emitting a heat that seemed to fill the room. She swallowed hard and watched as Emily closed the space between them. This wasn't how she had planned nor imagined this surprise playing out. The thought of taking Emily over the breakfast table, with a belly full of muffins, bacon, avocado and egg had sprung to mind but that vision was quickly fading.

"Are you okay?" Emily slipped her hands around Meredith's waist. The movement was small, but enough for the shorts to slip over Meredith's narrow hips and the bright blue bulbous head to spring out in welcome. Emily's mouth formed a perfect "O."

"I wanted to surprise you." Meredith explained stifling a laugh.

"Well, you did." Emily nodded sagely. "When I saw the cargo shorts I thought you were about to tell me you were going to attach a toolbelt and embark on some sort of woodwork project... but I think I might like this project a little better."

Allowing her hand to slide down between their bodies she grabbed the shaft, running her fingers over its length, and then as she became more acquainted with its texture, its weight, its balance, she fisted her hand around it. In slow, controlled movements she moved it gently causing the rough end of the length to rub against Meredith's now swelling clit. She let out a small gasp.

"I think I prefer this type of toolbelt too," Emily chuckled, her hand moving in easy undulation. The sensation made Meredith's eyes widen further.

Releasing the phallus, Emily turned nimble fingers to undoing the shorts fastenings allowing them to fall around Meredith's ankles. Taking two steps backwards she viewed her lover with an impressed nod and a seductive smile.

"Well, bless my heart, Dr. Asquith, I do believe you might have the most beautiful cock I have ever seen." Emily drawled in a faux southern accent that was almost verging on comical, but when she ran her tongue along her lips, eyeing the full length of the shaft, Meredith swallowed. Hard.

With her heart beating hard in her chest, unable to control her excitement any longer Meredith kicked the shorts from her ankles and wrapped her hand around the appendage. Watching a wicked smile cross Emily's face as her eyes darkened with desire was one of the most thrilling sensations she had ever seen.

"I liked it when you touched me... when you *stroked me*." She kept her eyes on Emily but the younger woman seemed mesmerized by the slowly deliberate movements of Meredith's hand.

"Fuck me, Meredith. You are so fucking hot." Emily's breath hitched. "I'm wet just watching you."

"It feels..." Meredith let out a small gasp as each unhurried, repetitive movement caused her clit to harden. "It's like... it belongs to me and having you watch me just now is just—so fucking erotic."

Meredith's gaze dropped down Emily's body taking in her boobs, the curve of her stomach, the white glint of panties below her tank. The metre of her movement was steady and growing in power.

Emily's ever increasing ardor burst forth and she pushed herself forward, crashing her lips against Meredith's mouth. The passion between them sent sparks flying and with the parting of lips, their tongues thrust forth, twisting and writhing in an all consuming dance. The hot, wet heat of lust drove them on.

The need to feel skin against skin saw tanks hauled over heads and thrown into the air with abandon. Meredith's head spun with hunger. She wanted to consume and be consumed all at the same time.

The dildo pressed hard between their bodies desperate for attention. Meredith felt its power, desperate to unleash it on the woman she loved. Her hand dropped to Emily's panties, sliding over the material, reaching to the molten heat between her thighs.

"You are so wet," she murmured cupping her centre.

Emily moaned and pushed her hips forward as she felt Meredith's fingertips trace the elastic towards her pleasure. Meredith's heart beat faster as the younger woman made no attempt to disguise how much she wanted her.

"Take them off... now." Emily's words came between panting breaths. "Please."

Four thumbs hooked into the elastic as they rapidly worked together to lose the material barrier. Emily spun Meredith backwards until her calves hit the edge of the bed. With firm pressure Meredith allowed herself to be lowered until she was lying flat on her back, the bright blue cock jutting into the air with a small tremor.

The sight of Emily climbing on top of her body, knees sliding down either side of her hips sent pulses of unbridled want through every cell of Meredith's body. She couldn't remember the last time she'd seen something so erotic, if ever.

Gathering her senses for a moment she reached out to the drawer at the bedside and pulled it open, grabbing a tube of lube.

"I don't think that'll be needed." Emily's tone was low and sexy as she took Meredith's free hand and placed it against her drenched centre.

A long appreciative moan erupted from Meredith's mouth and she exhaled fully.

"That feels so good." Their eyes locked. She took a beat to appreciate Emily's beauty before she went on, "Trust me this isn't about adding wetness. It's all about sensation." Holding Emily's gaze she clicked open the lid. It took effort to withdraw her hand from the hot folds but she knew it would be worth it. Squeezing lube over her fingers she then applied it to the blue silicon, in measured movement.

"Oh, fuck," Emily's voice tremored.

Squeezing from the tube again, Meredith coated her fingers once more. Straddled by the woman she loved, Meredith's only focus was on delivering the most bountiful amount of pleasure she could. The sight of Emily; legs wide; nudging her wet entrance against the toy was... incredible.

Reaching up she allowed her long, slick fingers to caress Emily's labia with the most tender of touches before sinking into the velvet hot folds beneath. The bucking of hips, desperately trying to gain purchase against her hand, sent shudders through her own body. Her thumb ran languid circles around Emily's engorged clit, enjoying the twitching growth. It was beautiful; slick and hard and full.

With a hand on each of Emily's hips she pulled her forward towards her mouth. She wanted to taste her, swirl her tongue around every inch of Emily's arousal. Drink in her juice.

Emily released an audible gasp and Meredith drew her into her mouth. The soft, plump luscious flavor of Emily coated her tongue and she tugged her deeper into her mouth. Her tongue swirled and flicked, before she returned to a few purposeful pulls with her full lips.

"Oh, Jesus, Meredith." Emily's thighs shook under her grasp. "I'm going to come."

Meredith withdrew her mouth and watched as Emily's jaw dropped. Suddenly bereft of tongue and lips, she looked as though she might burst into tears.

"Not yet. I want you to enjoy this." Meredith said in a soothing tone. "To *really* enjoy this." She gave Emily a quick wink and pushed the panting woman back down her body. "Rise up slightly... On your knees, beautiful." Taking the head of the toy she rubbed it against Emily's entrance, watching Emily's obvious hunger contort its way across her face. "Touch yourself."

Emily's eyes widened, and with a growing salacious smile her hand dropped, slipping between her thighs.

Meredith gulped. Her chest tightened in excitement, in hunger, in love. The beauty of her desire, her wanton pleasure; the unabashed confidence with which she wore her sexuality was magnificent. Meredith's heart soared.

The sight of Emily's fingers rubbing tiny circles around her clit and the sweet moans filling the air above her head had Meredith so unbelievably turned on she almost forgot her part in the activities.

"Are you actually going to share or are you just going to keep the toys all to yourself?" Emily panted, offering a small pout to emphasize her frustration.

"God, yes. Sorry I was just lost in... Sorry." Meredith was very British in her apology which only served to make Emily giggle. But giggling was quickly forgotten when Meredith placed the tip of the dildo at Emily's entrance ensuring she was wet and ready. They moved together inserting the head and linking their bodies.

"Are you okay?" Meredith asked as Emily, resting her hands on either side of Meredith's stomach, lowered herself gingerly down, inch by inch.

"Mmm-hmm, you bet." Deep concentration etched across Emily's face as she bit down on her bottom lip. "God, you feel good. So good."

Meredith squirmed in pleasure as the end of the dildo pressed hard against her clit. Overwhelmed by the exquisite pressure of Emily's weight pushing down through the dildo, rough and firm against her clit, Meredith's eyes rolled back, her eyelids fluttering closed. The loudest groans now filling the room were her own.

With a few tentative movements of her hips, Emily had taken everything Meredith had to offer.

This woman is utterly breathtaking, Meredith thought as she watched Emily grind against their toy; her beautiful long back arching, as her hips thrust forward and down. Her tempo was strong and steady, as it echoed against Meredith's swollen nub.

The riding motion as Emily fucked hard into her lap was unbuttoning Meredith inch by throbbing inch. The boxers she wore so snuggly were drenched with their wetness, and that alone felt glorious against her skin. Reaching up she captured Emily's hips pulling her down against her own rising hips. The power was intoxicating. Moving one hand across she strummed her thumb over Emily's undulating clit.

"Oh, fuck, Mer, don't stop. Just don't fucking stop," her panting breath was all the urging Meredith needed as she doubled down on her efforts. Their bodies slammed against the bed again and again and again. Every rough movement brought Meredith to the edge, as she raised her hips to slam her clit against the end of the dildo with as much force as she could muster. Her clit would be bruised but deliciously sated if she could just keep the punishment going to enable her to climax.

"I'm—I'm going to—" Emily screamed, then words were lost to the agonizing ecstasy of orgasm that jolted through her body. As the younger woman's back arched in spasm, Meredith felt her release flood over her centre, gasping in elation she came with one hard long grind against the hardness of the toy, letting out a guttural wail.

Panting, their bodies slid together in a slick of hot sweat. With Meredith still deep inside, they clung to each other in a long, tight embrace.

"I love you, Emily."

"I love you too... " Kissing Meredith's neck, Emily let out a chuckle. "If you didn't move out, we could have this sort of mind blowing sex every day."

"Every day?"

"Every—single—day," Emily whispered in her ear. The hot breath made Meredith's body shudder.

"If that's a promise then you'd better clear me a little more closet space," the murmur came with a sheepish grin.

"Really?" Emily's eyes were shining with hope. "You really mean that?" Easing herself forward, she moaned as the dildo edged out of her body.

"I kind of got the hint you liked having me here and I don't—don't want to leave you and Reno, even for a night so... if the offer still stands?

"Yes! Yes, yes." Emily bounced on the bed and sent the strap-on bobbing in delight, cheering them on. The sight made them both burst out laughing.

"I don't know which one of us is happier."

"Definitely Percival." Emily placed a kiss on Meredith's cheek.

"Really we are calling him Percival? Should we talk about this?"

"Nope. You make me so happy, Mer," she said and sliding herself to the side, she kissed her way down Meredith's body before placing her lips onto the happy toy, "as do you Percy," she murmured. Looking up at Meredith through hooded eyes, she ran the tip of her tongue from base to tip, tasting herself.

"Oh, Lord. Consider me 'moved in'," Meredith said her eyes wide in wonder and rising excitement.

What a journey they were about to have.

WANT A LITTLE MORE...

BONUS SCENES, FREE SHORT STORIES & OFFERS

To be offered bonus scenes (**including two bonus chapters for Healing of the Heart**), offers and more sign up to Ruby's newsletter.

https://www.rubyscott.com/freebies/

Thank you for reading. I hope you enjoyed the book and if you did, I'd love it if you could leave a review. Reviews make a world of difference to indie authors, they can quite simply make or break all the love and effort that authors including me, put into developing characters and stories. If you loved it then tell other readers so they can enjoy it too.

ABOUT THE AUTHOR

Ruby Scott was always an avid reader of #lesfic and lesbian romance and one day she got up had an extra cup of coffee and thought "I'm going to have a shot at writing a story." Her books, she jokes, are always a result of an extra cup of coffee. Born to a British parents, Ruby has lived in many places and loves traveling when it's possible.

Ruby currently lives in central Scotland along with best pal, Baxter, surrounded by family, friends and her girl, A.

Want to know more about Ruby and her antics?
www.rubyscott.com

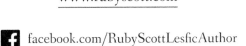 facebook.com/RubyScottLesficAuthor

 twitter.com/RubyScottAuthor

 instagram.com/rubyscottauthor

ALSO BY RUBY SCOTT

Stronger You Series

Inside Fighter

Seconds Out

On The Ropes

City General: Medic 1 Series

Hot Response

Open Heart

Love Trauma

Diagnosis Love

Trails of the Heart

Healing of the Heart

Evergreen Series

Evergreen

Printed in Great Britain
by Amazon